A SIMPLE
CARPENTER

A SIMPLE CARPENTER

Dave Margoshes

Editor: Susan Musgrave
Cover art: Tania Wolk
Book and cover design: Tania Wolk, Third Wolf Studio
Printed and bound in Canada at Friesens, Altona, MB

The publisher gratefully acknowledges the support of
Creative Saskatchewan, the Canada Council for the Arts and SK Arts.

Library and Archives Canada Cataloguing in Publication

Title: A simple carpenter / Dave Margoshes.
Names: Margoshes, Dave, author.
Identifiers: Canadiana (print) 20240340108 | Canadiana (ebook) 20240340132
ISBN 9781998926091 (softcover) | ISBN 9781998926107 (EPUB)
Subjects: LCGFT: Novels.
Classification: LCC PS8576.A647 S48 2024 | DDC C813/.54—dc23

radiant press

Box 33128 Cathedral PO
Regina, SK   S4T 7X2
info@radiantpress.ca
www.radiantpress.ca

for dee

One thing, and this is most important, remains to be said. Purity of heart is not the ultimate end of the monk's striving in the desert. It is only a step towards it. Paradise is not the final goal of the spiritual life. It is, in fact, only a return to the true beginning. It is a "fresh start." Paradise has never been lost and therefore is never regained.

–THOMAS MERTON, *ZEN AND THE BIRDS OF APPETITE*

God Moves in a mysterious way
His wonders to perform;
He plants His footsteps in the sea
And rides upon the storm

–WILLIAM COWPER

And the angel spake: "All will be revealed in time."

–REVELATIONS

Last night I dreamed that I was sailing
Out on the Sea of Galilee
We cast our nets upon the waters
And Jesus pulled them in with me

–LENNIE GALLANT, "PETER'S DREAM"

CONTENTS

BOOK 1

A Blank Slate

CHAPTER 1
FEVER

THE BLOOD IN MY VEINS sang and boiled. The sheets of my bunk were awash with sweat and other foul emanations of my body. I slept and slept, slipping in and out of consciousness. Through the haze of my own mind, I heard voices babbling in a stew of languages, their words clear and indistinct at the same time, their meaning incoherent. I heard the voices of men calling for their mother the way a child would, helpless and devoid of bravado. I heard curses, aimed at various gods, at poor choices and bad luck. And I heard the plaintive sound of men sobbing. Through that cacophony one voice eventually distinguished itself and became clear, the voice of the first mate, cutting like the serrated fisherman's knife he wore on his belt: "Come on, Carpenter, hold on," and while everything else was vague, in turmoil, suspect, I was certain of two things: I was Carpenter – *Najjar* – though whether that was my name or my occupation, I did not know – and I was holding on.

I could remember none of the details but I knew I was on board a ship and had been on it for many months – knew it because the voice of the first mate told me so. From where the ship had embarked I could not say, nor what business had occupied me prior to my taking ship. Indeed, my

3

entire life was a page devoid of writing. The likelihood, I sensed, even in my feverish fog, was that the men of the ship knew little more of me than I myself remembered, such being the nature of men at sea, strangers who come together for a certain task who are reluctant to reveal too much of themselves. And so a third certainty came to me, like a light beaming through fog to guide a puzzled mariner. I might not actually be Carpenter, whoever that poor wretch might be; after all, I was not the only one suffering – that was clear – so how could I be sure it was *I* who was Carpenter? To go further, I might be anybody, anyone of my own choosing. Who was to say?

My memory had all but disappeared – who I was, where I had come from, my childhood, my loved ones, all of that. Even the most recent events, those of the misadventure that had led me and my fellows to our sickbeds, were beyond my reach. It was the mate who, as I began to regain consciousness for more than just a few minutes at a time, told me the tale: engine trouble; our ship, the *Al-Aqba*, powerless and adrift, far off course, food and water supplies dwindling, even the radio unreliable; the sighting of an uncharted island; the mustering of a landing party, myself included, to retrieve a good supply of fresh water, and fruit if there were any to be had. We had landed on the thickly jungled island, the mate reported, to find not fresh water springs but swamps, their water foul, and the abundant trees and bushes bare of anything edible except for a waxy, putrid berry. As we stood on the shore assessing the lay of the land, suddenly the ground beneath our feet began to tremble, strongly enough that several of our number were knocked off their feet. A fissure appeared in the ground of this befouled island and from it flew a swarm of rapacious flies, which immediately fell on us, dining on us, infesting our blood. The seamen called them flies, the mate said, but unlike any flies any of us had ever seen. They were brutal things, big as a man's morning gob of spit with jeweled eyes that made them irresistible. One would land on your bare arm and you'd look at the filthy thing first with disgust, then, catching its eye, with fascination. As you stood mesmerized, the dreadful insect plunged its razored proboscis through your flesh and began to suck, though only after first, as one of the sailors from the tropics explained it to us, spitting its own ugly phlegm into your blood to thin it. That part would have been bad enough, but invisible parasites riding on the flies' juices soon were sailing through our own systems, and it was this that sickened us, a fine distinction.

Back on board the *Al-Aqba*, the men of the landing party were coherent enough to describe their nightmare but were quickly stricken with fever. Now the half dozen of us of that party, our good captain included, lay thrashing in our bunks, beyond the reach of the other men. They could comfort us, sympathize, whisper or even shout encouragements, as the first mate was doing for me; they could cool our brows, force liquid through our clenched, parched lips, but they couldn't reach us, couldn't come to where we were, so far were we from where we had begun, from where they still stood.

As the mate told me this story, as he had heard it, several times over the days of my recovery, he prompted me, "You remember this, now, Carpenter, don't you?" or similar words, but I did not, could not, though he assured me my memory would return. What I mostly remembered was *trying* to remember, for the flies had infested my memory, and I could not tell if this was a true memory or imagined, sparked by the mate's vivid description. Either way, the glowing eyes of those foul insects had begun to illuminate my dreams. Even now, more than two years later, those eyes still haunt me as I sleep.

How long this went on, I cannot say – for days, certainly. Eventually, though, I awoke and rose from this fever.

"Well, look who's awake. Look who's back from the land of the dead."

Those were the first words I heard as, after an indeterminate time in the grip of fever in my bunk onboard the *Al-Aqba*, I regained full consciousness.

The first mate was a giant of a man – well, so he seemed to me then. He was a Scot – his name was Fergus but no one referred to him other than "Mate" – who had traveled the world on a series of ships and was fluent in several languages, including Arabic, which most of the crew on our ship spoke. He was the first man I saw after awakening and, the first man I could recall *ever* seeing, so must Adam have felt when first he found himself in the presence of God. I looked down at myself, all sagging skin and hollow ribcage, then up at him and he was terrifying. If this was a man, then what was I? Or, conversely, if I was a man – "Be a man, Carpenter," the mate had exhorted me earlier, as I writhed in my fever – then what manner of beast was he? Later, I learned he stood no more than six foot two. Tall, yes, but hardly a giant; broad-shouldered, strapping, a well-built man who could lift a hundred-weight cask of whisky on his back with barely a puff of breathlessness. Imposing, yes, but a giant, no. Just an ordinary man. Even his moustache, which at first presented itself like a feral beast curled above his lip, was ordinary enough later on, when I sat across the table from him in the mess, that last morning, the day of the storm. While

I was still in the grasp of the fever, wild-eyed with it, I'd have sworn the moustache writhed, that it hissed, that it bared its fangs at me.

It was the mate himself who hissed. "Get a grip on yerself, Carpenter," out of his twisted, green-toothed mouth.

As the other men of our ill-fated landing party died off, including the captain, while I grew stronger, my mind clearing, the mate, who'd been skeptical, became convinced I really had lost my memory but that it would in due course return. He presented me with a notebook, the sort the ship's officers used to record weather, distance and time, and other observations. "Here, as you remember things, write them down," he told me, "as an *aide mémoire*," the expression rolling clumsily off his tongue.

But I didn't remember things, nothing from my past – my entire life prior to waking up on the ship, the fever gone, was a blank.

The men of the *Al-Aqba* looked at me with amazement, as if they were seeing a ghost. They assumed I would die as well. When I didn't, I became invested with a special mantle of honour: I was Carpenter, *Najjar*, as always and again, but I was also something, some *one*, else.

Behind my back, the men whispered in their own varied tongues; to my astonishment, I could hear and understand every word.

I also became some sort of celebrity. We were in the ship's galley among a group of sailors when the mate teasingly asked if I didn't at least remember my first time with a woman. I shook my head, having only the vaguest notion of what a woman was. His response was to brand me with shame: "A man who has not had a woman canna be a real man," he growled.

When I looked around me in bewilderment, another sailor, a lopsided man with blackened teeth but a sweet smile nonetheless, explained more simply: "It's a woman who makes a man a man."

"True enough," the mate replied, "don't you lads worry none of this fine fellow. He mayna' remember her, but he's had a fine fighting vixen of a lass just the same, and the battle scars to prove it." The men gazed at the mate with bewilderment until he burst into rough laughter. "Ah, but I'm forgettin', you lads hain't had the mixed pleasure I've endured of bathin' this poor wretch durin' his fever – and seein' the scratches on his ass. The kind only a woman's fingernails might make."

This brought on roars of laughter from the men, adding to my confusion.

WITHOUT MEMORY, I was a clean page, waiting to be written on, and more. I was a song waiting to be sung, a meal to be cooked and eaten, a seed to be planted. I was an idea, waiting to be thought of. I realized this, conflating myself with the thought of myself even as it was assembling itself in my mind.

Perhaps, as the first mate suggested, my memory would return – in days or weeks, maybe longer. If not, it came to me, I could be the author of my own future, I could fill that empty page – or at least begin the narrative written upon it. I could sing the song, prepare the meal, furrow the field of my choice, plant the seed and nurture it; I could begin the process of thinking the thoughts – the obvious, the brilliant or banal, the tedious, the thrilling – the whole panoply of possible thoughts, all the way unto the unthinkable thoughts, whatever they might be.

The repository of these thoughts was my journal, the notebook the first mate had given me.

What memories I'd had were gone, but the ability to accumulate new ones remained, like a pail drained of the water it once held. Dip that pail into a flowing stream and immediately it fills again.

So, I remember everything from the moment in which I awoke from the fever on the *Al-Aqba* to this moment now, a period of less than two years. Indeed, my memory now is excellent, unburdened as it is by so much that any other man of my age – whatever age that might exactly be – would necessarily carry: a mother's love, family, childhood, school learning, the scrapes and bumps of adolescence, the anguish of young manhood, first love....all of that, I have been spared. Indeed, I had to relearn how to do virtually everything, including to read – though that came very quickly and with remarkable results. Presented with a book for the first time, on board the *Al-Aqba*, I asked what this object was, just as I asked about a dinner plate, a cup, knife, fork and spoon, a toothbrush...an endless list. When I asked about the book, which happened to be the Koran – likely the only book on board the ship – the first mate, who, since the death of the captain, had assumed command, replied that it was "a box filled with knowledge in the form of words."

"And words? What are they?"

"See for yourself," the mate said.

I opened the book and immediately dropped it, much to the mate's amusement. The open pages were covered with what I first took to be some crawling insects. When I picked the book up again, the black specks, which seemed at first to be in motion, settled down and quickly came into focus in larger clumps of various shapes. The mate leaned over my shoulder, so close I could smell the garlic on his breath. "These big'uns here, they's words, the little ones, each little part in the word, they's letters. See how they's used over and over again?" I glanced up to see reassurance in the mate's surprisingly blue eyes. "They's only so many of them letters, but thousands and thousands of words. A miracle!"

Gradually, this intricate, complex system began to take shape in my mind, and within a few hours, I was reading. And once having cracked the code – I realized that's what it was, a puzzle to be solved – reading became easy for me. Writing too came quickly, though the mate laughed at my first clumsy attempts – "elephants dancing" is how he described those clumping words I managed to scrawl on the page.

I also had to learn how to do simple sums, how to stir sugar into my tea, how to blow my nose and wipe my ass – just as a baby must learn – and the rote litanies of history, geography and the physical sciences – like any student. I did learn quickly – I had no conscious memory of these things, but, apparently, that part of my brain employed for such learning was facile and muscular. I only had to be told something once, to read it once, to remember it; had only to try an experiment once to master its technique. I was a sponge, thirsty for knowledge, of the world, of my surroundings, of myself.

As soon as I was able, though, I was put to work, fashioning crude coffins for the departed seamen. I did remember the uses for various tools, once they were comfortably, familiarly, in my hands, but not their names, and the mate spelled them off for me, "hammer, saw, adze, screwdriver," and I dutifully wrote them down. He looked over my shoulder and shook his head.

"What language is that, Carpenter?"

I couldn't say.

Other sailors, from different countries, were summoned to look at my jottings, but none recognized the language in which I wrote except for one man, an Arab from Palestine, who said he thought it might be Hebrew.

CHAPTER 2
SHIPWRECK

THE TRAVAILS OF THE *Al-Aqba* and its hapless crew were far from over.

No sooner than the coffins I'd hastily constructed, with their mortal remains intact inside, been put overboard, with solemn words spoken by the mate, and tots of whiskey all around, then dark clouds began to roll toward us from the west. With the engine still not working and the radio erratic, we were helpless to flee from the onrushing storm or to call for assistance.

As the storm came upon us, battering the powerless *Al-Aqba*, the mate advised me to gather some tools in my carpenter's apron, "just in case." Along with a screwdriver, a small hammer and pliers, I'd tucked my notebook and a flat-sided carpenter's pencil, carefully wrapped in oilcloth, and a handful of wooden matches into a zippered pouch, along with a flint.

The storm, "the worst I've ever seen," the mate said, pounced on the ship "like a lion on a gazelle." I had no knowledge of either animal, but I took his description to be accurate. Thunder rolled overhead, blanketing us with deafening noise, and the sky was ablaze with lightning. With each flash, I could see the terrified faces of my fellow shipmates.

Rain pelted down, drenching us before we could take cover below deck, and unimaginably huge waves, powered by over-powering wind, battered the ship, threatening to turn it over, which it eventually did.

We managed to lower two lifeboats, with some men in them, others hanging on. From the safety of one of the dories, I along with half a dozen others, watched as the ship floundered and sank. We tossed life preservers to men bobbing in the water and rescued a few. Other men were being hauled into the other lifeboat as well, but there wasn't room for all.

A few others, no room for them in either overloaded boat, held fast to the gunnels. I could hear the piercing voices of men still in the water calling for help, uttering prayers, and the shouts of encouragement from our boat and the other as the oarsmen battled to come closer to those helpless wretches. But if even one more was pulled from the water's clammy embrace or given purchase on the side of the boat, I was not aware of it. Gradually, the voices grew weaker, then died out entirely, and all our energies became focused on our own plight, keeping our small boats aright, and still the storm howled around us. The grip of men holding on to the gunnels weakened and soon they slid from view without a sound. In the storm's fury, we lost sight of the second boat, and its fate, and that of the men aboard it, including the first mate – what a stalwart man he was – remains unknown to me.

The storm was passing, the thunder becoming more muted, the lightning flashes still seen but in the distance. We were enveloped in an eerie silence.

By dawn, the storm had fully abated and the sun arose on a sorry crew of survivors, crowded into the dory. We took stock: thirteen of us, in a boat built for no more than eight, crammed shoulder to shoulder, all in weakened straits. No water, no food, no weapons, not that we had any immediate use for them. No tools other than the few basic ones attached to my carpenter's apron, which I still wore and containing the notebook that would become my journal. And, we were quite sure, we were far off our course, in waters unlikely to be part of any regular shipping lanes. Our distress calls the previous night had gone unanswered, then the radio died, so there was no reason to think anyone even was aware of our plight. We were on our own. We were adrift in a becalmed sea, the sun beating down on us relentlessly, the only evidence of our ill-fated ship a thick coating of oil on the water.

Horrific though the storm was, though, our ordeal was just beginning. We had only one oar, suitable for going in circles and not much else, no map, no compass, no food or water. The sea was calm, there was no wind, and the sun merciless. We dozed in heat and exhaustion. From time to time, the silence of the lifeboat was broken by a sailor calling out "land, I see land." But always it was a mirage.

Twice, we awoke in the morning to find ourselves engulfed in thick fog, giving us temporary relief from sun. But soon it dissipated and the sun resumed its assault on us.

At some point a sailor named Amoud, noticed that we had a visitor: a black bird, circling above us. It appeared in every way to be a seagull, much like the gulls that routinely followed the *Al-Aqba*, but this one was black as coal, drifting above us like a pirate flag. And once in a while, a curious whale rose from turbulent waves to gaze at us with sympathetic eyes, then dropped silently below again.

One by one, the survivors of the shipwreck succumbed. When the first man died, there was talk of eating him, and one fellow, armed with a knife, was ready to begin carving. But without the means to build a fire, the thought of raw human flesh was too much for us all, and the body was gently lowered overboard.

There was a flurry of activity in the water, followed by a red stain floating to the surface. 'Sharks," one sailor said.

By the fourth day, our number was reduced to six, then four on the fifth day.

Finally, just two remained, me and an engineer named Mohan, a once-shy, now oddly talkative fellow from India. His mother tongue was Hindi, but in deference to me he spoke a surprisingly cultured English.

We amused ourselves by telling stories – his were much better than mine – and riddles. I, of course, knew none, but the engineer had a seemingly endless store of them, and after I heard a few, I was able to fashion one or two of my own.

"What is full of holes and still holds water?" was one he posed that I liked, though I had no answer. 'A sponge," Mohan said smugly. The irony of that one was not lost on either of us – we were surrounded by water but had none to drink.

Eventually, Mohan cried uncontrollably at the thought of never again seeing his wife and children. "Oh, God, why have you forsaken me?" he cried out, while I, with only the haziest notion of who or what God was, remained silent. But I cried as well, over my own losses, whatever they might have been: mother, father, wife, children... I didn't know who it was I would probably never see again.

I noted this in the journal of our ordeal I had started to write on the second day in the dory. Writing about it made the loss somehow easier to bear and yet, simultaneously, more heartbreaking.

The evening of the sixth day, Mohan and I sat across from

each other in the wide belly of the lifeboat, gazing at each other, telling riddles. I had finally come up with one I felt proud of.

"What rides on the sea, flies through the air and walks on the land?" I riddled.

"That's too easy, a seagull," the engineer laughed feebly. We were visited by several of these birds in the last few hours, giving us hope that we might be approaching land of some sort.

"No," I protested, "man. We surely walk on the land, we fly through the air in airplanes – or so I've been told – and here you find us, floating on the sea."

"Masters of all we survey, is that it, Carpenter?"

"Yes, masters," I agreed, laughing bitterly.

"Then I must be master of my own fate as well,'" the engineer said. "This is unbearable. Goodbye, Carpenter."

And with that, he struggled upright, leaned himself over the gunnel and, with a final burst of effort, and before I could respond, threw himself into the water.

Why I was spared, I couldn't fathom. I assumed it was only a matter of time before I too would perish.

I had heard my shipmates callout to Allah, and other gods, but I knew nothing of god so I said no prayers.

Then, as if I had prayed and my prayer answer was coming, clouds began to form on the horizon and a breeze sprang up.

A group of silvery fish no larger than my hand began to circle the dory, some of them leaping playfully into the air. To my surprise, one of them landed in the boat, right at my feet. It flapped then for a moment, then lay still, looking up at me, its eyes black and soulful. I reached down and picked the fish up, with every intention of returning it to the sea, hut instead, overtaken by my hunger, I banged its head against the gunnel until it lay still in my hand. Then, taking care to avoid the bones, I devoured it.

The wind picked up and it began to rain.

As darkness fell, waves were battering the sides of the boat, and the rain grew stronger, falling in sheets, both a blessing and a curse. The former because, with my mouth gaping open, I was able to slake my thirst. I was still powerless to steer the boat or to protect myself in any way. Eventually, a wave tipped the dory over and I was thrown into the sea. I thrashed and righted myself, began to swim – I found to my amazement that I knew how. I swam and swam, though I had no way of knowing the direction or what might be ahead of me, if anything. I was carried aloft by wave after wave, pushed along by an incessant current. If there is one thing as strong as a storm at sea, it is the determined force of a tide. I swam and my arms weakened, and just as I was certain that within a few strokes I would reach the limits of my strength and be overpowered by exhaustion, I felt something soft beneath my feet. I attempted to stand, stumbled, fell, righted myself again, and staggered onto a beach, then collapsed, falling face first onto a soft, granular cushion – sand. The waves that pushed and pulled me into the comforting arms of the island beach now receded, and I slept.

Dawn found me there on a beach, so weak I could barely move. I was alone, except for the black gull, still circling above me as if it were my guardian.

Time passed, I know not how long, eventually I mustered the strength and will to move. The black clouds that unleashed the previous day's storm softened to grey, with occasional shafts of sunlight penetrating though. And gradually, I became conscious of a pleasant sound, the singing of birds not far away, songbirds, not just gulls, and I thought that I could smell the presence of sweet water nearby.

I dragged myself across sand toward the sound of those birds, and found myself lying beneath trees and beside a pool of water, into which I thrust my head and drank. Drank and drank, until I could drink no more.

Such was my arrival on the island that would become my home for some time. And, once again, I was alive.

CHAPTER 3
ALIVE

ON THE SECOND DAY of what would become an extended stay on what I came to think of as Shipwreck Island, I awoke dazed and drained beside the pool of water in a grove of trees. I fell into an exhausted sleep there as soon as the sun went down the previous evening and slept fitfully, disturbed by a dream of a ship passing in the dark.

The storm that brought me to this place was just a bad memory now, rain and wind having exhausted themselves, and the sun came out, filtering through the leafy branches of the trees. On my knees, I drank my fill again. When I managed to stand up on wobbly legs, I discovered that the trees were laden with fruit I hadn't noticed the day before, fruit which I had no memory of, yet was immediately able to apply names to: bananas, dates, figs, oranges. I picked and ate, first tentatively, then ravenously, filling myself till my shrunken stomach felt bloated. And, indeed, I threw up most of what I'd just eaten. But after an hour or more's sleep, I felt hungry again. This time I ate slowly and more prudently.

The pool of water and the fruit trees were in a clearing in the centre of a larger woods of various types, filled with singing birds and whooping monkeys. The pond appeared to be spring-fed and out of it flowed a number of streams, like the arms of an octopus. Shrubbery and flowers grew on the pool's fringe in abundance but there was no other sign of life, except for a large number of bees drawn to one particular flaming red flower. I was reluctant to leave this protected spot, with its abundance of food and water, yet felt compelled to return to the beach from which I'd be able to spot any ship that might happen to be passing.

I spent the remainder of that day on the beach, alternatively dozing and awake, and when awake straining my eyes for signs of a ship. I was battered and, apparently alone, wearing only ragged pants that were cut off above the knees and a tattered pullover shirt.

Night fell and I continued to lie on the beach, mustering my strength. The sky was once again clear and the great canopy of stars revealed itself to me, just as it had during the nights in the lifeboat. Then, the stars seemed to be mocking us – Mohan had made that observation and I agreed with him – and now they took on an entirely different countenance, like that of an interested, sympathetic onlooker. I interpreted each winking of a star to be akin to a nod from the heavens – I had no concept of a god to attribute this to. I lay awake for some time, attempting to count those stars, to understand the meaning of their crude communication. At the first light of dawn, as the stars faded, I finally allowed myself to sleep. I shivered, waking frequently from terrifying dreams filled with blood-sucking insects and drowning men.

The third day brought blistering heat and I made several trips into the cooler woods for fruit and water but always, after a brief interval, returned to the beach. The night was milder than the previous one and I stayed awake for hours, vast arrays of stars and occasional flashes of lightning my only companions, the stars moving and forming oddly shaped combinations as I watched. When I did finally sleep, I was undisturbed by dreams.

And so, I developed a routine: frequent visits to the oasis for food and water, and quickly back to the beach where, at night, I sat up staring either up at the sky or out toward the sea until sleep overcame me. I was haunted by the notion that, while I was at the pool, a ship should come by and – its crew seeing no one – pass on, so I wanted to be visible. Yet, until the day of my rescue, I never did see any sign of a ship, though one day a school of porpoises swam close by, a couple dozen in tight single-file formation like soldiers on parade, their cries still ringing in the air even after they passed from sight. That night, as on several others that followed, lightning lit up the sky, but there was no thunder, no rain.

I had no real sense of time – hours were the same as days. So I cannot say with certainty what the timetable of my stay on the island was, but if I were to think in terms of a week, then the day I washed up on shore in the midst of a storm might have been a Monday. In which case, the day I struggled to the pool where I was able to drink and eat was Tuesday. And the following day, then, would have been Wednesday. That evening I again visited the oasis, drank, ate, and fell asleep there, and upon waking the next morning, the fourth day, Thursday, found myself back on the beach. This puzzled me. Had I awoken and stumbled back to more familiar surroundings only to sleep again? Walked in my sleep? Had the landscape somehow changed?

The next day, feeling my strength returning, I decided to explore the island – what I thought of as *my* island, since I was its only inhabitant – and set off.

Not far from where I'd been sleeping, I discovered the shattered dory I'd spent more than a week in and other detritus from the wreck of the *Al-Aqba*, that seemed to have followed me here, including a blue enamel cup, chipped and cracked but still usable, and a battered tin pot.

That was the day, too, that I began the record of my time on the island.

Wedged beneath one of the dory's seats, I found my carpenter's apron and, secure and dry within one of its pockets, wrapped in oilcloth, the notebook and pencil – still sharp – the mate had given me.

The apron remained on my waist during the cruel days on the lifeboat, but I'd lost track of it after the dory capsized and I swam blindly through the dark. Now, I took inventory of the apron's contents: as well as the notebook and pencil, there were several hand tools that would perhaps be of assistance on this island – the thought of building a raft occurred to me – as well as the matches and flint, for lighting fires.

Immediately, I began to jot down observations and thoughts in the notebook, a practice I'd begun during the ordeal on the lifeboat, where I'd learned that recording events and my thoughts had a settling effect on my mind. The journal became both my companion and my confessional.

"I am alive," I wrote, "and utterly alone." And then I wrote down my resolve to write in the journal every day.

Had I known what mischief it would later be used for, I doubt I would have begun it.

CHAPTER 4
A KINGDOM OF SAND

LATER, DURING WHAT I NOW think of as my sojourn of sand, I had ample time to ponder the implications of my lack of memory. In between that time and what my shipmates thought of as my miraculous recovery, I experienced several other unforgettable misadventures which now vied for attention in my otherwise uncluttered memory: the terrible storm that sank the unfortunate *Al-Aqba*, long painful days in the lifeboat and the slow death of my fellow shipwreck survivors, a death only I managed to escape. I thought of all of this as I lay in the sand of the small island I had washed up on, the second island to play a role in my story, but I thought also of sand.

I've since heard that snowflakes are all different – millions, no billions of snowflakes fall gently to earth each winter in northern climates, and, due to the peculiar nature of the crystallization process that forms them, each one is different – or at least as different as each person is, as different as each person's fingerprints are. Now consider sand. It too is a crystal and it too is unique. Think how many trillions of grains of sand there are on this Earth, on every beach and every desert, from the Sahara to the Negev, trillions upon trillions of grains of sand, some composed of quartz, some of gypsum, some limestone, some shells and other organic material, and to the naked average eye each grain indistinguishable from its siblings, but to the eye of the expert as unique, as distinguishable as the portraits in a rogue's gallery. I became just such an expert, a connoisseur of sand with an intimate knowledge of its structure, its composition, its personality.

But I was a discrete authority – not a pompous ass blinded by his own brilliance, no, I was nothing like that. I was deeply, broadly, profoundly knowledgeable about the subject of sand. Not that there was anyone present who might have sought my opinion. No, I was totally, completely, impossibly alone.

And like a grain of sand, I was unique, though I didn't know it then. And I did not have even the slenderest inkling of who I was.

I lay, often for hours, in a bed of sand with a view of the sea, each portion of the back of my body, from skull to shoulder to buttock to calf to heel of foot, developing a deep intercourse with those crystals, my fingers threading through the sand at my sides, my lips engaging deeply in conversation with the grains of sand upon them, my eyelids and the hairs of my nostrils tugging and pushing against their incessant current. For several weeks, though it seemed much longer, day after day, except when I'd rouse myself and walk the short distance to a pool of water for a drink and to pick fruit from the surrounding trees – except for these brief interruptions, sand was my companion, my colleague, my lover, the endless object of my study, my interest, my ardour, sand was my passion, my obsession. Surrounded by sand, how could it have been otherwise?

Sometimes, as I lay in my cradle of sand, its touch, smell, taste and essence oozing its way into my being as though through osmosis, I allowed my mind to wander, all the better for sand, in its complexity and duplicity, to take me unawares, to ensnare me, and often, on those occasions, I would find myself contemplating the absence of my past, or, that is to say, the absence of any known past earlier than the recent disasters connected with the *Al-Aqba*. Known to me, that is. In my isolation, I was the universe, the audience complete, and what was unknown to me was, simply, unknown.

Lying in the sand, I was always conscious of the irritation on my buttocks, and would wonder if the scratches, if that's what they were, hadn't actually been made by a woman, as the mate insinuated. I would often lie on my side or my stomach and allow my fingers to explore the raised welts. They felt to be thick, the width of a narrow rope, say, and hard as callous, not really like scratches at all. More like the scar from a burn – I had seen such scars on several of the sailors.

Though I remembered nothing of the initial disaster beyond which was related to me by the first mate, I remembered every moment of the second disaster – the storm, the shipwreck, the lifeboat and its dwindling party of doomed seamen – and suspect I will for the rest of my life. Thinking backwards, I ticked off the final storm that washed me ashore, the agony of the lifeboat, the shipwreck, the first storm, the illness that preceded it – and then a blank wall. Beyond that, I – my life, my self – was a blank page.

I was, in a very real sense, the sum of zero, and no more.

THE DAY AFTER my discovery of the dory and my apron with its treasures, what I reckoned to be Friday, I continued my exploration of the island. It was no larger than the estate of many a rich man, or so I have come to discover. It was roughly round, fringed by a circumference of sandy beaches, like links of gold chain in a necklace, one leading to another, only occasionally interrupted by brief rocky outcrops or streams that meandered toward the sea, and enclosing a circle of dense forest and the pool of sweet water from which the streams emanated. Despite that oasis, I came to think of this as a desert island. In every way, it was different from the jungle island I visited only a few weeks earlier, with its swamp, its withered shrubbery and vines, and its swarms of biting insects. The Isle of Flies.

My beach, what I came to think of as Shipwreck Beach, was narrow, perhaps a hundred metres wide from shore to where the woods began. I took a bearing on the sun and headed north, walking slowly through hot sand on bare feet. Gradually, the beach narrowed and petered out entirely at a stream. It was shallow and smooth-bottomed and I waded across it easily to a second beach, which gradually widened, curving toward the northwest. This beach was much the same as the first, except that it was here where on the previous day I'd discovered the wrecked dory.

I carried on. This second stretch of sand also narrowed, ending at a rocky outcrop which took me some time to cross. On the third beach, I discovered the tracks of an animal, a small, four-toed imprint in the sand. I attempted to follow them but they abruptly disappeared. Otherwise, this beach was the same as the previous two, except for the position of the sun, for I was now walking west.

As I walked, I observed that I was being followed from above by a silent black bird, a gull in appearance except for its colour, much like one I'd seen at sea trailing the lifeboat.

There was really nothing on these three beaches, or the several more I'd traverse before returning to where I'd begun, identifiable only by the detritus of shipwreck still littering the sand.

On the fourth beach, I thought I saw something slithering away into bushes further inland, and on another I came upon the jawbone of an animal with sharp teeth. Finally, moving west and south, I came across what I first took to be a large white rock.

I drew closer to inspect it. Shading my eyes from the blazing sun, I gazed down and realized the object was the skull of an animal. It was larger than a man's head, broad at the back, narrow at the front, smoothly rounded on top, and crowned by large curved horns. The upper and lower jaws, still intact, were studded with teeth as long as my fingers and sharp as bird feather quills.

I stepped back, marveling and looking around, as if expecting a herd of the animals possessing such magnificent heads to suddenly appear. I noticed then a sound I hadn't heard before, which I first took to be caused by a swarm of flying insects. I noticed bees near the pool, attracted by the brilliantly coloured flowers blooming there, and the sound I heard, I decided, was surely the buzzing of bees. But there were no flowers anywhere near where I stood. I stepped closer again, and bent closer to the skull. Then I stepped back abruptly, almost falling. What I had taken to be bees buzzing was a whispering sound coming from the skull.

I took a deep breath, mustering my courage, and squatted down beside the skull. The whispering continued, distinct yet indecipherable.

DAYS PASSED, days that felt like weeks, weeks that felt like months, years. I no longer felt hunger but still I forced myself to eat of the fruit that grew from the few trees of my oasis – dates, figs and other exotic fruit all, inexplicably, from the same trees.

I would have liked to eat one of the small animals that came to drink from the spring, but they were too quick and nimble for me to catch. Most were small creatures that walked or ran on four legs, with bushy or long hairless tails and pointy snouts. (I should say something here, perhaps, about snouts, inasmuch as it reflects on my memory. Should I put a finger to the front of my face, the word "nose" comes to my mind. But seeing these animals that I had no memory of, that, as far as I knew, had never seen before, the word "snout" appeared. Nose, snout, different words for what is essentially the same part of the body, with subtle differences. And "subtle" – how had a word like that found itself into my vocabulary? The depth and breadth of my abilities with language had not yet become apparent to me, but I continued to be surprised by language's complexities.)

I had no better luck spearing fish with a sharpened stick in the surf that pounded against the rocks edging my island. I recalled the fish I'd eaten raw, on my last day in the lifeboat, and thought longingly of enriching my stew of roots, fruit, berries, leaves and grasses I ate almost daily with the soft, flaky flesh of fish. After using up the few matches I'd found, I'd become adept at starting fires with my flint, rubbed against a rock to produce sparks that easily ignited a handful of leaves and twigs. So my meals, except for fresh fruit I ate right from the trees, were always cooked in the battered pot I'd salvaged from the shipwreck debris. I was fortunate indeed.

In the back of my mind – the front part, the active part, was preoccupied only with sand – I considered that this abundance of fruit was a miracle (a term I'd heard the mate use upon my recovery), that my continued existence was a miracle, and I didn't question either. The greater miracle, I thought, was that the sea storm that washed me up on this benign island had not left me stranded on that earlier, malignant island, the Isle of Flies.

YEARS PASSED, or so it seemed. In fact, it was only a few weeks before I was rescued. The sand and I communed. I say my memory was virtually blank, but no, not quite. Memories did come, they haunted me, in fact, but they were hollow. Memories of the horrible days on the lifeboat, the slow agonizing death of my companion Mohan. Memories of the storm and the terrifying *crack* of our ship as it split in two. Memories of the brief period of camaraderie on board the *Al-Aqba* between my awakening from the fever to the storm – was that a day or two? A week? I couldn't tell. Memories of the first mate, who nurtured me back to life, and my other shipmates, who constituted the sum total of the population of my small known world, now, alas, all gone, thrown into the treacherous sea and presumed drowned. These things I remembered, yes.

And when I slept, memory slipped into my mind in the form of dream... a woman, even though to my knowledge I'd never even seen a woman. In my dreams, yes, a woman, pillowy-breasted, white-haired, her hand on my face soft as rose petals... my mother? Grandmother? I didn't know, still don't know. A man, colourless sagebrush hair, gnarled face not dissimilar to that of the first mate, a limp... my father, grandfather? Again, I don't know. And this... a girl, a young woman, duskyskinned, dark-eyed, raven-haired, looking at me with what I could only describe as adoration...was she a lover? Certainly not a sister, not with that look on her face. An utterly unforgettable face, and yet I had forgotten her.

A face that, to my shock, I would encounter within a couple of months, in a room behind a sweetshop on a busy street in the Old Quarter of Beirut.

There is no logic to dreams. In another one I had repeatedly on the island, I could see but could not be seen, could hear but not be heard. I was there but it was as if I were not. I was on a sandy beach, not unlike the beach upon which I lay sleeping, but I was awake. I saw the boats while they were still far out, little more than specks on the horizon, then as they began to approach I could see there were two of them, and as they came closer still that they were inflatable dinghies, crammed with people – I thought I counted ten or a dozen between the two of them. As they came closer still, I saw the guns these boatmen carried, and the masks they wore. And as they scrambled onto shore, bloody footprints in the sand. Then I awoke, totally baffled, to the sound of a baby crying. Was that part of the dream? It must have been.

As I lay on the sand of Shipwreck Island, my eyes closed against the burning sun, or open to the wonder of moon and stars, my mind replayed those few memories over and over again, attempting to find meaning in them. There was no meaning beyond the facts of the memories themselves: actions, words, the story of my brief life from the moment I awoke from the fever – and, in effect, was born, or reborn. A very short life indeed.

Not having a past I knew for a certainty, I had to invent one.

People always ask you, where you're from, school, family, friends. And, of course, what do you do. That much I knew – I was a carpenter. I was told that on the ship, and in the few days between my recovery and the storm, my familiarity with the tools supposedly mine and my evident skill with them as I fashioned coffins for my less fortunate shipmates, all spoke clearly as to my occupation. As for the rest, I imagined it all: the colour of my mother's hair, the time I fell out of the palm tree and hurt my knee, first day of school how I cried, the missing finger, up to the second joint, on my father's left hand. I was born, I would say, in Bethlehem, the eldest of two children, just another brother, my father a carpenter who took us to Judea, in what is now the West Bank, where he earned a reputation for the finesse of his woodwork. I apprenticed to him until I was in my thirties....

"But Yusef, you are only in your thirties now," someone will always say at this point.

" – yes, of course, I mean my twenties, when the Israelis...."

And so it will go. Occasionally I stumble, make an error, but rarely one I cannot quickly, smoothly recover from. I have become adept at telling these fictions – that's what I think of them as, not lies. It has been almost two years since I fell into that fever and lost my memory and, except for the occasional fragment lurking in my mind on waking – a face, a gesture, a scent, a strand of music – nothing has returned. My memory of everything since then – the storm, the shipwreck, my isolation on the island, my rescue, my new life, first in Lebanon, now here, on this small farm in Israel – all of that I remember as well as the next man, maybe better, since I have so much less clutter in my memory than most people. But meeting someone new requires a retelling of the fictions. I know them so well, after so many tellings, that they might as well be genuine memories, might as well have really happened.

CHAPTER 5
ANIMALS

THERE WERE MANY animals on my island, as I've said. Surprisingly many, considering how small was the wooded area where most of them lived. I had no names for these creatures then, and later learned I'd been in the company of rabbits, squirrels, and monkeys, as well as few unidentifiable animals.

One creature had large rear legs, shorter front ones, pop eyes and huge ears, something smaller, akin to a kangaroo, though I didn't know that then, of course. There were also a number of bashful snakes that quickly slithered away as I came upon them, with one exception: a large black serpent that stood its ground, giving me a baleful look until I retreated.

A few larger animals, creatures that, like me, hunted and fished, also lived in the woods. One in particular caught my attention. It stood at perhaps calf height and had a long reddish furred body, a flaring tail with a white tip and a long sharp snout. I've since seen a fox; this animal was similar but considerably larger. It moved gracefully, silently through the woods and along the beach. For the first week or more, I caught only fleeting glimpses of it, or occasionally found what I took to be its footprints in wet sand near the shore, an oval central pad with four clawed toes, the whole thing no larger than half my own palm. As time went on, the creature – I'm sure there was only one – grew accustomed to me, and bolder. As I washed my face or gathered water from the spring, I would become aware of eyes upon me and, raising my head, would see it sitting on its haunches beneath a tree, calmly observing me. Other times, as I walked through the trees gathering fruit and firewood, the creature followed me, at a respectful distance, its eyes large and luminous. Sometimes, at night, as I sat before my fire on the beach, the animal would creep out of the woods and approach, pausing to sit and watch, then zigzag a bit closer still, one night coming close enough that, had I reached out, I might have touched the ruffled fur of its head.

I took comfort from this companionship. I was disturbed when, one day, I realized I had not seen this creature for some time. I watched for it, the flash of red out of the corner of my eye, but there was no sign of it, no print on the ground. After many more days I had to conclude that the beautiful animal was gone. Had it died? Swam away? Met some other fate? I had no way of knowing.

Some time after that, I began to be aware of another animal, a much larger one.

I awoke abruptly at dawn, feeling eyes on me. But when I looked around, there was no one, nothing. Walking to the stream, I heard a rustle in the brush – again, nothing. That night, just as I was falling asleep, I heard a growl. I sat up, eyes wide, ears open, listening, the hair on the back of my neck bristling. Nothing. Surely my imagination. Then again, a distinct growl, low and rumbling, something I would have recognized as feline if I'd had any knowledge or memory of cats, something halfway between a warning and a purr. The sound gradually diminished, then was extinguished. I fell into an uneasy sleep, wondering if

I was in any danger, glad that the sharp stick I used for fishing was nearby. In the morning, I searched the area for tracks but found nothing.

That night, the same thing, the growl coming just as I was drifting into sleep, thrusting me wide-awake, but this time, the sound seemed less threatening. I sat up listening for a few minutes and heard it settle into a steady low drone, like the chanting I'd heard coming from the storage room on board our ship where the Muslim sailors prayed. I lay back down and fell into a comfortable sleep filled with vivid dreams through which several animals of various sizes and shapes benignly appeared. Again, in the morning, no tracks or other sign of my visitor.

This went on for another night or two. Then, I was awoken at dawn by the tide, unusually high, lapping against the soles of my feet. I scrambled up and began to move backward, something caught my attention and I waded back into the retreating water. There, in the wet sand, were prints much like those of the animal that visited earlier, an oval central pad with four claws, but twice the size. I whirled around, but nothing, turned again to the prints, but they led nowhere – or, rather, they seemed to have come from and returned to the sea. Impossible.

Shaken, I walked off the beach and into the trees to the stream. I drank and washed my face. When I rose and turned around, the animal was there, sitting on its haunches the way the earlier creature had, calmly observing me.

This creature was as large as a man but configured with four long and muscular legs, clad in short, sleek lustrously brown hair. The paws were adorned with long, sharp-looking claws. The legs supported a barrel-shaped body covered by a tawny, shaggy coat and a massive head with flaring nostrils and an even shaggier mane, and topped by a pair of large curving horns. Having since scoured books containing photographs of various animals, I can say this creature seemed to be an unlikely combination of lion and bull, something akin to the Minotaur of Greek myth. I had never seen anything like it in my waking life, yet I instantly recognized it as having visited me earlier in my dreams. Perhaps it was this familiarity that allowed me, despite the creature's size and evident strength, to feel no apprehension.

We gazed at each other for several minutes. Then, feeling hungry, I reached for a fruit hanging from the tree to my right, a fruit I had previously seen on a tree with branches higher than I could reach. My eyes were off the animal for only a moment, and when I turned again toward it, it was gone. The fruit was something like a peach, juicy and delicious. I ate it standing there, picked two more, sat down and devoured them. Then I rose, stretched and turned back toward the sea, intending to have a short swim and, as was my custom, a short nap on the sand. I wanted to lie still for a while and consider my new companion. But ahead of me, as I came out of the trees onto the beach, was the creature, standing as if to greet me.

And then, to my utter surprise, the creature spoke.

CHAPTER 6
RESCUE

AS IT TURNED OUT, this encounter occurred near the end of my time on the island, only a few days before the arrival of Syrian fishermen whose boat, like the *Al-Aqba*, was adrift for some time.

During those few days, the Creature and I spoke together several times. Its initial words echoed through my dreams that first night and haunted me on awaking. I stood at the edge of the beach, my feet in water, gazing out to sea, wondering if what the Creature said could possibly be true.

"You will have a long life and see wondrous things," the animal said. "Do not be afraid, now or at any time. Whatever there might have been to fear is behind you."

I didn't hear the Creature's footsteps but rather felt its presence and turned around. It was as tall as I was, so we stood eye to eye. Its eyes fluctuated from deep blue to grey and back again.

"What did you mean, 'wondrous things?" I asked. "What wondrous things?"

"You will see," the Creature said. "All will be revealed in time."

Did it really speak? I should say, the Creature's lips didn't move, yet I heard its words clearly. But were they actually spoken, and heard? Or did they fly directly from the Creature's mind to mine?

I cannot say.

As I stood in the rising tide, reflecting on the Creature's words, I reached down, cupping my hands to splash water on my face, and to my complete surprise, a fish swam into them. It appeared to gaze at me, and made no effort to wriggle out of my hands. I brought it ashore and that evening ate better than I had since washing up on the island.

My sleep that night was troubled. In my dream, I am in a city somewhere, the streets wet from a steady rain but crowded nonetheless, people dashing along the sidewalks under a canopy of brightly coloured umbrellas. I'm sitting on the patio of a café, completely dry despite the rain, sipping a strong black coffee, nibbling on a flaky pastry. I hear snatches of conversation from the tables around me, a language I haven't heard before but know to be French. I see the motorcycle approach, slow down and stop in front of the synagogue across the street. I know that's what it is even though I have no knowledge of such things. Earlier, I saw bearded men in black coats and hats congregating on the sidewalk in front of the building, then going inside. Now I watch as the motorcyclist gracefully swings his leg over the seat, dismounting. Light from the streetlamp catches in the folds of his slicker, shining. He turns around, looking up the street and down, then across toward the patio where I'm sitting. The eyeshade of his helmet is lowered so I can't see his eyes, yet I can feel them on me. He nods, as if signaling me, then he turns and walks away in the direction from which he came. At the corner, he turns his head to look back, then disappears. I finish my coffee and am about to get up to go when the air is shattered by an explosion.

The force so strong it awoke me.

I lay on my familiar sand in complete darkness, except for the ceiling of brilliant stars above me, conscious of where I was but at the same time feeling entirely removed, as if while I slept I'd been lifted and moved – to where? Another part of the island? Another island altogether? I didn't know. As I grappled with these questions, the stars directly above me coalesced into a giant wheel and began to spin.

I drifted back to sleep and in the morning I awoke to familiar surroundings, feeling myself again, but found the Creature seated beside me. I sat up – all sense of apprehension I'd originally felt was gone by now – and again we gazed into each other's eyes.

"It is almost time," the Creature said. "You should prepare yourself."

"Time for what?" I asked. On the island, time seemed to have little meaning. "Prepare myself for what?"

"You will see," the Creature said.

I was reminded of the riddles Mohan and I told each other on the lifeboat as we grew weaker and weaker. Some of them were clever, but others defeated themselves with their cleverness – they were beyond meaning, as the Creature's predictions seemed to be.

"What do you mean?" I asked, then turned my head away for a moment, alerted by a sound, and when I turned back the Creature was gone.

WAVES LAPPED AGAINST the shore not far from where I lay sleeping. This was a sound I heard every night as I fell asleep, every morning when I awoke, and through the night in my dreams. This night, though, something was different. In my dream, I listen closely, hold my breath, concentrate. Of course, it's not the shore the waves are lapping against, but the sides of a ship. Has it been that long since I heard that sound, a sound that must have lulled me to sleep for many, many nights – how long had I been a sailor? Months? Years? I hear it again now. But how? There is no ship, just sand, endless sand.

The following morning, the morning of the day of my rescue, the Creature walked with me on the beach in silence. I looked behind me and saw the companionable sets of footprints, my two bare feet, the Creature's four paws. I felt remarkably at peace in its presence.

"Brother," I said to it, "are you angel or demon?" On board ship, I had heard of both of these things, and, though I had only the haziest notion of what they might be and which was which, I knew one was good, the other evil.

The Creature gazed at me impassively. Then, though I thought it impossible for such a countenance to show emotion, it seemed to me that the creature smiled. I could see its black gums, and bright shining teeth.

"Perhaps a bit of both," it said. "But you have no need to fear me." A gull flew toward us from the sea and we both raised our heads to watch it circle above us, chattering noisily. "Brother, I am full of fear," I said, without willing myself to do so. The words merely appeared on my lips and were transformed into sound. "Can't you tell? I've been ill, shipwrecked, abandoned. I've lost everything. I am alone, adrift. Every rustle of leaves behind me frightens me, every slap of wave on the sand. Even my hopes frighten me, for who can tell what they might bring?"

To this outburst, the Creature gave no reply, merely continuing to gaze at me with a mixture – or so I felt – of amazement and compassion.

Within minutes, the sky, which had, as always, been clear, grew dark, clouds racing overhead, and I heard thunder for the first time since the night of the storm that brought me here. It was then that I saw a sail on the horizon.

"You have nothing to fear," the Creature said. "Goodbye." And with that it disappeared.

I felt both elated and bereft.

CHAPTER 7
A FACILITY FOR LANGUAGES

IN TIME, I DEVELOPED a facility for languages. Or, rather, I discovered that I'd had it all along.

During the several weeks of my recovery, with much time to merely think, I began to ponder the way languages echoed through me, like wind through a shell you hold to your ear. On board the *Al-Aqba*, our working language was Arabic. Even the first mate spoke it. At least, that was the way I remembered it. When I tried to recapture conversations, I couldn't be certain of the language. I remembered the meaning, not the words, their cadences and rhythms, not their sound. I thought of the mate, of his thick accent – yes, there was an accent, I was sure of that, but what kind?

I remembered the mate's name to be Fergus MacBay, and that he'd claimed to be a Scot. What strange circumstances might have led a Scotsman to take ship with a crew made up mostly of Arabs, I had no idea, and now, thinking of it again, I decided his name might really have been Macabee, or even Mahoud. And that perhaps he wasn't a Scotsman at all.

Whatever the everyday language of the *Al-Aqba*, I was sure that there were other languages spoken privately among the sailors. Jhamin, a stoker, was a tall pock-marked Algerian, a battle-scarred veteran of the FLN campaign against France, who, at night, in his bunk, would play the accordion and sing French love songs he learned from his mother, who'd worked in a café. I understood these simple laments but had failed to remark upon it, any more than my ability to understand the curses of several other men – a Serb, a Chechen and a Bosnian among them – who reverted to their native tongues when angry or fearful or in pain. One big black sailor from deep in Africa, a man with ribbed pink scars upon his muscled chest, whether from fights or religious ritual I didn't know, was particular fluent in oaths of his native Swahili. I understood them all – "son of a perverted camel," "may the python take your penis as its tongue" – and I remembered them. Oh, yes, I could remember nothing of my earlier life, but of those days on the *Al-Aqba*, following my recovery, it seemed as if much of it was imprinted on film, available for me to watch again and again on the screen just behind my eyelids. I remembered faces, the colour of eyes, the particular slant of the third mate's left eyebrow. He was Chinese, I was certain, who spoke both Mandarin and the local dialect of his home village. Yes, and now I began to doubt that Arabic was the language we spoke on the ship after all, rather – as it came back to me in sharper and sharper focus – that we were a floating Tower of Babel, men from various lands speaking a cacophony of languages and yet somehow all understanding each other. Could that really have been?

And the Creature that spoke to me on the island – what language did it speak? Again, I didn't know.

One thing I was certain of was that Arabic was the language of the *dhow* that rescued me from my island, the appropriately named *Dallal*, which means "going astray." The fishermen who rowed ashore were Syrians, swarthy, hook-nosed men with broad, furry eyebrows. It had been so long since I'd seen another of my species even these ugly brutes seemed beautiful. And they, fierce as they were, once they got a good look at me, more skeleton than man, only half-conscious and probably raving, treated me with respect, even deference. They didn't know I had survived the fly-bitten fever, yet they could see with their own eyes that I had survived Shipwreck Island. And, though I hadn't realized it, I was once again in the grip of a fever, not unlike the one through which I suffered earlier, as if the fever, or the malignancy that caused it, remained hidden in my body, seeking an opportunity to reassert itself. Although I'd usually had as much to eat as I wanted on the island, or so I thought, I was thin as a stick and just as hard, and the look in my pale eyes, they told me, was wild.

Yes, Arabic was what they'd spoken, these men, a rough Arabic of the streets – of the sea – and I'd understood it, fell into it, assumed that it was my own. What reason did I have to think otherwise?

They rowed back to the *Dallal* and hoisted me aboard. One of them volunteered his own berth for me and, after eating as much of a thin lentil soup as I could force down, I fell into a deep sleep and, during the several days sailing before we made land, drifted in and out of consciousness. When I finally awoke fully, I was on dry land, and in bed, between sheets dry and electric with static. The first face I saw when I opened my eyes was that of Sister Mark, a woman several years younger than I, with deep brown eyes and fair eyebrows but not another hair on her head. Across her smiling face was an irregular-shaped birthmark, a port-wine stain almost the size of an open hand, extending from just left of her nose to her right ear. She wore a loose-fitting gown that swung open when she bent over me, giving me an unobstructed view of her breasts, but I was in too weakened a state to appreciate them.

"Welcome, stranger," she said in a cultured Arabic, though she was too fair-skinned to be Arab. "You're alive, you're safe, you're all right."

I was, of course, immediately reminded of waking from that earlier fever on board the *Al-Aqba*, the face of the first mate hovering above me, his voice, urging me to live. But Sister Mark was no rough-talking sailor.

"Can you tell me how you feel?" she asked. "Do you have pain? Any discomfort?"

It took me a minute to take stock of my body. No pain, no discomfort, just a moment of blurriness upon opening my eyes that quickly passed. I was suddenly conscious of being hungry. "No, nothing like that," I said finally, and observed the concern written vividly over the nun's face ease. "Just..."

"What?" She leaned closer and I realized my voice was barely a whisper.

"Bereft."

The nun cocked her head and looked at me quizzically.

"You asked how I feel. Bereft. Alone. Lost. Frightened."

"You are no longer lost or alone, my friend," she said. "And there is nothing to be frightened of," reminding me of the Creature's last words to me on the island.

I learned that I was in a sort of hospital, a clinic in Jounieh, a small city on the Lebanese coast run by an obscure order of Maronite Catholic nuns, the Sisters of the Divine Crucifix. It was there that my talent for languages really began to emerge, though it wouldn't be until a month later, when another woman – certainly no nun - I visited in Beirut would decipher the mystery of the markings on my backside, and the implications of language and my mastery of it would hit home. Language, it turned out, would prove to be a way for me to make a living, to make my way in the bewildering world and to begin to find my way back to my self.

SISTER MARK ASKED ME what I could remember of my ordeal. I didn't tell her, not right away, that before a certain date I remembered nothing. In the attempt to describe to her my time on Shipwreck Island, I was surprised to discover that what memories I had, recent though they were, were unreliable. Almost two years later now, that has not changed.

Often, my memories disagree. I have two very different memories of my days on the island.

In one, there was a sandy beach, no more than fifty feet from the shoreline, grasses and bushes began to grow, leading into woods and to a stream, from which I was always able to slake my thirst. And the fruit growing on the trees by the stream and mushrooms which grew in abundance there provided me with plenty to eat. I never suffered from hunger or thirst or the elements, and my life on the island was not altogether unpleasant. I recorded some of these details and feelings in my journal, and have just recounted them again in this testimony.

Yet I also remember that the island was almost all sand, desert, with only a few sparse trees offering shade near an almost-dried up stream, which, even at its best, never provided more than a trickle. There were few animals and those there were eluded my snares, as fish eluded my spear, and I existed almost entirely on a stew of bitter roots and salt water, and, if I was lucky, handfuls of ants I scooped out of the sand. The sun was merciless, and I fell into a fever, not unlike the one I'd suffered on board ship after venturing onto that earlier island, the Isle of Flies. This too is recorded in my journal.

Which is the true memory? One or the other, surely, or are they perhaps both true?

I do know this: when my second fever broke and I awoke in clean, cool sheets in a bed in the Sisters of the Divine Crucifix's clinic, I was emaciated, weighing barely a hundred pounds, and too weak to walk.

"Where am I?" I asked Sister Mark, and she explained. We both spoke Arabic.

"How long have I been here?"

"Three days."

BOOK 2
Sisters

CHAPTER 8
THE JOURNAL

THE SISTERS OF THE Divine Crucifix were a formidable group of women. As I would learn from them, they not only sought to be brides of Christ but to embrace the pain of his death and the ecstasy of his resurrection. As such, they wore no habits. In fact, they wore very little in the way of clothing, going about their daily business – both prayers and tending to the sick of the community – much as God had made them, heads shaved and naked but for loose white poncho-like robes, made of sackcloth and open at the sides, worn more for the convenience of their pockets, filled with tongue depressors, stethoscopes and other medical apparatus, than for the scant modesty they provided. They showed no sign of modesty, or shame, and their appearance and demeanour dared men to look on them with either desire or reproach.

I asked Sister Mark about those peculiarities of their appearance and she answered matter-of-factly, as if reciting from a memorized script:

"The better for God to see into our minds," she replied to the first question.

"And the robes?"

"The better for God to see into our hearts."

The Sisters all took the names of men who were important to Jesus: Matthew, Mark, Luke and John, and the other apostles and disciples. Sister Paul, the abbess, was the oldest and was a formidable presence. She was a tall woman, six foot easily, with broad shoulders, wearing a tunic no more modest than those of the other nuns but trimmed with red piping. Thick tufts of white hair were visible under her arms. Her eyebrows, which grew like hedges above her thick-lensed, wire-framed spectacles, were completely white, and her face was deeply lined, with bristly white hairs in her nostrils. She appeared to be someone not to easily cross.

The sisters' clinic administered to women and children only. Many small families, the survivors of men killed in the civil war I learned, had been sputtering along for a number of years, living in a makeshift camp of tents and rough-hewn shacks that had sprung up around the clinic.

The working language of this order was Italian, Italy being the place of origin of the order's founder, and it was with great delight that they discovered I both understood and could speak it. Before that, they'd spoken to me only in Arabic. Communication between us having been eased, Sister Mark, my prime caregiver, took it upon herself to relay to me the strange tale of my rescue.

The seamen who had come upon me and delivered me unconscious and just barely alive to the care of the Sisters were fishermen, half a dozen strong, but not locals. They'd said they were Syrians, but rather than Arabic, had spoken a language unfamiliar to the nuns, or so Sister Mark said, which surprised me, as I remembered it as Arabic, but perhaps it was Turkish. One of the fishermen, though, was schooled by nuns and priests and retained enough Latin that he'd been able to convey the fundamentals of what had transpired. Still, Sister Mark told me, she was sure she hadn't properly understood much of what he had tried to tell her. There was no way to confirm what they told the nuns or to acquire more information, though, as, having taken on fuel and supplies, they set off again, and I was never able to thank them properly.

Several days out of Baniyas, their home port, the fisherman told Sister Mark, they'd been caught up in a violent storm – this was weeks earlier, so quite possibly it was the same storm that sunk the *Al-Aqba* and shipwrecked me. When the storm abated they'd found themselves far off course in unfamiliar waters, on a becalmed sea, the single-masted lateen sail of their *dhow* useless. They floated for days and days, seemingly endlessly, their provisions and water growing perilously low. Finally, weak, dehydrated and desperate, they floated within sight of an island that appeared on none of their charts and two of the men set off in a dinghy to seek water and food. Hearing this, I became agitated, fearing that the misadventure which led to my initial fever was about to be repeated, but no, these fishermen found no infected insects, just an emaciated man dressed in filthy rags, all but incoherent. There was no sign of anyone else on the island.

The fishermen found my stream of fresh water, fruit-laden trees, and the embers of a fire in my pit. And dried fish, hanging from a tree. "They thought this was strange," Sister Mark said, "because they were casting their nets for days but had seen no sign of any fish in those waters, or so he told me." Stranger still was a bowl of wine set by the fire.

"Wine?" I interrupted. "You must have misunderstood. I had no wine."

"No, he was most insistent that it was wine, and good wine, sweet and dark. They assumed a bottle or two had washed up with you from the shipwreck, and that you'd saved some, yet they found no bottle."

"No, no bottle, no wine," I insisted. "And no bowl."

Sister Mark turned her face away, leaning over to plump my pillow.

"At any rate," she said, "the fisherman told me they found enough food and water to provide for them all for several days." Remarkably, no sooner had the small party returned to the *dhow* with their castaway than a wind sprang up, filling their sail, and they began to be blown at a rapid pace in an easterly direction. Within a day, they were in familiar waters off the coast of Lebanon. They came ashore at the first landfall they found, Jounieh, not far north of Beirut, with the hopes of taking on supplies and finding a refuge at which to leave me. That accomplished, and their story told, they'd set off again.

The nuns, Sister Mark told me, had examined the journal in the carpenter's apron that accompanied me, in hopes of learning something about their new patient, but they could make no sense of its strange language.

"Let me see it." I said, "Perhaps I can decipher it for you."

Sister Mark looked at me warily. "Sister Paul has it," she said, referring to the abbess. Then, perhaps thinking that I might try to reclaim it by force, added, "Under lock and key." She pursed her lips and I could tell she was trying to decide something. "Wait," she said, and bustled away. A few minutes later, she was back, journal in hand. It was half the size of an ordinary book, with a dark brown leather cover to distinguish it – not the sort of thing a carpenter would ordinarily carry among his tools. The pages were dog-eared and stiff with salt. I opened it to the first page and began to read, effortlessly translating into Italian for Sister Mark's benefit.

"February 3. Terrible storm blew in from the east. Winds stronger than any my shipmates have known. Despite all our efforts, we could not keep the ship aright. I fear multiple lives were lost. I write this the following day from the safety of a lifeboat."

I would have continued but Sister Mark interrupted me. "You read with no difficulty at all. What language is that?"

I laughed, and assured her, taking pains not to seem boastful, that I appeared to have a peculiar talent for languages. Then I glanced down at the page. The words were written in an alphabet I had no memory of having seen before, not Arabic but similar, yet I had no trouble understanding it, and I was able to identify it. "It's Aramaic."

"Ah," Sister Mark said. Her face registered surprise and she looked away briefly. When she faced me again, she had composed her features into a mask of calm. "Read more."

"February 5: To my continued astonishment, I am alive."

"This is the second time I've died, or seemed to, and been resurrected."

I paused and looked up. Sister Mark's eyes had closed and her discoloured face had taken on a look of deep concentration.

I continued, telling of the attack of insects, the fever they gave us, and the death of all the infected sailors but me. And how the first mate pronounced my survival as a miracle.

I glanced up from the page, saw Sister Mark's smile, her lips describing a bow, her teeth shining and white.

I read on, relating the details of the storm and the sinking of the *Al-Aqba*. And how I and a number of others wound up in a lifeboat, and how, with neither food nor water, we managed to survive for several days until, one by one, my companions died.

I stopped reading and looked up. Sister Mark appeared completely absorbed in the tale I'd been recounting. She smiled when she noticed me looking at her. I asked for a glass of water and she brought it immediately.

"Should I read more?"

"Yes, please."

Once again, I picked up the journal.

Sister Mark grimaced when I read of how some of us grew mad with thirst, and she made a sound of disgust when I came to the attempt by a few to eat the flesh of our fellows who died. She was frowning, wringing her hands.

"Should I go on, Sister?"

She nodded.

Her eyes filled with tears as I read how Mohan cried uncontrollably at the thought of never again seeing his wife and children.

I paused to allow her to compose herself.

"We're coming to an end of this," I said. "A sad end, I'm afraid. Perhaps..."

"No, read more, please," Sister Mark said.

I read on, relating how Mohan had chosen to end his life on his own terms. "He sank immediately and the waters where he disappeared calmed. I stared, amazed at that square of water, certain that he would surface in a moment and that I might be able to reach over the gunnel and grab hold of his collar, but for him there was no resurrection. He was gone, I was alone in the boat, alone in the wide expanse of calm ocean and sky."

"God have mercy on his soul," Sister Mark whispered.

I paused, feeling overwhelmed by the memory. Sister Mark raised her head and recited a prayer in Latin.

"You know," I said, "I don't think I'd even known Mohan on the ship, not that I remember, but in the few days we spent together on the lifeboat he became – what's the expression? – my best friend in the world. Then he was gone. Just like everyone else."

I wiped my eyes to clear them before continuing.

"Night is falling and the wind has picked up again," I read. "I can write no more."

Sister Mark was looking at me with a countenance that combined pity and surprise, not dissimilar to that of the Creature the last time we'd been together. I looked away, then down again to the journal.

"There's no more to this entry," I said, and thumbed through the rest of the journal's pages. "There are many more entries, but from this point on they were all written on the island where I washed up."

"Enough," Sister Mark said abruptly. She got to her feet, reached out and took the journal from me. "I can't hear any more. You rest now." She turned sharply and left the room. I lay quietly, gazing up at the crack in the ceiling I was becoming so familiar with, my thoughts with Mohan. And wondering idly what I knew of airplanes, to have used one in my riddle. But within a few minutes Sister Mark was back.

"Here." She offered me the journal, and resumed her spot in the chair at the foot of my bed. "I'm sorry, that was rude. Carry on."

"Not at all, Sister."

Sister Mark and I gazed at each other. I could see she was eager to learn what happened to me next. And, as my memory of my landfall was hazy, I too was curious to see what I'd written.

Sister Mark closed her eyes and I found the proper page.

"This picks up a few days later. Should I...?"

"Yes, go ahead."

"February 15 (though I can only hazard a guess as to the true date): I write a few days following the events I will now record." I recounted how the storm grew wilder and the dory capsized, leaving me to blindly swim until, miraculously, I found myself only half-conscious on the beach of an island. And how, in the morning, following the sound of singing birds, I crawled to a stream from which I was able to drink.

I closed the journal and sighed, having suddenly grown tired. "I was alive, and grateful for that," I said. "There's more, but..."

"Another day," Sister Mark said. She took the journal from my hands to return it to the care of Sister Paul.

"Don't worry," she assured me. "It will be safe."

I'VE DESCRIBED THE TIME of my seclusion on the island, my shipwreck period, in terms of months, even years. That certainly is how it felt, an almost endless period of loneliness and total isolation. Devoid of memory, I truly was alone, as alone in my body and uncluttered mind as a man can be. Yet perception can be deceptive. My impression was that I lived fairly well on the island, that water was plentiful, that trees were laden with fruit, that meat and fish were easy to acquire. And yet, the shipwrecked survivor those fishermen delivered to the nuns at Jounieh was emaciated, his ribs a cage of bone from which skin hung like wind-deserted sail. So too can the passage of time deceive. The journal I kept and which the fishermen brought with me in my carpenter's apron makes that quite clear.

The entries written in the lifeboat and the first from the island are dated. Those that follow are not. The first of these describes the island from the vantage point of the beach where I spent most of my time and the pool of water, and records my surprise at having found my leather apron and the notebook and pencil.

I smiled when I read of my resolve to write in the journal every day.

It was a reasonably reliable record of my time on the island, a time that felt as if measured by months, perhaps even years. And yet, thumbing through its pages, I saw there were only forty entries.

CHAPTER 9
SMALL MIRACLES

AS FAR AS I KNEW – could remember – the Sisters of the Divine Crucifix were the first women I'd ever known or seen. It was inevitable that I would fall in love with one of them. That was Sister Mark.

She was among the youngest of the nuns, with dark, flashing eyes and seemingly no self-consciousness about the stain on her face, or the glimpses of her body her costume afforded. She'd grown up in a devout Catholic family in a small town near Naples and joined the Sisterhood at sixteen, with very limited exposure to men.

In some ways, she was the perfect woman for me to fall in love with, since I had even less experience with women than she with men.

You must understand that for the immeasurable time on the island, I had the company only of myself and, briefly, the mysterious Creature. And during the undetermined time prior to the shipwreck, aboard ships, the company only of men. And beyond that, no memory. My knowledge of women, therefore, was completely blank. I had no memory of a mother, a sister, a favourite aunt, a doting grandmother. No memory of the village girls at play, their laughter and song rising above their heads like

swirling birds. No memory of the girl who first enchanted me –
I say this with the certainty that there was such a girl, based on
my subsequent knowledge of human behaviour and emotion,
based on my own limited experience, observation and the voluminous reading of novels. No memory of the woman who first
instructed me in the art of the flesh – if there even was such
a woman. Whatever carnal knowledge I may or may not have
had in the period prior to the loss of my memory, I was in every
real sense of the word a virgin. Indeed, before my first sight of
Sister Mark I had only the haziest notion of what a woman was.
I had not seen one, had not been in one's presence. All I knew of
women was based on glimpses of the giant mermaid carved into
the prow of the ship, grainy photographs in an old yellowing
newspaper from Cairo that circulated in the galley, and part of
a deck of pornographic playing cards, the prized possession of
a Sinhalese sailor called Sunil – twenty-three black and white
photographs of naked women performing various poses, alone
or with men, images that both excited and confused me. All of
which was fodder for lewd jokes of my shipmates, who were
infinitely amused by my lack of knowledge. This same lack
of knowledge in other areas, table manners and hygiene, say,
caused curiosity and some amusement, and the blank page that
represented my family provoked sympathy, even compassion.
Yet the subject of women was one of endless hilarity for the men
of our ship. So their jokes, their ribald tales, their crude hand
and arm gestures in attempts to evoke the image of women in
the air – that, and my imagination, was all I had.

Despite this lack of knowledge, I burned with desire. Echoes of
the sailors' taunts and my imagination produced in my slumber
during the endless days and nights on the island dreams of
furious passion from which I would awake soaked in sweat and

other secretions which, at first, terrified me, then, perversely, reassured me – once I realized what the sticky, slightly sweet and salty emanation was. I took it as a periodic reminder of my mortality and, hence, proof of my existence. I dreamt, therefore I was alive. And, though I had no knowledge of women, they populated my dreams in abundance, evidence, I imagined, of memory bursting to break free of its bonds. But just as surely I knew that I was bereft of one other essential: "A man who has not had a woman canna be a real man," the first mate had growled during one of those moments of hilarity among the crew at my expense. When I'd looked around me in bewilderment, another sailor, a lopsided man with blackened teeth yet a sweet smile nonetheless, explained more simply: "It's a woman who makes a man a man." I still hadn't really understood, no, not really, but on the island, where I lived so intimately with my thoughts, that exchange haunted me, and I was determined to discover what I could, as quickly as I could, should I ever be restored to the larger world.

Now, having regained consciousness and was on the way to regaining my health and strength, that was among my earliest thoughts: salvation, a life to resume, a woman to know, manhood to acquire.

And Sister Mark became the object of my desire.

On the day after I regained consciousness, she asked my name and I had to confess I didn't know. "I'm a carpenter, and that's what they called me on ship, *Najjar.*"

"That's not a proper name," Sister Mark said, and she began to call me Adam – an appropriate name for me, she said, as "he was the first man." Soon the other nuns adopted that name for me as well.

Whenever Sister Mark called me Adam, she would blush, and the banter between the first mate and the black-toothed sailor would come rushing into my mind. I had only the haziest notion of what either of them meant about what makes a man a man, but the sight of Sister Mark's breasts swinging free beneath her tunic stirred me in a way that was foreign to me, and frightening.

I knew no better, so one day, as she sat on the edge of my bed, I reached out, without thinking, and touched her breast. She recoiled as sharply if she'd been touched by fire but said nothing. After a moment, she sat down again and our conversation continued as if nothing had happened. But I knew better than to repeat that gesture. Instead, I began to dream of women.

In one such dream, I was back on my island, my empire of sand. I was lying on the beach, dozing, the feel of sand on my limbs and back, the hot tongue of the sun on my chest and face, the sound of waves gentle in my ears. I felt a presence, opened my eyes, raised my head. Beside me sat the Creature that had briefly been my companion, this time it had the face and deep-breasted chest of a woman, of Sister Mark. I woke with a start, bathed in sweat.

AFTER I'D BEEN at the clinic for several days, I was visited by a doctor. I awoke to find him standing at the foot of my bed, a short, pudgy man with a dark complexion but remarkably pale hands, wearing a white linen suit. A stethoscope and a large silver cross hung from his neck. "I am Doctor Shamaoun," he announced when he noticed me stir. "And how is our patient today?" Although I understood him perfectly, I didn't immediately recognize the language he was speaking.

"I'm alive," I said, with a weak smile.

"Ah, you speak French, good, good. And alive, yes, alive is good, very good indeed."

"I didn't know there were any men here," I said. "I've only seen the sisters."

"Oh, I come and go. The good sisters tolerate me." He gave me a smile that showed white, even teeth. He sat beside me on the bed to take my pulse and feel my neck just below the ears, revealing that his hands were as soft as they were pale. He peered into my eyes, nose and throat, listened with the stethoscope to my chest. "More than alive," he said with satisfaction. "Rest and food, that will set you right. You're skinny as a rag, my friend."

He glanced over his shoulder, then back at me. "Tell me, sir, what is your name?"

"I don't know. The nuns here call me Adam, a little joke of theirs, I guess."

"I see. I was told your memory is poor."

"Not poor. Nonexistent."

"Completely?"

"Almost."

"Do you know what year this is?"

"Nineteen eighty-one. Sister Mark told me."

"Ah. And the month?"

"March. I'm sorry, I forget the day. No, April, I saw Sister Mark turn the page."

"Very good. And where you are?"

"Lebanon. A place near Beirut."

"And your home?"

I shook my head.

"Your family?

Another shake of the head.

"You speak French beautifully. Are you French?"

"I don't know."

"This is not so good." He consulted his wristwatch. "Perhaps we should have a neurologist see you. There are some good ones in Beirut."

"Will such a doctor restore my memory?" I asked in frustration. "Bring back my family? Bring back whomever else I may have loved or may have loved me?"

The doctor stood up, smoothing the creases of his pants. "We'll see how you progress. Now, rest, eat."

I didn't see him again until my last night at the clinic, almost a month later, and on that occasion his only words to me were "You look fine. Goodbye and good luck."

DURING THE FIRST WEEK that I stayed with the sisters, slowly recovering my strength, I had many talks with Sister Mark. She was fascinated by my loss of memory and equally so by my language abilities. I restrained myself from touching her or pouring out my adoration of her. I had already learned that nuns forsake marriage and sex and realized such behaviour would only embarrass her.

"Tell me what you do remember," she said, like a child begging for a story.

"Not very much," I said. I intuitively felt, though, that some things were best not mentioned. "Just the little I relearned on board ship after my fever and until the storm that wrecked us."

"Like what?" Sister Mark had a mischievous smile on her face.

"Personal things, how to do this and that. How to read. The

Qu'ran was my textbook. And our history: the ship was called the *Al-Aqba*, out of the port of Muscat in Oman. Our cargo was barrels of crude oil. But that time was so brief, and I was weak, lying in bed for a few days, just as I am now, then gradually regaining strength. I was just about normal when the storm hit."

"And of your time on the island?"

"Again, not much really. I was weak, after so long in the dory, and the days were much the same. I wrote in a journal, as you know, but there was little to record: 'walked to the beach, tried to catch a fish, picked fruit from a tree.' That sort of thing. Thinking back, I can't really distinguish one day from another."

That was not entirely true – there were some things that occurred on the island I remembered very clearly, yet I hesitated to tell Sister Mark about them.

"So my memory is not a completely blank slate, but mostly so. Now I'm stocking it with memories of this place, the wonderful soup you brought me last night, this morning's coffee, your many kindnesses."

I wanted to add, *and the touch of your breast, the sight of your lips, your eyes,* but I knew better.

"And your ability with language?"

"I have no idea. That goes back to the ship; it just appeared when I woke from my fever. I remember I heard a clamour of sounds, then suddenly something changed and I understood everything I heard. I wasn't even aware that different languages were being spoken." Sister Mark brought a portable radio into my room, tuned to a Beirut station that played a variety of music, which was a wonder to me – both the radio and the music. I pointed to the radio now. "Like fine-tuning that station dial – the sound is fuzzy, then suddenly clear."

She was eager to hear more from the journal, so I read a few passages to her every day, when I came to the skull that appeared to be speaking, I thought it best to warn her. "Some of what you'll hear, well, you may think these are the ravings of a madman. Maybe I *was* mad, when I wrote them, maybe I'm mad now."

Despite my disclaimer, or perhaps exacerbated by it, I could see she was upset when I read about the skull and the first appearance of strange animals. "Perhaps I imagined them, I told her – and it occurred to me that perhaps I had. After that, I was careful to leave out any references to the Creature.

SISTER MARK ALSO became fascinated with, as she put it, my "relationship with God." She was shocked that I had no knowledge of God, nor even a clear sense of the idea of God.

"God was looking out for you," she'd said when I told her, on one of my early days in her care, about the shipwreck, and I immediately thought of the Creature that had become my occasional companion there. Was the Creature God? No, that idea was preposterous. We'd been speaking Italian and she used the word *"Dio."* Another time, saying a prayer in Latin, I heard her invoke *"Deus."*

On another day, in all innocence, I asked her about the stain on her face. "Some of my shipmates had tattoos," I told her, "but I haven't seen anything like this."

Her smile was wistful. "No, nothing like a tattoo. This was the hand of God caressing my face."

"He does that?" I asked, genuinely surprised. "He touches people?"

"Of course. He touches us all, in different ways."

"What is this God you speak of?" I asked her. "On board ship, I heard many of my mates refer to a God of some sort, with different names – I heard 'God have mercy,' 'God damn,' 'Allah be praised,' 'the will of Allah.' I overhear your prayers – forgive me, Sister Mark, for listening – and your talk of a just God, a loving God, a vengeful God. How can God be all these things?"

This came pouring out of me and Sister Mark was taken aback. "You have no knowledge of God, Adam, really?"

"How could I, Sister? You know I lost my memory."

"But since then, have you not come to know God?"

"No." Again, though, I thought of the Creature.

"How can that be?"

"I don't know. Wait, let me think. Is God an animal? A wild creature?"

"Certainly not. What are you thinking?"

"Nothing, Sister. No, I have no knowledge of God."

Sister Mark grew silent, obviously thinking deeply. "God is the Creator," she began, slowly, gently, as if talking to a child. "He created the whole world – the heavens, the land, the sea – and all its creatures. He created man – the first man, Adam, your namesake, and from Adam's body he created Eve, the first woman. We all" – she waved her hand to indicate everything we could see around us and beyond – "are their descendants." She paused. "And He is, as you said, a God of love, but also a vengeful God and a just God."

Despite the simplicity of Sister Mark's explanation, I still had only a hazy notion of what God was. "Love and vengeance. How can that be? They're opposites."

"That is not for us to know," she said simply, bowing her head.

"So also a God of contradictions."

"It might appear that way to us, but for God there are no contradictions."

"So a God of mystery."

"Yes, life is full of mystery, my dear Adam, and God is the greatest of them. And he work his wonders in mysterious ways."

She rose and left my room, returning in a moment with a book, the *Bible*. She opened it to the first chapter, Genesis. "Here, read."

Which I did, fascinated, until my eyes grew heavy. In my sleep I returned to my island. I'm walking on the beach. Above me, in the cloudless sky, the black gull circles, slowly descending. It flies so close I can see the brightness of its eye, then it ascends again. I feel the presence of the Creature beside me. "Are you God?" I ask. There is no reply, yet I persist: "If you are, if you are God, why have you done this to me? What have I done to offend you?" The Creature remains silent and takes my hand in one large paw. Despite the claws, the touch is gentle, and I feel a flow of warmth rising through my hand, my arm, into my chest and belly.

EVEN MORE CONFUSING than the nature of God were the various ways people had established to worship him, what Sister Mark called "religion." Counting on her fingers, she mentioned Judaism, Islam, Hinduism and the various arms of Christianity, ending with an explanation of the Roman Catholic hierarchy, from priest to bishop to cardinal to pope. And Jesus Christ, whom, she said, sat at the right hand of God.

"Jesus is His son?" I was confused.

"Yes."

"And all these other people, the priests and so on, what do they have to do with God?"

Sister Mark shook her head. "They're all God's servants, as are we sisters."

"I thought you said we were *all* God's servants."

"Yes, but in different ways. We all serve God, in many ways. The Church exists to give glory to God but also to instruct people, to bring comfort to them..."

"Like a ship," I said, suddenly seeing. "The church is a ship. The pope is the captain, but a captain can't sail a ship on his own, he needs the mates, the seamen, all the way down to the lowliest deck hand."

"That's it exactly," Sister Mark said, beaming.

"I still don't understand," I said, confused again. "The church isn't really a ship. A ship needs all its hands to function. If we all worship God as individuals, if we all serve God, in different ways, then what do we need all these others for? This 'church' you speak of? Can't God instruct us directly?"

"Yes...." She began, then shook her head again, this time in exasperation.

I NOTICED THAT the sisters gathered regularly in a chapel in the centre of their complex for organized prayer, which Sister Mark explained to me was "communication with God. It's our chance to speak directly to Him.

"When we pray together, we speak with one voice, and our voice is louder."

I couldn't help smiling. "God is hard of hearing?"

Sister Mark frowned. "No, you silly, blasphemous man. But God is pleased by our harmony."

That answer pleased *me*. "But you, Sister Mark, you're not with the others right now for Matins, and I've noticed other times when you were not in the chapel with the others. Why is that?"

"Our lives are more than just prayer, Adam."

"Is God displeased by the absence of your voice in the harmony?"

"No, of course not, because I pray even when I'm not with the others. I'm praying right now. I pray for your recovery and for God to restore to you all that you've lost – if that is his will. God hears my voice as clearly when I'm here as when I'm in the chapel." She paused. "Just as He hears your voice, Adam."

"My voice? But I'm not praying, Sister Mark."

"Yes you are, whether you know it or not. Our lives *are* prayer."

I ASKED SISTER MARK what she meant by God's will. "You said you prayed that God restore things to me, if that was his will."

She smiled, happy to have another opportunity to instruct me. "We don't know what's in God's mind, his plan. A sick person might pray to be made well, and sometimes God will grant that prayer – but God may want this person to be sick and so the prayer goes unanswered." She held up a hand. "I know what you're going to say – 'why would God want someone to be sick?' It sounds awful, I know, but we don't know God's will. Maybe the sickness serves some purpose that will reveal itself later. Perhaps it's a punishment, perhaps a test. In your case, restoring your memory seems like a simple, logical thing, but God may have reason to have your mind a clean slate. Again, we don't know. He works His wonders in mysterious ways."

I mused on this. "What possible purpose could my loss of memory serve?"

The exasperated tone crept into Sister Mark's voice again. "As I told you, we don't know. Think, Adam...there were eight of you in the lifeboat? Is that right? And one by one God took them, until only you were left. Do you think that was an accident? Can't you see that God must have had a reason for sparing you?

"You know that with certainty because you know with certainty, or believe, there is such a God," I said. "I don't know that, so I can't believe in the reason."

A look of mild shock crossed Sister Mark's face. "That knowledge, that belief that I have, is called faith," she said. "You've lost yours, I'm afraid."

"Or never had it."

"Oh, we all have it, Adam. We're born with faith. The evils of the world, or the trials of the world – and you've certainly had your share of the trials – rob us of it. Right now, Adam, you are much like the original Adam – with your mind a blank, you are as if you were brand new." She paused, hesitating. "You are without sin. Maybe *that* was God's purpose. To erase all your sins, to restore you to innocence."

I wasn't sure what exactly she meant by sin, I was getting tired, too tired to continue this conversation. "I don't know, Sister Mark. You asked if I thought my survival was an accident. Couldn't it be that God is just another word for accident? For coincidence?"

As I drifted into sleep, I wondered idly what sins I might have had, sins so bad some God felt the need to erase them.

ON ANOTHER OCCASION, I asked Sister Mark if God was a person, as she and I were.

She seemed shocked. "Certainly not. Where do you get such foolish ideas?"

"You call Him 'him.' And Heavenly Father, our Father in Heaven."

Now she was vexed. "These are figures of speech, do you understand? Ah, it's too complex for me. I'll ask Sister Paul to explain it to you. Should I fetch her now?"

"No, there's no hurry. But Sister, what about Jesus? He *is* a person, isn't that right?"

"Yes, Jesus was a man."

"And the son of God?"

"Yes. But born of a woman, the Blessed Virgin Mary."

"But God can do anything, isn't that what you said?"

"Yes, but..."

"Then he didn't need Mary. He could have created Jesus himself, the way he did Adam. Isn't that right?"

"Yes, of course, He could have. But He didn't." Sister Mark's smile turned into a glare. "This is another of God's mysteries." She paused, thinking. "You know..."

"What is it, Sister?"

"I've hesitated to mention this. You were weak, confused. You're much stronger now."

"I am. Tell me."

"The fishermen who rescued you, who brought you to us, I told you, one of them was a Catholic. He said their boat was laden with fish..."

"Was it?"

"But that before they found you, they'd caught practically nothing. He said... everything changed when they found you.

Their nets filled with fish, more than their boat could hold. A wind sprang up and blew them quickly to port. It was, he said... like a miracle."

"I've heard that word, Sister, but don't really know its meaning."

She looked at me gravely. "Something Divine. Something from God."

We sat in silence for a minute.

"He said he thought you were perhaps the One."

I shook my head, smiling. "The one what, Sister Mark?"

She too shook her head.

By the time I left the Sisters, a couple of weeks later, I had learned much more about the various religions different peoples believed in, and their gods, but my idea of God Himself remained hazy.

I LAY IN BED at the nuns' clinic for a week, gradually growing stronger. Finally, I mustered the strength and courage to get up. I walked shakily down a corridor and out into a garden of fig trees, not yet in bloom. It was early April. Two boys were playing hide and seek among the trees and when they saw me walking there they abandoned their game and came to investigate me. I already knew that few men ever came onto the sisters' property, so the sight of me must have piqued their curiosity. The older of the two introduced himself, Antun, and his brother Jergyes, sons of one of the widows living beside the clinic. We sat down on a bench beneath a fig tree and Antun jabbered in Arabic. They seemed like likeable boys, perhaps twelve and ten years old, and, Antun told me, often helped out with odd jobs at the clinic.

Jergyes said not a word, and after a few minutes, I turned to him. "You're the quiet one, aren't you?"

"He doesn't like to speak," Antun said quickly, as Jergyes looked down at his dirty bare feet.

"Oh, and why is that?"

"People make fun sometimes."

"Oh? Does he make jokes?"

"No, he… my brother talks funny, that's all."

"Jergyes, if I promise not to laugh or make fun, will you say something to me? I'd like to hear."

The boy's eyes were fixed to his feet. I said nothing more and waited. Gradually, he raised his head. His eyes were black pools that seemed to pull me in.

"I c-c-c-c-ca-ca-can't g-g-g-get…," he began, and those pools filled with tears.

I reached out and touched his hair, then his forehead. "Slow down, Jergyes. Take a breath. A big breath. Another." I let my hand wander down his face, over his cheek, along his nose, to his mouth. I let the tips of my fingers rest on his lips for a moment before dropping my hand. I had nothing in mind, just the impulse to touch him. "I too had an affliction once," I said, surprising myself, for I had no memory of an affliction, no idea what it might have been. The words had just come, and continued: "I overcame it. You can too."

The boy looked up me, his eyes wide.

"Now just stand there and breathe. Think about what you want to say, imagine yourself saying it. Can you do that?"

The boy nodded.

"Can you see yourself?"

Again, a nod, tentative.

"Can you see yourself talking? Can you hear yourself?"

"Yes."

I stood up and put my hands on the boy's shoulders.

"Speak then."

"What, what should I say?" Those words came out of his mouth perfectly, but he seemed unaware.

"There, see?" I said. "That wasn't so hard, was it now? Say anything you want. Say, 'my name is Jergyes.' Say 'this is my brother, Antun.' Say 'I am very happy to make your acquaintance.'"

The boy took another deep breath. "My name is Jergyes," he began.

WORD SPREAD QUICKLY. The next day, when I ventured out for a walk, the garden was filled with widows, calling my name: "Adam" and another, unfamiliar name, "Isa." But even before that, Sister Mark had come into my room, where I lay dozing, and fell to her knees beside my bed.

"Sister Mark, what are you doing?" I swung my legs over the side of the bed and got to my feet. "Get up."

She did, but she wouldn't look at me. "The fisherman was right," she said.

FATHER LORENZO, a Maronite priest whom Sister Mark referred to as the nuns' confessor, without explaining, paid me a visit. Aside from me, the priest and Doctor Shamaoun were the only men to penetrate the cloistered world of the clinic.

"I hear you're feeling better, that you're up and about," the old man said, without bothering to introduce himself or greet me. He sat himself down gingerly on the edge of my bed. Wisps of thin white hair splayed across a mostly bald head. His scalp, narrow face and hands were mottled with age spots. His body was concealed beneath a loose-fitting black cassock with a row of white buttons down the front and a stiff-looking white collar.

"I am, Father," I replied. I'd heard Sister Mark and other nuns refer to him that way, the word "father" felt odd on my tongue, false. I had no idea who my father was, but it certainly wasn't this old man.

"Would you like me to hear your confession?"

"Confession? I don't understand."

The priest leveled his gaze at me, brown eyes softened by a milky veneer. "Confession of your sins. Surely, you…"

"Perhaps *you* don't understand, sir. I've been ill, I've lost my memory. If I've sinned, I have no knowledge of it." I gave him a rueful look. "I have to admit I have only a vague idea of what sins even are."

"None of us is without sin," he insisted, frowning.

"That may be so, but…" I raised my hands in a gesture of help-lessness. "Gluttony. Sister Mark told me that was a sin. Perhaps I've eaten too much? On the island where I was shipwrecked, I was sometimes hungry, so perhaps I can be forgiven for eating too much here."

"You're mocking me, young man," the priest said, rising. "I understand you have some high and mighty notions about yourself. You'd be wise to tend to your mortal soul." He turned and left without another word.

BY THIS TIME, I'd regained my strength and some weight, but the Sisters of the Divine Crucifix allowed me to stay a while, giving me some simple tasks to perform – chopping wood, tending to the fire – and paying me a small wage. I was comfortable there, and learning things every day, yet I was burning to see more of the world – all the more so after walking along the beach and, once out of the cover of the canopy of trees, I saw the skyline of Jounieh – not so much a village, as I'd thought, but a town - and beyond the gleaming white statue of Our Lady of Lebanon. As soon as I felt I was able, I announced that I was ready to go, would leave the following morning.

Sister Paul nodded her head gravely. "Yes, you must leave us," she said. "You've been resurrected, Adam, Now you must go out into the world and preach your gospel."

I looked at her curiously. "I have no gospel to preach. I don't even know the meaning of the word."

But Sister Paul had already turned and was walking away, and didn't hear me, or pretended not to.

Kitchen duty rotated among the nuns, and in the afternoon, Sister Luke told me that she and Sister Andrew, in charge that day, had planned something special. They'd even invited Father Lorenzo and Doctor Shamaoun. I volunteered to help prepare the meal.

"We need enough fish for eighteen," Sister Luke told me, and I set out along the beach with fishing pole and baskets, and the young brothers Antun and Jergyes, who had become my constant companions when I was outside. We were heading for a pier where fishermen often had good luck, on the way we passed a shallow lagoon where several men were picking oysters.

We stopped to watch them. "That looks easy," Jergyes said. "And fun."

I put down my pole and we stepped into the warm, shallow water, which was studded with oysters. Within a few minutes we'd filled our baskets.

When we got back to the compound, we found a large group of widows and children milling around outside the gates. They fell silent when they saw me, and some of them dropped to their knees. Inside, Sisters Andrew and Luke were cutting up vegetables.

"No fish," I said, "but look."

The nuns' eyes grew large. "Just the thing," Sister Luke said. "We'll make a stew." The nuns looked at each other. "But did you see the people at the gate, Adam? They've heard you're leaving."

"That's all right. Why not invite them to eat with us?"

"Oh! Did you see how many are outside? And more are coming, I fear. We can't feed them all."

I looked at the boys – Jergyes was grinning. "Yes, we can, Sister. Get more pots. And we need some pails, as many as we can carry."

The crowd outside had grown as the boys and I left with our empty pails. I swung the gates open. "Come in, come in, all are welcome."

CHAPTER 10
A CITY OF WOMEN

THE MORNING AFTER my farewell meal with the nuns, Sister Mark walked me to the bus stop. As we waited for the bus, I told her something of my jumbled feelings: "I'm like a child leaving home for the first time, excited but frightened. Who knows what awaits me? Maybe I'll step off the bus and an old woman will approach me, exclaiming 'my son.' Maybe I'll be able to reclaim my old life. But what are the chances of that? No, I believe today is the beginning of my life in a real sense."

Sister Mark nodded and squeezed my hand. "New beginnings are good, Adam. Either way, no matter what happens, God will be watching you."

That didn't seem too likely but I nodded and squeezed her hand back. When we saw the bus approaching, she kissed me on the cheek and turned away in tears. "Go with God, Adam," she said.

I'd left the journal, wrapped in the same oilcloth that protected it in the cold water of the Mediterranean, in Sister Paul's care. Sister Mark had suggested it and it seemed like a reasonable thing to do, since I wasn't sure what lay ahead of me, yet I came to regret it later.

And so I set out down the coast and into Beirut. I had heard that it was a city of many nationalities and languages, and I hoped to find some clues to my past there.

I entered the city, as I'd told the nun I would, like a child. With so little in my memory – just a jumble of images from the *Al-Aqba*, the storm and shipwreck, the lifeboat, the island and the events and lessons of my time at the clinic – I was, as Sister Mark put it, a blank slate, waiting to be written on. I had replied to her, only half joking, "I have to learn again to be a human being," and I learned much, including the niceties of eating with knife and fork and spoon, and brushing my teeth. I'd heard the radio, seen newspapers, observed the curious operation of the telephone in Sister Paul's office. I'd learned to button a shirt and tie shoelaces, how to thread a needle. And more importantly, how to talk to people. But I still had so much more to learn. I had never been in a bus, or any moving vehicle other than a boat, and had no idea how to drive a car. I had never been in a restaurant or a store. Nor had I ever been with a woman, not in the way I'd come to understand, however hazily, that to mean.

I was wearing ill-fitting hand-me-downs, donated by some of the clinic compound widows, clothes of husbands killed in the civil war, and Sister Mark admonished me to buy new clothes as soon as I could. I had a bit of money, earned from doing chores for the sisters, but that, and building coffins on board the *Al-Aqba*, was my only knowledge of work. I had no concept of the value of money, Sister Mark had told me I had enough to buy some clothes, find a place to stay and feed myself for a few days. Beyond that, I could only imagine, but after my experience with the Sisters I had faith in the kindness and generosity of people. "That kind of faith I do have," I'd told Sister Mark.

During the several weeks that I'd lived at the clinic, I'd been in the company of a number of nuns much of the time, all in careless, immodest attire, with the exception of Sister Mark, there was nothing sexually attractive about them, and in the case of Sister Mark, I forced myself to refrain from sexual thoughts. It wasn't until I arrived in Beirut and saw various women on the street, women of all ages and types, in skirts and slacks and blouses, that I began to appreciate the power they wielded just by their physical presence and I was seduced by the sight and aroma of them.

Sister Mark had prepared a pita stuffed with falafel for my journey and I'd eaten it on the bus, so when I stepped down onto a crowded Beirut street I had no hunger, and thoughts of finding shelter for the night vanished from my mind. Instead, I found myself swept up by a need I could neither understand nor put a name to, and no knowledge of how to satisfy it. I took a chance and approached an old man at a market whom I thought looked worldly. He laughed and directed me to a nearby district. "The women there are of the lowest type, but a fellow can afford one," he said, wiping his hands on the long tails of his shirt. "Be wary – these girls are all liars and cheats. You'd be wise to neither believe them nor trust them."

I followed his directions and there, in the midst of a warren of stalls selling all manner of food, I stood on a street corner, transfixed by the sight of passing women, and perhaps my desire was so obvious that even a child could see it, for presently a young boy, about the same age as Jergyes and with the same large dark eyes approached me. I looked into the boy's eyes and was shaken by the reflection of myself I saw.

The boy led me from the street, to the rear of a two-story

building and up a rickety flight of stairs, through a door, its paint peeling, into a dark hallway and then, without knocking, through another door and into a dimly lit room. When I saw the woman for the first time, and when she undressed, it was a revelation that left me speechless.

I entered her room as a child and, without shame, told her as much. She nodded, seemingly unsurprised, and proceeded to instruct me in the art of which she was practiced. It didn't take long, but longer than it might have as she insisted that I slow down, that I follow her lead, which I was more than content to do.

Then, having done what I dreamed of doing for so long, I lay in a state of sated exhaustion and disbelief, but the woman remained restless. She rose from the makeshift bed for a long drink from the pitcher of tepid water on the nearby table, then sat beside me, stroking my naked skin, murmuring. Only moments earlier, during the height of our passion, her fingers had caressed my backside – not raking it with nails as I feared might occur once more – and she had remarked on the raised welts. Now those fingers, slender and skillful, went to them again and she leaned over me, drawing her face closer. She paused, her fingers hovering above my flesh as a hummingbird might above a blossom.

"What are these strange markings?" she asked. Whereas before, she had spoken only in soft murmurs, now her words were clear and precise,

"Not markings," I said. "A scratch."

Immediately, my mind raced back to that night on the *Al-Aqba* when the first mate remarked on what he called scratches, "the kind only a woman's fingernails might make," he'd said.

The mate's words remained a mystery to me. Why would a woman rake her fingernails across the buttocks of a man?

"No," the woman said. "Not...." She paused again and her fingers traced the outline of the welts. "My god." She said it in Arabic, which we were speaking, then repeated it in Hebrew. It did not occur to me to be surprised that I understood her.

"A scratch," I repeated.

"No," the woman said, reverting to Arabic. "It's letters, a word. A Hebrew word. I've seen it before." And here she switched again to Hebrew. "It's 'Reuel.' It means 'child of God.'"

CHAPTER 11
A PROSTITUTE WITH A GOOD HEART

THE WOMAN I FIRST took to be a prostitute was actually a saint, though it would be some time before I would know that. As soon as I saw her, she seemed familiar somehow. "Do I know you?" I started to ask, then shook my head, knowing that couldn't be – then I realized with a shock that I had seen her face, a number of times, in one of the dreams that haunted me on the island.

She was a woman of contradictions, dark-haired but blue-eyed, a prostitute of the lowest type, or so I'd been told, not to be believed or trusted, but her patience and gentleness – tenderness, even – surprised me, since, based on things I recalled the sailors on my ship saying, I'd expected something rougher, both more physical and indifferent. The result was that, though I felt tender toward her in return, I remained wary.

She was a Jew, although I wouldn't know that for several weeks, as she first represented herself to me as a Druze, and she was dressed in a simple black robe with a white headdress that trailed down her back. Her name, she told me first, was Maryam, then Mary, and later still, Maryam again. I took her to be about the same age as Sister Mark, mid-20s.

Over the next few weeks, as our friendship deepened, I heard her refer to herself as well as Miryam, Miriam, Mira and Meira, as if she, like me, wasn't sure who she was.

That first day we were together, after she made her pronouncement about the markings on my backside, I told her she was crazy and I paid her. The boy who'd led me to her had set the price, and I had just barely enough.

"I would pay you more if I could afford to," I told Mary. "I am in straitened circumstances."

"There's no need," she said. "I asked a price, you've paid it."

"I would like to give you more," I replied. "I would also like to see you again." My hand was in the pocket of my cheaply made trousers and I jingled the few poor coins within to underscore my predicament.

I hadn't meant for this to happen, but against all expectations, she took pity on me. Rather than cast me out, she took me in. Fed me a feast of bread, honey, cheese and goat meat. Sweet wine. Gave me a place to sleep, just a thread-bare carpet on the floor in her humble quarters, a set of two adjoining rooms in the back of a shop selling sweets in a bazaar. She slept in her own bed, which she sometimes shared with two small children, daughters of her cousin, who owned the shop, then she came to me in the early hours of the next morning, and many mornings to follow, always shaking her head in refusal when I reached into my pocket.

Still, I didn't know she was a saint, and took her to be a prostitute with a good heart, no more.

What should have been my first hint was when she declared, on our second day together, that her name was really Maryam. "Men prefer to call me Mary," was her simple explanation. I was impressed by this small offering of honesty. It too seemed to go against expectation.

She also told me that, by her own count, I was the one hundredth man she had lain with. That was her term for it, what she did. Not *slept with, went to bed with*, certainly nothing more vulgar, terms she heard the other women of the quarter using. "I think maybe you will be the last," she said, without elaboration.

I didn't know what to make of that. I was still so new to the world, everything was a marvel to me, I knew so little. Was she telling me she loved me – love being a word and an idea I'd begun to understand dimly – or something more practical?

"That's very sweet," I replied. "But you shouldn't change your profession because of me."

"It's hardly a profession. I fell into it by accident, against my will. It would be nice for me to leave it. And to make that decision on my own."

CHAPTER 12
MY BRIEF CAREER
AS A CARPET MERCHANT

A FEW DAYS AFTER I settled into residence in Maryam's small apartment, she took me by the hand and led me to the front of the sweets shop and introduced me to the owner, a large woman with a hawk-like nose. "This is my cousin, Ghada. And this," she turned to me, hesitating, "is my friend Reuel."

"Ah," the woman said. She looked at me closely, without hostility, causing me to wonder if she'd been introduced to many of Maryam's "friends." Apparently I was found acceptable because I was then ushered onto one of the handkerchief-sized chairs circling a small white table, and offered rich dark coffee and date-and-walnut shortbread cookies, *maamoul*, so sweet they made my teeth ache.

The following day, Maryam led me down the narrow streets of the old quarter to the shop of a carpet merchant, a friend of her cousin's and also, not coincidentally, a client of hers on occasion. Before she could again refer to me as Reuel, I introduced myself to him as Yusef, a name I heard one child in the street calling another. It had a nice ring to it and sounded familiar enough that it might actually have been mine. The merchant's name was Mohammad. He was an old man, though not as old as

I first took him to be, with a lazy left eye. His good eye looked me up and down as I told him my story, as truthfully as I could: "I am a sailor, a ship's carpenter, with neither ship nor tools. I was shipwrecked and lost everything, all but my life. I'm sick of the sea. I have no family, no friends except this good woman." I could see he was skeptical so I plunged on. "I have nothing to offer except my willingness, if you have work for me I will do it and you'll have no cause for complaint. I'm a good carpenter" – I looked around the shop – "perhaps you are in need of some shelves? Cabinets?"

"No, nothing like that," the merchant said. "You are, in most likelihood, a liar, but I can see you are not a thief. Arrogance is not becoming in the young. But self-confidence need not be arrogance. I will afford you the benefit of the doubt."

He put me to work immediately. He would retire to the back of the shop where there was much to do, he said – I never learned exactly what – and I was left in charge, to look after customers. Before he slipped behind the curtain, he gave me this lesson: "The customer must be wooed, seduced, then seized. You must be like a woman, promising nothing but pleasure, producing a small portion of it, then delivering pain and regret." I failed to understand this metaphor and I looked at him with amazement, but he was gone before I could ask a question.

Almost immediately the bell above the door tinkled and a large red-haired woman in a floral dress and with a florid expression came in, chattering loudly to a short man with a set jaw who trailed behind, carrying an umbrella and her handbag. She went directly to a pile of carpets Mohammad had indicated to me were the least expensive, with the poorest craftsmanship and quality of material. "Try not to sell these," he'd cautioned.

"Madame has excellent taste," I said. "Exquisite. You will be the envy of your neighbours with a carpet like that on your floor in...."

"Minneapolis," the small man said.

I was amazed at myself, my forwardness, yet I plunged on. "Yes, Minneapolis. There will be no finer carpet in Minneapolis than yours."

The woman gave me a look as skeptical as Mohammad's was. Her gaze then moved quickly around the shop, pausing here and there, then settling on the most expensive display. Even before she said a word, I shook my head. "I wouldn't consider those, Madame. Oh, yes, I can see you are intrigued, but I advise against it."

The woman went directly to the carpet I was eyeing and fingered it critically. Within moments, the expression on her face softened. "Why would you say that, young man?"

"It is always best to know one's limitations," I said simply.

The woman laughed, a forthright, open laugh that made me reappraise my feeling toward her. "You're suggesting this carpet is not just more than I can afford yet of better quality than I deserve? Is that it?"

"I said no such thing."

"He didn't say that, dear," the man said. "I'm sure he meant to imply no such thing." He had a resigned expression on his pinched face. The woman looked at him – she turned her back to me so I couldn't see her face – and the man reached into his jacket for his pocketbook.

Though I wasn't aware of them, Mohammad's eyes were on this scene the whole time. As soon as the couple left, the woman carrying purse and umbrella, the little man struggling with the rolled carpet, he emerged.

"Bravo," he said.

"I considered what you told me," I said. "I believe what you meant was first soft lips, then teeth."

"Ah, you are a quick student."

He counted the money they left, crisp American dollars. "Your English is excellent, by the way," he said.

"English? Is that what we were speaking?"

Mohammad gave me a room in the back of the shop where I could sleep, not on a bed but a bundle of carpets, and he provided me with a small wage, enough to allow me to eat my fill in my choice of the souks and cafés that honeycombed the old quarter. I ate voraciously and within days the sepulchral look that the Sisters hadn't been able to eradicate began to fade from my cheeks. My employer commented on this, and asked if I'd been ill.

"I was," I admitted, and, because he had shown me only kindnesses and given no reason for me to distrust him, I told him my whole sorry story, as much as I knew. "Beyond the little that I've told you," I concluded, "there is nothing more I can relate. When I say 'loss of memory,' I mean complete. I have no knowledge of my home, my parents, wife or sweetheart, children, nothing."

Mohammad listened in silence, his face an impenetrable mask, even the lazy eye uncharacteristically still. When I reached the end of my tale, he nodded his head gravely. "Better that than the other thing," he said.

Mohammad also gave me a name, an identity. After I'd told him my story, the rug merchant quietly arranged through a friend of his who trafficked in such things for a set of identity papers. To the name Yusef I had adopted for myself was added the family name Masoud, which meant lucky or fortunate – that certainly applied to me, I thought, lucky to be alive. Both names were typed on several documents, along with a birthplace, Jarara, a tiny village in Gaza, and a birthdate, May 14, 1948, which, as of that day in late April, 1981, made me almost thirty-four years old. I didn't know if that was older than I should be or younger, but it felt right. "Nineteen forty-eight," I said, trying out the sound of the year of my birth.

"Al-Nakba," Mohammad snorted. "The year of the catastrophe."

I gave him a puzzled glance. "Yusef Masoud, from Jarara," I pronounced, as if introducing myself, and feeling vain as a child in a new suit of clothes. But Mohammad frowned.

"With your accent, better not to proclaim your birthplace," he said.

"I thought my Arabic was good," I said. We were speaking Arabic, of course, and the sound of my own voice rang in my ear with authenticity.

"Yes, yes, it's fine, excellent, but you speak it like a professor of classical literature at the university in Cairo."

I was crestfallen.

"Better to be a listener than a talker, at any rate," Mohammad said.

Good counsel, which I've tried to remember.

MOST NIGHTS I SLEPT on the carpets in Mohammad's back room, reluctant to abuse Maryam's generosity, but once or twice a week I met with her and she either cooked for us or I treated her to a café meal, and we would always end the evening by tumbling into her bed.

As she'd predicted on our first meeting, she had forsaken her former life and taken a job in a clothing shop in a bazaar, though I didn't realize that the first time I visited her. I went to the house where she lodged and her cousin Ghada, after looking me over from top to bottom, directed me to the street where she said Maryam worked, not far from Mohammad's carpet shop, and I found her haggling with a group of tourists over the price of silk scarves. Gone was the robe and headdress she'd worn when I first met her, replaced by a simple black skirt and a button-up white blouse, a bright green scarf not covering her chestnut hair but around her neck. Her face lit up when she saw me and she stepped aside from the women and enfolded me in her arms. She offered no explanation, just told me she was glad to see me and that she would meet me in an hour at a nearby café. After tea, she led me back to her rooms and to her bed. Only afterwards, after I'd dressed and was reaching into my pocket for money, did she reveal her new situation.

"No, Reuel," she said. "I don't do this for money anymore. I thought you knew that."

Her meaning wasn't immediately clear to me. "What for, then?"

"For love."

We looked at each other, the look quickly transforming itself into a gaze, and I felt something move through me I'd never felt before – at least not that I knew of. I sat down on the bed bedside her and took her hand.

"I don't really understand," I said.

Maryam smiled. her startlingly blue eyes serene, her shoulders slowly moving up and down. "I had no hope, which is why I did what I did. Now I do."

"Hope of what?" I asked, still feeling confused.

"Of you, silly. Don't you know who you are?"

"Who I am, yes, of course. Yusef Masoud, a ship's carpenter, temporarily landlocked, working as a carpet merchant."

She smiled again. "And you say you have no memory! You've learned that sentence by heart. You recite it almost as if you believe it."

"I do believe it, it's the truth." I couldn't mask the frustration in my voice. "It's the only truth I have."

We looked at each other, me bristling with irritation, she serene. Then we were in each other's arms again. Afterwards, lying in the darkness that had settled down on the evening, I mustered up the courage to ask one of the questions I still had.

"All right, since you seem to know something about me that I don't, tell me, who am I?"

Maryam's laugh was liquid. "You're Reuel, a child of God. But we know that, you know it."

I started to protest but she silenced me with a kiss. "No, you're right, you're Yusef Masoud, a ship's carpenter, etcetera etcetera. As you say."

'Except you think otherwise."

"Who you are is not for me to say," Maryam said.

"I'VE BEEN SCHOOLED lately in the mysterious ways of God," I told Maryam on one of these nights together. "Did God send you to me?"

"This is as close to heaven as either of us will ever come, Reuel," she said, smiling, light glinting in her eyes, wet with tears. "Well, as close as I'll ever come."

It was then that she finally told me she was really a Jew after deciding that I was probably one.

"And if you really are,' she said, "you're the first I've been with, since..."

"Since what?"

"Nothing." She lifted a hand to wave the question away.

"And what makes you think that I'm Jewish?" I was genuinely curious.

"You're circumcised."

The term meant nothing to me and she had to explain.

Without thinking, my hand went to my groin, as if to feel confirmation. Then, feeling self-conscious, I pulled my hand away.

"And is that proof positive?"

"No, but in this part of the world, it's mostly Jews who do it."

"But I could be from anywhere."

"Yes."

"So it could be meaningless."

"Yes...but, Reuel...I thought you wanted to know who you are."

"I do. I do."

"Then why resist this clue?"

I couldn't answer.

At this point, I knew next to nothing of Jews. If Maryam really was a Jew, as she said she was, she was the only one I knew. I'm quite sure there were none aboard the *Al-Aqba,* and certainly there were none at the convent of the Sisters of the Divine Crucifix. The little time I'd had so far in Beirut had exposed me to Muslim and Christians, but I barely heard the word Jew, let alone met any. Even Maryam's cousin Ghada, presumably as much a Jew as Maryam was, dressed and comported herself like any other Arab woman in the bazaar.

"And what exactly is a Jew?" I asked.

Maryam laughed. "Oh, nothing special. Think of a Christian but without the guilt."

Guilt was something I did know a little about, from my conversations with Sister Mark. It led from sin, and could only be healed through confession. "Why no guilt? Aren't Jews as susceptible to sin as Christians?"

"Yes, but our God is more forgiving. The guilt doesn't last long."

Just as I knew nothing of Jews themselves, I knew nothing of their history of suffering, nothing of the Spanish Inquisition, of pogroms, of the Holocaust. I was aware, of course, though only vaguely, of the conflict between Arabs and Jews over the neighbouring country of Israel which slipped across the border into Lebanon, but thought of it more as a dispute over land, not something connected to either sin, guilt or forgiveness. So I had no reason to question Maryam's assertion of the Jews' forgiving God.

Our conversation soon drifted off and we dozed. Lying with her, our arms and legs entwined, I felt a peace I'd not known before, something I supposed was happiness or something akin to it. I wondered if this was love; did I love Maryam, was I *in* love with her – a distinction I didn't really understand – or was this merely another infatuation such as I'd experienced with Sister Mark? "Infatuation" was Maryam's word. She'd tossed it lightly at me when, early in our friendship, I blurted out "I love you," three simple words freighted with a danger I couldn't then imagine.

Maryam was reluctant to talk about her own past. She'd told me she came from a kibbutz on the shores of Lake Kenneret, the Sea of Galilee, and that her parents were dead. But that was all, and if I asked about her family or her childhood, or how she had come to Beirut and become a prostitute, she was adept at deflecting the question.

But for my part, I felt grateful that she had, for how would I have met her otherwise?

BOOK 3

Speaking In Many Tongues

CHAPTER 13
PEACE IN "THE UNHOLY LAND"

MY CAREER AS AN APPRENTICE carpet merchant lasted less than three weeks. Mohammad was good to me, and I was happy enough in his shop, but fate, if that's what it was, had something else in mind for me. A United Nations office was nearby and, within days of starting at Mohammad's shop, I made the acquaintance of several men employed there, a Canadian, a Belgian who spoke French with an odd accent, and a Swede, each of whom came to the shop with instructions from their wives. Although they first attempted to speak to me in a jerry- rigged Arabic, I surprised them, and myself, by quickly switching to their own languages: English, French, Swedish. This happened in separate incidents, one at a time, but the first man told the second and so on. The Swede, Carl Hedberg, was an official with the UN mission. He offered me a job as a translator on the spot when he heard my Swedish and shortly I found myself riding in the passenger seat of a jeep driven by a Swedish soldier wearing a peacekeepers blue helmet, the white armband of the UN blazing on my crisp new khaki shirt, on the way to the border, where the peacekeeper force had their headquarters at the city of Naqoura. I had barely the time to say goodbye and many thanks to Mohammad, who seemed not the least bit surprised.

Maryam was surprised, though, and tearful. "Are you crazy? People run away from that sort of thing, not toward it. You could get killed."

"I could get killed here too."

"Yes, God could strike you down, but why would He? The Israelis will strike you down because you're PLO, the PLO will strike you down because you're Israeli."

"I'm neither," I protested.

"And how will angry men with guns know that?"

She had a point, but Hedberg, who was serving as political consultant to the UN force commander, assured me the peace-keepers' white jeeps rarely came under fire and were perfectly safe. I only learned later that several dozen of the UN soldiers had been killed since they'd arrived three years earlier, tasked with keeping the Muslim and the Christian warring factions apart, their job made all the more complicated by Israeli and Syrian involvement.

Although there had been a ceasefire since April 1978, the Israelis periodically shelled the Lebanese south with big guns, and bombed it from the air. No one could blame them; the PLO was shelling Israeli settlements just over the border from refugee camps, and, under cover of darkness, sappers and snipers would creep across the border and wreak as much damage as they could before withdrawing by dawn. No one could blame *them* either; conditions in the Palestinian camps were terrible. Some of the older people living in them could see through the barbed wire the roofs of Israeli settlement houses built on the ashes of what had once been their own homes. Each side was intractable, the situation seemingly insolvable. Those were the words of Hedberg, who was becoming my mentor.

"Our job isn't to defuse the situation but prevent its

deterioration," he told me. "They call us peacekeepers, but there is no peace to keep."

And indeed, despite the ceasefire, fighting continued, and the Blue Helmets were powerless to prevent it, often taking fire themselves. Some of the peacekeepers had even been taken hostage.

"And they can't be talked to?" I asked. "The Jews, the Arabs, they can't be brought together? There is no common ground?"

Hedberg looked at me the way one might at a child, with a mixture of amusement and wonder. Perhaps pity too, for my ignorance, perhaps envy, for my innocence. "Where have you been?"

I explained that I was at sea for some time.

Over the next few weeks I proved myself invaluable. I could speak Arabic to the Palestinians, Arabic and French to the Lebanese, Hebrew to the Israelis, the national languages of all the contingents making up the United Nations peacekeeper force, even the Nigerians, and English to any and all. All sides found me trustworthy and I was sent back and forth across the Litani River into the area occupied by the South Lebanese Army, through various checkpoints, even across the Israeli border with messages.

The more I saw, the simpler the situation seemed to me, but every suggestion I made to Hedberg was greeted with a condescending laugh. "You don't understand, but that's all right. You have to be here a long time before you can."

By this time, Hedberg and I had come to know each other better and were almost friends. When again I made a comment that demonstrated my ignorance, I mentioned that I had been ill, that it had affected my memory.

"You're fortunate," he said. "Memory is a curse."

"So is its absence," I replied.

We looked at each other – we were riding side by side in a jeep over a bumpy road, Hedberg at the wheel, as he preferred, though his rank entitled him to a driver, me trying not to fall out of the open-sided passenger seat. I wondered which one of us was more right, and I suspect he was wondering the same.

Hedberg was a tall, morose man in his fifties, with gaunt cheeks and watery eyes. He wore loose-fitting khaki trousers and bright sport shirts, often red or green prints, to demonstrate that he was not military. On his feet, he wore sandals, not boots, with thick wool socks. One of the first things he'd learned as a peace-keeper, he'd told me, was to shed his jacket and tie. In his career, he had been a soldier, a school teacher, a bureaucrat, a politician and a diplomat – either the ideal background for peacekeeping work, or the worst, he liked to joke. He worked in the Mideast for years, since Suez, and spent some time in Yemen and the Golan Heights. He called it "the Unholy Land."

He was divorced and his children were grown, so he had no ties. "These people are my family," he said on one of our first trips together, gesturing vaguely at the people on the street we were driving down, Lebanese Christians and Muslims and Palestinians, it was impossible for me to tell the difference, though I would learn to. I wondered if his gesture included me. I liked the idea of being part of Hedberg's family.

"The only solution is time," he explained. "These people" – he waved his hand, this time to indicate the Palestinians in the camp we were driving through – "have hope, too much of it. They remember their homes, their lives. They live in hope of reclaiming it. Peace is out of the question for them. The Jews must be driven out. Into the sea better, but out for sure."

"So we must wait for the next generation?" I asked.

"No. The next generation, these ragamuffins you see playing here, they have hope too, a second hand, hand-me-down hope. They weren't there, they have no memories, but they've heard the stories. They too hope to return. They won't make peace either."

"So the third generation?"

"The third generation will be without hope, yes. But peace-makers, no. They'll have no memories, and the stories will have faded. Israelis? They won't even know what they are, the third generation. That's if we do our job and keep them apart." He grinned at me, flashing large, rounded teeth and reddish gums. "It'll just be the idea of them they'll hate, each on their own side. That's the worst, when you hate an idea. That and no hope." Hedberg's face resumed its usual morose countenance, more morose than usual. "This will be the worst. It will be terrible. No hope, nothing to lose, and not human beings as enemies, just an idea."

"The fourth generation then?"

"You *are* an optimist! Who can say? Perhaps. By then, no one will remember even what the fight is about. The Palestinians, some of them anyway, will look around and say, why are we here? They'll move on, to Jordan, Syria, Egypt, England, the United States, anywhere that will take them. Some will stay. They'll make inquiries regarding peace. But it will take a peace-maker, a Gandhi. Not this Arafat. Some people say yes, Arafat, but I think no." He paused to take a swallow from his canteen.

"Some of my colleagues, officers, agree Arafat's not the man for it, but disagree with me that a Gandhi is needed, a soft man. They say a hard man's what it will take, like Collins in Ireland, say – you know of him?"

I nodded, though in fact my knowledge of the Irish troubles was almost zero.

"A hard man who won't flinch, won't be influenced, who sees what's needed and does it. That's more likely to be a soldier than a politician, but politicians are what we're stuck with, though plenty of them here are former soldiers, on both sides. Maybe they're right, two hard men, on both sides, who can talk to each other, then make their own people swallow the deal they make."

He fell silent, thoughtful, and after a minute I said, "That all makes sense, a perverse kind of sense."

Hedberg turned to me, grinning. "Yes, hard men to make peace, that is perverse, isn't it. Well, I'm not convinced. I still think a Gandhi's what's needed, a peace-maker." He narrowed his watery eyes. "Perhaps you?"

"What I think of Arafat? I..."

"No." Hedberg's laugh was as guttural as his spoken voice. "I mean maybe you're the peace-maker. I've heard some things about you."

"Me? What you've heard is probably not true. And as for me as a peace-maker, I'm not even sure which side I'm on." Nor which side I was part of, though I didn't say that. In my initial, cursory interview with him, Hedberg was careful not to ask my nationality or religion – he felt it better not to know, I assumed – and the subject hadn't come up since.

"All the better, maybe." His face broke into a rough equivalent of a half-smile. "Well, it doesn't matter. You and I, my friend, will be long gone by then. Long gone."

WHENEVER HEDBERG and I got to Beirut, I would steal an hour or two, sometimes more, to see Maryam. On these visits, if there was time, we'd go to her room. Otherwise, we'd go for walks, through the narrow streets of the Old Town or along the waterfront, sometimes holding hands, talking or being silent. On these occasions, I would feel almost happy. I told her so.

She laughed. "Why almost?"

"I don't know. I don't think I can be happy, not with the hole in my life. There's so much missing, I can't be myself."

"But you are yourself, Reuel," she insisted., "You are who you are, not who you once were."

"But what if...?

"If what?"

I was thinking of some of the men I'd recently met, Palestinians, Israelis, Muslims, Christians alike, with blood on their hands. "What if I was... a monster? An assassin, a bomber...."

She laughed again. "Do you really think that might be the case?"

"I don't know, don't you see? I could have been anybody, anything."

"And do you really want to know?" she asked. "I don't believe for a moment that you were ever a monster. But let's say you were. Would you want to know that? You're not a monster now. Isn't that what's important. You are who you are, Reuel. Be satisfied with that. Be *happy* with that."

I wanted to believe her, wanted to do as she bade, wanted to be content with who I was then and forget the past. I wanted to, but I couldn't.

CHAPTER 14
HOMELESS

LIVING ON THE BORDER, as I was, among so many homeless people, only served to underscore my own feeling of homelessness – home*sick*ness was something to which I could only aspire. I didn't pretend that I had suffered as they had, these Palestinians. They had lost their homes, lost everything. The memory of the sun on their faces as they stood in their doorways, the feel of the smooth pump handle in their hands, the sound of birds in the lemon trees and the scent of basil, each of these was a knife to the heart. For me, having no memory of such things, no catalogue of loss, it was much different. For me, there was nothing, a vacuum in my heart. How I yearned for the pain of these people, something to fill that void.

I mentioned this one day to Hedberg as we drove through a camp – not my loss but these people's, how hard it must be to endure – and he replied that many of the Israelis had lost everything too. "Loss on both sides."

I looked at him inquisitively. My knowledge of the Israelis extended little further than what I'd heard on the street and in the UN quarters.

"Before they were Israelis, they were Jews," Hedberg said. "Persecuted, hounded, hunted. Pogroms, anti-Semitism, the outcasts of Europe for centuries....you've heard of the Holocaust? The Inquisition?"

I had to admit that I had, but that they were just words. I knew nothing of them.

"You like to read, Yusef, I'll lend you a book." He was smiling, yet there was a slightly judgmental tone to his voice, and I knew he was thinking, how could anyone not know about these things? I told Hedberg about my loss of memory, and I was aware that he viewed it with more than a touch of skepticism. How can one lose something as fundamental as memory? What tormented me was merely a rhetorical question for him.

"Please. I'd like that. I want to know more, I want to know... things."

Indeed, I was a sponge, absorbing everything I saw and heard, as much as I could from both sides – no, all sides. "In Palestine," I'd heard Hedberg observe more than once, "there aren't two sides to every story, but a million." I wanted to hear them all. I felt as if I was one of that million – and how I longed to hear my own story.

A UN OFFICIAL FROM NEW YORK came to make an inspection. A meeting was held, in a small room at a border observation post. It was not to make peace, or even as Hedberg said, to talk about the possibility of talking about peace, but rather to talk about the possibility of holding such talks, talks to explore the possibility of talking about peace.

The official was a Swiss named Berg. Hedberg also attended. The Israelis were represented by an army officer named Greenberg, the Lebanese Christians by a Maronite named Burque, the Muslims by a Shia named Burki and a Sunni who called himself Abu Burkhan.

The Palestinians, who at first threatened to boycott the meeting, sent a masked man called Abu Burghouthi. And I was there, to translate.

Hedberg was right. There was no making sense of it.

AND, IN THE MEANTIME, I was a chameleon. The Palestinians took me to be one of them, but the Israelis I dealt with thought me a Jew, in part because of my flawless Hebrew. I had no idea who or what I was, and I was circumspect, noncommittal. Often, though, my silence was taken as assent, and people saw in me what they wanted to see.

I had no real home. Naquora, a small city about a three hours' drive south of Beirut on the coast and just a stone's throw north of the Israeli border, was our home base, but Hedberg and I were constantly on the move, going from one camp to another, checkpoint to checkpoint. I had no driving skills, or no memory of such a thing at any rate, so he was always the driver, I the navigator, the creased and dirty map in my hand, though Hedberg knew his way on these desert roads and through the warrens of the camps better than the map-makers.

I did have a name, though, even if only newly acquired. And now I found I was among multiple people who had assumed new identities. Stateless people are always at the mercy of their hosts, and there were many in the camps who had pasts the less known of the better, not criminals, necessarily, but in some cases people who overstayed their welcome elsewhere, in other camps, other countries.

Others were guerrillas who had taken on *noms de guerre*. "Call me Abu Minon," one Palestinian man said to me. He had a grip like a vice and eyes that penetrated me.

I joined a group of men at a Beirut coffee stall within sight of the DMZ. They all wore Fatah's checkered *kaffiyeh*, either wrapped around their heads or on their shoulders with a colourful knit Arab cap. "Yusef Masoud," I replied. The other men nodded but offered neither their names nor their hands.

"Masoud," the first man said thoughtfully. I feared he would question me but he merely looked me over, his eyes lingering on the UN insignia until he seemed satisfied.

"Do they call you Abu?" I asked innocently, just to make conversation. I was still feeling my way through the tangle of conventions, nuances and niceties of my new society.

The men burst into rough laughter. "For a man they say is clever you are not so clever," Abu Minon observed, but not harshly.

"Hardly clever," I protested, though I was pleased to know that these men had heard something of me.

One of the other men spoke up. "As clever as an empty bottle, reflecting the sun." He was a full-bearded man who looked more Jewish than Arab, wearing a dirty checkered *kaffiyeh*. He leaned back in his slightly tilted chair, and I noticed that the cup of black coffee in front of him was full, seemingly untouched. His eyes were sharp as those of the Creature that watched me on my island.

"Now there *is* a clever man," I said.

The men laughed, except the man who had spoken. He continued to observe me, his shrewd eyes unwavering. I gazed back, willing him to blink first but he did not. Finally, and only because the man who owned the silk shop next to Mohammad had the same affliction, I realized he was blind. What I had taken to be a glint in his eye was merely, as in his own metaphor, reflection.

I saw Hedberg waving from the jeep and I said goodbye. "You should stay clear of that Fatah crowd," he cautioned me as we drove away.

"Isn't it good for us to be on good terms with everybody?" I protested.

"Everybody but them. You never know where you are with that bunch."

I told him about the blind man, describing him. "Ah, that's the sheikh, Sheikh Al-Qatar," Hedberg said. "You don't want to know how he lost his sight."

I did, though. "He's a planner," Hedberg said, "doesn't usually get his hands dirty. Black September, the Olympics, half a dozen skyjackings, he had fingers in them all. But one bombing, he carried the dirty thing himself for some reason. Went off early so all he killed was the men with him. People revere him because he wasn't killed himself, Allah protected him. Took his eyes so he could see better, his followers say. Stay away from that fellow, Yusef, I'm telling you."

I was impressed by the vehemence in Hedberg's voice and we drove in silence for a kilometre or more. Puzzled, I asked, "Why would Allah protect a bomber?"

"Ah, that's the question." Hedberg produced a half-laugh as if he were clearing his throat of phlegm. "You're finally getting the hang of things here, my friend."

I chewed on this for a minute, then I asked if he knew anything of the other man, Abu Minon.

"Ah, that one's a nasty piece of work. Have you ever come across a snake, Yusef?"

"Yes, there were a few on the island I've mentioned."

"Cold-blooded as a snake and as deadly, that's Abu Minon. None of this is proven, of course, but he's got plenty of blood on his hands. I mentioned Black September, he was part of that crowd." He turned to me. "You do know of them?"

I shook my head.

Hedberg laughed dismissively, reluctant as always to believe my lack of knowledge of the world around me.

"He's a good shot, that one." Hedberg said. "A crack shot. They say he fired a shot two hundred metres across the border that struck a 10-month-old baby in the arms of her mother. Killed the baby, the mother unharmed, if you call having a baby killed in your arms unharmed."

"Why on earth would anyone do such a thing?" I demanded.

Hedberg gave me an appraising look. "To produce exactly what I see in you at this moment, my friend, just hearing of it. Horror. Revulsion. Terror." We drove on, each of us deep in our own thoughts, but after a minute or two, Hedberg turned to me again. "You know, they don't see it that way at all. That shot, to the man who fired it, was a strike for freedom. And so many Palestinian babies have died, what's one Jewish baby?"

I shook my head. "That's a terrible arithmetic."

Hedberg laughed. "Now you're getting it, Yusef."

"I don't know if I ever will," I said with resignation. "Not really."

"Oh, yes. You know, we Blue Helmets can only do so much, can only understand so far. Israelis, Palestinians, this is their war." Hedberg shook his head. "We're just tourists. But you, you're part of them, Jew or Arab, I don't know which you are."

I didn't reply, thinking, suddenly of a dream I had while on my island, a man with a rifle, a shot... and Hedberg too was silent, thoughtful, then observed, "You know, there are no villains here, evil though some of them may seem. Just simple people homesick, longing for home." He turned to look at me. "Like anyone."

"But why here?" I asked. "Palestine is a small space. Why not give the Jews Siberia? Or the Australian Outback?" These were places I knew nothing of, really, but heard or read about. I was reading voraciously by then, newspapers, magazines, books, listening to the radio, soaking up as much knowledge as I could. A garbage can full of facts and ideas was constantly rattling around in my head. "All those wide open spaces in America. Or, I don't know, some empty place in Sweden, if there is such a place. Why here, where there already are people? And so many of them."

Hedberg laughed. "Yes, and why not give a sailor a home in a desert?" He gave me a sharp look. "No, this is home to both people. The British botched it – they were supposed to guarantee homelands for both Palestinians and Jews. Once they walked away, those guarantees blew away with them. Don't repeat that, Yusef – I'm supposed to be a diplomat."

"But you know, they're not so different, Arabs, Jews. Have you heard Arabs referred to as Ishmaelites?"

"I have."

"Descendants of Ishmael, whose father was Abraham – you know who I mean?"

"Yes."

"So half brothers to the Jews. They're the same people really, though they'd never admit it. Speak practically the same language, as you know so well."

"Yet they seem to hate each other," I objected. "How can that be?"

"They're brothers, you know. You have any brothers? Brothers squabble."

"This is some squabble."

"Yes," Hedberg said. "Remember Cain?"

I knew that story, of course, Sister Mark and I talked about it once. I remember wondering then if I had a brother, and the same question came into my mind now as I rode beside Hedberg. And if I had, might I have slain him? Might he have wanted to slay me? Questions which, to my torment, seemed unlikely to ever have answers.

CHAPTER 15
THE SHEIKH

I WOULD HAVE GLADLY followed Hedberg's warning to stay away from such people – his advice was usually sound – but the sheikh himself had other ideas. A week later, we were in Damascus for a meeting with Syrian officials, when I was approached by two men, both clearly Fatah. I had gone with Hedberg to a meal with other UN people, then left them to their whiskeys and talk and was making my way back to our hotel on foot. The sun had gone down but the heat was still stifling. The men stepped unexpectedly out of a doorway and were on either side of me. There was no way to elude them, even if I'd wanted to, and aside from the momentary fright their sudden appearance caused, I had no fear.

"The sheikh wishes to speak with you," one of the men said.

"Very well." I didn't ask which sheikh they meant – that title is common here – but I expected to be ushered into the presence of the blind man, Sheikh Al-Qatar, even though Damascus was a good three hours' drive from Beirut, where I first met him. And sure enough, after a brief blindfolded ride in what sounded like an ancient vehicle, I was. So apparently, the sheikh was as much at home in one city as another.

"You interest me, translator," the sheikh said. There were no introductions, no offers of food or drink, not even a curt invitation to sit. "You could be of use to us. And we perhaps to you."

We were already inside when the blindfold was removed, in what I took to be the kitchen of a tarpaper and tin house. A counter ran along one wall, laden with dishes and utensils and an old-fashioned tabletop clock in a polished wooden case that seemed out of place. In the middle of the room stood a table with chairs ringing it, but the blind man sat cross-legged on a mat on the hard-packed dirt floor, next to an open fire.

The two men who delivered me took chairs at the table but I chose to join the blind man on the floor, which was cold through the cloth of my trousers, despite the heat in the room.

"And why should I be of use to you?" I inquired.

"He who is of use to me is of use to Palestine," he said without hesitation. "And to himself. Does that interest you?"

"Of course."

A woman entered the kitchen and served coffee from a pot on the stone tray above the fire, strong black coffee so hot it burned my tongue. She was swathed in robes, only her ferret eyes and the bridge of her nose visible. She looked at me with a dangerously prolonged glance, not with curiosity, I thought, but something more like desperation, as if I represented an abandoned possibility. When she served the sheikh, he leaned forward as she brought the demi-tasse to his lips and I realized that he had no arms. One of the men lit a foul-smelling cigarette and brought it to him, holding it close so he could take a puff. For several minutes, the two of them, man and woman, waited on the blind man, alternating sips of coffee and puffs of cigarette.

"I suppose you think," he said suddenly, "that you see a broken man."

He nodded and the attendants stepped back. The stub of the cigarette was thrown into the fire. The woman left the kitchen, giving me one last glance. The two men also withdrew.

"Your will is impressive," I said.

"That is Allah's will, not mine."

I sipped my own coffee and considered the man's implacable view of the world.

"Is everything Allah's will?" I asked. "Man takes neither credit nor blame?"

"Allah gives us choices. What we make of them is for us to decide."

"Regardless of what happens, that is Allah's will?"

"Yes and no," the sheikh said.

I'm afraid I laughed. "Allah gives us dice, allows us to throw, but the dice are always loaded."

The blind man seemed to smile, though his lips were concealed within his mustache and beard and it was hard to tell. The hair around his mouth was moist from the coffee and glistened as his lips moved.

"And that's a gamble you're loathe to take, translator? You are not a betting man?'"

"I don't know if I am or not. I surmise you've made inquiries about me. You may have heard, I lost my memory some time ago. I'm like a young child, learning his way in the world. I don't know what I am."

"That's part of what interests me about you. No memory, no preconceived notions. No biases."

"Yes," I agreed. "I try to take life as I see it, as it comes. Often I have no choice but to do just that."

"Still, you hesitate?"

"As I say, I take life as I see it. Some things, I can't see."

The blind man's shoulders lifted slightly in a weak shrug. "All of life is a gamble."

"Of course. That much I know."

This strand of conversation having wound down to its logical conclusion, we sat in a silence broken only by ticking from the clock on the counter. I studied the sheikh and, if I didn't know that he was blind, I would have sworn he was studying me. What did I really know of him? I first thought him to have sight, was sure his eyes were on me, then discovered he was blind; I'd assumed he had arms, then found he lacked them. What of his legs? I had only seen him seated, at a table and now, apparently, cross-legged. Had I seen any motion in those legs? Was anything about this man as it first appeared?

"We would want you only to do what you are already doing," the sheikh said suddenly. "That is to say, going about your duties with the United Nations, translating, accompanying the man Hedberg...." I noticed that in his cultivated Arabic he somehow made the Swedish name sound Jewish. "And perhaps just one other small thing that would cause you no inconvenience."

"I would carry no bomb," I said emphatically.

"No, of course not. We would not ask you to. Only messages. Messages which, I can assure you, will produce no harm."

I considered his request, a little surprised at myself for not immediately rejecting it.

"And why should I do that, what you ask? I'm UN, we take no sides."

"Yes, you're UN. But before that, you're Yusef Masoud" – he paused – "if that's who you really are. You've suffered, I can see that."

"What do you know of my suffering?"

"Little, I admit. Just that it was real. And that you continue to suffer. We too suffer. Even the Jews suffer, I grant them that. Maybe our effort will ease suffering on both sides." Again he paused. "With your assistance."

We sat in silence for a minute or two. The sheikh cleared his throat. "Perhaps even your suffering will be eased."

"Oh? And how would that happen?"

"By your having a purpose. And..." – he paused for a moment, then continued – "as I said, perhaps we could be of use to you."

"Oh? How?"

"We know your past is a mystery, that this bothers you. We have some contacts, and many sources of information. Information is our stock and trade, in fact. Perhaps we might learn something of your past."

Up to this point, I was both curious and sympathetic. Now, I became intrigued as well. And so I determined to take him at his word and I agreed. "If at any time I believe that there *is* harm," I said, "harm flowing from my actions on your behalf, then I will cease them immediately."

"That is understood," the blind man said. "I would expect no less."

And so I became a messenger for what I believed was Fatah, although the sheikh was in fact an agent of an entirely different agenda. I finished my coffee and rose. Again the blindfold was applied – "with a thousand apologies," I heard the sheikh saying, as my own sight disappeared, mimicking his, "but we have many enemies" – and the two men led me to the car. Within what seemed just minutes, I was dropped off in exactly the same dark stretch of street where I had encountered them, just a couple of blocks from the hotel.

"Remember, not a word," one of the men said ominously, to which I could only laugh inwardly. Who would I tell? And what, exactly? Then the car drove away, its tailpipe sputtering.

As I crossed the hotel lobby on my way to the elevator, I noticed Hedberg in the bar having a solitary whiskey in dim light and puffing on his pipe. He looked up with surprise. "I thought you were already in bed. Where have you been?" The question was not demanding, the question an employer demands of an employee, but rather one of idle curiosity, so I felt no threat.

"Gambling," I said.

CHAPTER 16
A MESSENGER

AS I LAY IN BED that night trying to fall asleep, I went over and over my conversation with the sheikh. I realized I had no idea why I agreed to become his messenger, other than an impulse. His dangling of the slim hope of discovering something of my past struck me now as a very slim hope indeed, and by morning it had grown even slimmer. The feeling of intrigue – of *hope* – I'd immediately felt when the sheikh mentioned it was the deciding point, I knew, and in the bright light of day, it seemed like a far-fetched fabrication, yet it remained, quivering in me, and I clung to it. In the days and weeks to come, I would continue to question my decision, and later to regret it. Eventually, long after I ceased to carry messages, I came to understand that there was a purpose to it after all.

And so the next stage of my life began, my brief moonlight career as a messenger. Throughout it, and afterwards, I continued to wonder why I agreed. It seemed clear to me then. Wherever I looked, I saw despair – homelessness, poverty, hunger, idleness, humiliation. Suffering, as the sheikh put it. At the same time, I was reading the history of the Jews Hedberg had loaned me, and it was filled with despair – persecution, slaughter.

More suffering. I was angry and wanted to do something. And, I understand now, confused.

I was given messages and I delivered them. With each message, I was given the name of the person to deliver it to or the place to go. I went to that place or sought out that person, and then delivered the message. That was all.

I paid close attention to the words of the bargain we'd struck – "no harm." I kept track of where I'd been and the pattern of bombings and attacks, both within Lebanon, as the civil war rumbled on like a low-grade fever, and across the border in northern Israel, where kibbutzes and settlements often came under fire – to see if there was an intersection, but there was none, not that I could see. As far as I could tell, I was a neutral vessel, my activities as innocent as those of a postman. In the back of my mind, though, and in my dreams, I knew that couldn't be true.

The messages themselves seemed innocuous, though certainly they were in code. In the morning, as I walked from the billet to the jeep, I would pass a certain man who would say to me, quite openly and in thick Syrian-accented Arabic, "Another good day, Allah willing," or "Windy again. The sand will shift beneath your wheels." I would say nothing in reply, merely nod my head in greeting and walk on. In the webbing of my water bottle I would find a scrap of paper, the words "Nablus, the date stand." How they knew where I would be going that day, and to what exact location, I have no idea, though I was reminded of the sheikh's comment that information was their stock and trade. Hours later, we would be in Nablus, I would stop to buy a few dates, and a man would say to me, "Allah is great," and I would reply "Another good day, Allah willing," or he would say, "The drive must have been difficult" and I would agree, "Yes, it was windy again. The sand shifted beneath our wheels." The words were not exactly as they were given to me, and I wasn't certain that I was acquitting myself properly, but I was not corrected.

A few times, there was something more tangible. Once, an almost-empty packet of Turkish cigarettes. At a certain time, in a certain place, I withdrew the last cigarette, lighted it and took a few puffs before stubbing it out. Then I crumpled the packet and threw it carelessly away at a pre-arranged location. Another time, an envelope appeared under my door at the billet. It wasn't sealed and I succumbed to temptation, but the folded piece of paper inside was blank. Was this a test? Could there be words written in invisible ink? Was the message somehow secreted on the envelope itself? I didn't know, and I allowed myself to be carried away with the intrigue of the game. "Just let it be harmless," I whispered, folding the envelope and putting it in my pocket. Three days later, in Mays al Jabal, near the western blue line with Israel, as I left a meeting, a man with a limp brushed against me. "Ah, a thousand pardons, *Sayyid*. I was looking for the postman." I took the envelope out, unfolded it and smoothed it, and I could tell from the set of the man's eyes that this was what he'd been waiting for. "A thousand thank-you's," he said, mimicking himself. *Just let it be harmless*, I thought again, and, as far as I could tell, it was.

THE BOOK HEDBERG loaned me, *The History of the Jews*, was a thick paperback, its pages already much thumbed. The early chapters sent me off on a detour to read the Old Testament, which of course led me to the New. I browsed in both after

Sister Mark introduced them to me, several months earlier, now I devoured these books in full, better able to assimilate what I read with my expanding view of the world. It was a few weeks, my eyes as widened as the expanse of sky over the Mediterranean Sea, before I came back to the history. I read compulsively, every evening in my bed, wherever we were staying, late into the night. I carried the book with me and would read a page or two whenever I had a few minutes to spare, although, at Hedberg's suggestion, I fashioned a plain brown paper jacket to mask the cover. The chapters on the Inquisition, the pogroms, the Cossacks, the Pale, the Holocaust...they all shattered me, electrified me.

I asked Hedberg if there was a similar book on the Palestinians. He laughed.

"They wouldn't want to hear me say this, but they're not a people, really, they have no history of their own."

"The Arabs, then?"

"Certainly. The libraries here are full of such books. Some probably have a chapter or two on the Palestinians.'"

And so my reading expanded, and with it, my understanding.

On both sides – on *all* sides – there was inequity, cruelty, grievances.

I WAS ESPECIALLY interested in the differences between Judaism and Islam. It seemed remarkable to me that two peoples living side by side had developed such different religions, but Hedberg disagreed. "Not a dime's worth of difference between them," he said with a gruff laugh. "Jehovah? The Jewish God? And Allah? Twin brothers, I figure. I imagine them playing chess and laughing at the folly of man."

'So this dispute between the Jews and the Arabs, it isn't about religion?" I asked.

"No, though some think it is. Some Muslims think Jews are infidels, and some Jews think Muslims are no better than pagans."

"If not religion, what then?"

"Power. Some would say land, too. And culture, just the way different people live. Mostly power, I'd say."

"GET YOUR GEAR, YUSEF," Hedberg said early one morning. "Have to be in Gaza City in six hours."

I was lying on my bunk in Naqoura, which had become our more-or-less permanent headquarters, not just for the southern region but the overall Lebanon mission. Our compound was bristling with Blue Helmets, the faces beneath them of all hues, and civilians like Hedberg and I. Our job in Lebanon – the UN's job, as I was merely an employee with no say – was fairly simple: try to keep the various sides apart, try to keep the starving from perishing. Gaza was a different story altogether: part of Israel, or occupied by it, since 1967, the Palestinians there relatively quiet.

As soon as I heard the word Gaza, though, I thought about my papers, about my supposed birthplace, Jarara, not far from Gaza City. The chance of it being my actual birthplace was almost nonexistent, but the idea of going there and seeing for myself was irresistible.

We were assigned a driver, a young American Marine, his blue helmet and white armband prominent. I sat beside him, in the passenger seat as usual, Hedberg in the back, his nose deep in a briefing book. The jeep jolted and rolled over the gravel road, and I imagined that the words on the pages Hedberg was attempting to read must be dancing before his eyes, the way I remembered they had for me the first time I attempted to read after waking from my fever at the Sisters' clinic, my mind as blank as an open sky.

After we crossed the Israeli border, the road became a smooth highway that followed the coastline, the Hills of Galilee in the distance on our left, the calm Mediterranean on our right as we traveled south, past Acre and Haifa and Tel Aviv. Maryam, I knew, came from a kibbutz somewhere on the other side of those hills. Several hours passed, mostly in silence, and as I gazed at the Mediterranean, the sea which had once been my home, I allowed my mind to wander, in a way it rarely did.

A few weeks earlier, the jeep Hedberg and I were riding in was involved in a small accident – not a bomb or an ambush, just a minor collision with another vehicle as might occur on the streets of any city anywhere. Neither of us was hurt, just shaken up, as a precaution we were sent to a hospital in Beirut for a quick look over. It occurred to me, as I sat on a high cot in the examination room waiting for the doctor, that I had never – as far as I knew – seen one before, except for the cursory examination by the French-speaking doctor, Shamaoun, at the Sisters' clinic.

The doctor turned out to be a young Canadian woman with shining blonde hair and an aquiline nose, as different from me in every way that we might as well have been from different planets as countries, or the head and tail on either side of a coin. She was quite pleasant, though, and briskly efficient as she ran her hands over my ribs, peered into my eyes and ears with an instrument, measured the rhythm of my heart.

"What do you see?" I asked

"What do you mean?" She let the stethoscope fall against the breast of her white jacket and regarded my face for the first time.

I laughed. "I'm sorry, I didn't mean to be mysterious, or rude. It's just that I have such limited experience with doctors – I can't remember the last time I saw one. I can't help but wonder what your professional opinion of this specimen is."

The doctor frowned, studying my face. "My professional opinion is that this specimen is a healthy young male of some thirty-odd years, displaying no evidence of disease, no cuts or abrasions, no sign of broken bones, now or in the past. In other words, a splendid specimen, in the prime of life and peak of health." She picked up the stethoscope and turned to my back, placing its cold head on my skin.

"Thirty-odd years," I repeated.

"You don't know your age, Mr....?"

"Masoud. No, I don't."

She came around to my front again and took my wrist in her hand, a gesture that struck me as both clinical and intimate. "I'd say you were somewhere between thirty and forty, perhaps thirty-five, maybe even a year or two younger." She checked her watch, let go of my wrist and placed her hands on my jaws, applying just enough pressure that my mouth opened of its own accord, and she peered in. "No sign of dental work of any sort, no visible sign of decay...in fact, Mr. Masoud, you have a remarkable set of teeth for this part of the world." She stepped back and regarded me again. "Yes, thirty-five tops, I'd say."

She examined my eyes again, holding the lids wide apart with her fingers while shining a bright light onto my pupils. "And blue eyes," she said. "That too is unusual for this part of the world."

I replayed this conversation as we drove south. If I was no older than thirty-five, or even forty, then my parents could easily still be alive. I thought of them often in the weeks since seeing the doctor, And thought turned to desire, desire to compulsion. I burned to see my mother, my father, my sisters and brothers if I had any, yet had no idea where to look.

I'd asked the doctor if she could discern any clue as to my nationality. "Semitic, probably, but that's not a nationality really, is it? And that's not a professional opinion, just based on a few months here. You could be Jewish, could be Arab. Palestinian, Israeli, Lebanese..." She laughed. "With those blue eyes, you could be European, from anywhere. Do you really not know?"

I shook my head. "No, no idea. Your examination – no offence, doctor – failed to reveal that I was very ill some time ago. I lost my memory."

She stepped closer and looked into my eyes again, fingered the back of my head with strong, supple fingers. "No blow to the head?"

"No, an insect bite, on a strange island, and then raging fever, coma. Others who'd been with me died. When I regained consciousness, I had lost all sense of who I was."

"And there's been no return of memory?"

"None. But I didn't mean to trouble you with this tale of woe, though it's hardly that, doctor." I laughed. "As you said yourself, I'm in the peak of health. I just don't know who I am, not really. Your time is too valuable to be wasting it..."

"It's no trouble," she interrupted. "But I can't really help you. We do have a neurologist here. I can schedule you a time with him. He might be able to help."

I remembered that Dr. Shamaoun had also suggested I see

a neurologist and that then, as now, my reaction was sharply negative. Despite my strong desire to know my past, there might well be secrets locked in my head best left alone, I thought.

"No." I got up, reached for my shirt, suddenly uncomfortable. I had said too much. "Please. I didn't mean to burden you, I don't want to take up anyone else's valuable time. Believe me, it's not such a terrible thing, not remembering."

The doctor nodded. "It's true. Some people long to forget."

Not I. I burned, not to remember exactly, but to make contact. This was something new, I realized.

And now, remembering my reaction to the suggestion of seeing a neurologist, I wondered what I might be afraid of learning?

Calculating again, as I had so many times already, I estimated that my parents could easily be in their fifties, early sixties, perhaps, maybe late sixties. There was time to find them, not all the time in the world, no, not too much time, especially not in this dangerous land. Would they know me? I wondered. Recognize me? "Yusef, where have you been?" Is that what my mother would cry? No, certainly not. What was the chance that my name really was Yusef?

And could it be possible that I actually was from Gaza, as my counterfeit papers proclaimed, that I'd really been born in the village of Jarara? My name, that place of birth, they'd been chosen arbitrarily, but could there possibly have been some greater hand guiding that of the forger?

These and quite a few other thoughts crowded my head as we drove south through Israel, Hedberg and I and the young marine at the wheel, far from the tumult and shouting of Lebanon. We came to the checkpoint at the Gaza border and I took a deep breath. Nothing was familiar, nor was there anything in the crowded, rabbit-warren streets of Gaza City that spoke to me.

We had driven almost five hours for a meeting, that included diplomats from Egypt, that lasted less than an hour and, as far as I could tell, accomplished nothing. I'd told Hedberg about my private mission, of course, and afterwards, while he and other UN representatives had a whiskey, the Marine driver and I took the Jeep a few miles south to Jarara, a gathering of houses so small as to almost be unnoticeable. Again, there was nothing familiar. We stopped so I could speak to several people, they knew of no family named Masoud. That was a disappointment, but no surprise.

"The people who lived here in the '40s and before, they're all gone," an old man told me. "We're refugees, newcomers here."

I asked the driver to wait and spent ten minutes walking around, looking at houses, many of them no more than tarpaper shacks, and alleyways, choked with burned-out old tires and other trash, it was clear that there was almost no trace of the pre-war village. Nothing about the place, not even its smell, was familiar.

No, I was certain this was not my home.

"You look downcast, Yusef," Hedberg said when I sat down across from him in the hotel restaurant. "No luck?"

"A wild goose chase," I said with a wry smile. I'd learned that phrase from him not long before and liked the sound of it. "I knew it would be. Jarara's not really my birthplace, just a name pulled out of the air to put on my papers." Hedberg already knew all this, so I was not revealing a secret. "But I thought that maybe...."

"Disappointing nevertheless," he said.

"Yes."

The waiter came and I gave my order. "I just wish...," I began when he'd left, but the words failed me.

"Wish?" Hedberg prompted.

"I wish there was something," I said. "Some clue, some thread... I feel like a kite that's lost its grounding cord, flying loose." There was a hint of a whine in my voice that I didn't like.

Hedberg must have heard it too. "Some day, maybe."

"Yes, some day. Maybe."

Driving back to Lebanon the following day, as we approached the border, I found my eyes increasingly turning to the right, toward the Hills of Galilee, brown smudges on the western horizon. A strange sensation had begun to grow within me, an urge I couldn't quite identify. Those hills, it seemed, were calling to me.

Was that where my home lay?

CHAPTER 17
DAYS OF MIRACLE AND WONDER

THE BUS TRIP NORTH from Beirut to Jounieh took less than half an hour. I got off a kilometer or so before the stop near the nunnery and walked through a light rain down toward the beach, where the makeshift buildings of the Sisters' clinic nestled among ancient olive trees. As I approached the clinic, the rain suddenly stopped and the sun came out.

That morning, I'd accompanied Hedberg to a meeting in Beirut with a dogs' breakfast of people, Lebanese Sunnis, Shias and Maronites, Syrians, Israelis, Palestinians – including one man I'd encountered several times in my message-delivering, a swarthy man called Abu Niger – and UN officials. I was the only translator there – even the Syrians, whom I'd had only occasional dealings with before, and spoke Arabic with an odd French-inflected accent, had heard of me by reputation and were content with this arrangement. It was an intense if fruitless couple of hours.

Afterwards, Hedberg was ensconced in a gathering of his UN colleagues that would keep him occupied the rest of the day and he wouldn't require my services. I'd mentioned to him that I'd hoped to get down to Jounieh, but not my reasons, and he offered the use of jeep and driver.

"Go ahead, Yusef, I won't be needing them."

But I preferred to be on my own.

I'd been thinking about my journal ever since my disappointing trip to Gaza. I had every expectation that it would be exactly as I left it with Sister Paul.

I prided myself that my memory was excellent, within the narrow scope of its context, but I could not recall exactly what was in that journal any more than anyone could remember what they said or did or observed on a certain day months or even years in the past. My sojourn on the island of sand was less than a year behind me, yet I remembered very little of it, just its broad strokes, with the exception of some of the smallest and oddest of details which still came to me in dreams. Was there a chance that somewhere in the journal, that record of my forty days – if that's what it was – on the island, there was a clue, some scrap of information that might lead to my origins?

That's what I wanted to see for myself.

I retraced the same steps I'd taken only months earlier, shaking my head that so much time had passed. On that day in late April, with my strength and clarity much restored, I'd left the clinic and walked up the hill to the road, accompanied by Sister Mark, who claimed to be adept at flagging down the bus. I'd worn my carpenter's apron, strapped to my waist, and carried a knapsack containing a few pieces of hand-me-down clothing. I was headed first to Beirut and then on to either Tel Aviv or Jerusalem or Ramallah, or staying put – I hadn't yet decided – and I didn't know what lay in store for me.

Much had occurred in the months that followed, including, most momentously, my relationship with Maryam, and my education in diplomacy and the nuances of Middle Eastern politics, yet I was no closer to discovering any truths about myself, not even my name. My recent visit to Jarara in Gaza left me feeling unsettled, restless; the lack of a past, I'd realized, had become a wound that would not heal. I hadn't had any real expectations that I would find any link to my past in Jarara, so I was surprised by the deep feeling of disappointment that followed. Now, I was pinning my hopes on the journal. It was unlikely there'd be any clues in it, but I wanted to see.

I could hear voices as I drew close to the clinic, women and children chattering happily and one disconsolate infant crying, but when I stepped through the trees into the clearing, it suddenly fell silent. Even the crying child fell mute.

The clinic is a rather make-shift affair, from the outside appearing to be no more than a clutch of shacks and lean-tos, with a larger villa-like structure, which serves as the nun's living quarters and chapel, behind it. But within, the clinic is clean, orderly and stocked with modern medical equipment. None of the sisters are physicians, two or three are qualified nurses; the rest, like Sister Mark, are capable assistants and midwives who, under supervision, can handle most situations they're likely to encounter, including childbirth, inoculations, flues and other minor ailments. Anyone appearing at the clinic with gunshot wounds or other really serious ailments is sent on the Jounieh hospital or one of the larger hospitals in Beirut. The patients are primarily women and children, mostly from the Palestinian refugee camp nearby, though a few Maronites from the area, drawn by the religious connection, are also regulars, and they form the majority of widows and orphans who have set up semi-permanent camp in tents on the clinic grounds.

Sister Luke and Sister Peter were sitting outside on plastic web lawn chairs, plump, happy-faced women, pendulous breasts plainly visible beneath the loose folds of their tent-like, open-air gowns, their bald heads shining. They were surrounded by children and a handful of women dressed in the Palestinian manner, with robes and scarves covering their heads. All of them turned their heads toward me as I stepped into their sight and they all stared at me as if I were an apparition.

The silence hung above us all like a cloud of gnats for several seconds, then rapid murmuring began, in Arabic and Italian, too low for me to hear more than a few words: *Najjar, Isa, Yeshu, Yeshua, Yehoshuah, Mahdi, Mustafa.*

Sister Peter stood up abruptly, the child on her lap falling to the ground with a thump. "We didn't expect you, Gesù," she stammered, slipping into Italian.

"Yusef," I said. "Yusef Mahoud, remember?" Then I remembered that I hadn't yet chosen that name when I was last here. "Adam, I mean. It's me, Adam, the castaway you nursed back to health."

"Yes, we remember, of course. I must get…"

Just then, Sister Mark and Sister Paul, the abbess, appeared, drawn by the commotion, their mouths falling open at the sight of me. They were quickly followed by the other nuns, altogether eight or nine. Sister Paul fell to her knees, and the others followed suit.

I was astonished by this reception. "What on earth? Sister Mark, sisters, it's just me, Adam, the shipwreck, don't you remember? You nursed me back to health."

"Yeshua," Sister Mark said. "We remember you very well. How could we forget? We are honoured to have you among us again, blessed."

"Sisters, there's been a mistake. I'm not who you think I am."

I said this even though I wasn't really sure *who* they thought I was, just that I was not. "I'm Adam, well, no, Yusef, I've remembered my name, it's Yusef Masoud, a ship's carpenter who was shipwrecked and almost died, rescued by Syrian fisherman, nursed back to health by your graciousness. Yusef, not Yeshua, a simple man, a carpenter, now working as a translator. That's all. I'm not..."

"You are," Sister Paul spoke up, bold now. "You are The One. *Yehoshuah*. It's in the book. In your own hand."

SISTER TIMOTHY, thin and birdlike, poured tea, looked nervously to Sister Mark and Sister Paul, then withdrew. We were in the courtyard behind the villa, again in the shade of olive trees, the caress of the sea on the shore – a sound I was so familiar with – gentle on our ears.

"I don't understand," I said.

Sister Paul took off her glasses, used a fold of her tunic to carefully wipe them clean, and replaced them on her bony nose. Her eyes avoided me during this procedure, then, after blinking several times, they focused on me. "We were told there might be a reaction like that." Her Italian was precise, but with a slight German accent.

"Told? By who?"

"The Vatican," Sister Mark said. She was the same Sister Mark I remembered so well from my convalescence in her care months earlier, slim and athletic, and a remarkably pleasing face, serene and almost beautiful despite the port wine stain, or perhaps because of it.

"Someone *in* the Vatican," Sister Paul corrected her. "There are protocols, procedures, chains of command. The Holy Father has not yet been told."

"Nor anyone close to him," Sister Mark said. "But someone with authority."

I looked from one to the other. "Told? Told what?"

"About you," Sister Mark said.

"What *about* me?"

"Who you are," Sister Paul said. She took a sip of tea, never moving her eyes from me. Then, correcting herself: "Who you may be, that is. Only the Holy Father can determine that. And only after much more study."

I was speechless for a moment. "Who I am?" I finally asked. "I told you, I'm Yusef Masoud, ship's carpenter..." I faltered. Ship's carpenter, yes, at least I had been that, for how long I didn't really know. Was my journey on the *Al-Aqba* my first, or the last of many? And how long had the *Al-Aqba* been at sea? I didn't even know that. We had set out from Oman, I remembered the first mate telling me that, yet which ports we visited, and what our destination was at the time of the storm – I had no idea. Ship's carpenter, yes, at least for that brief time, but beyond that? I didn't know, that was the bitter truth. Yusef Masoud, no, that was an invention. I had no idea who I was, really, but surely not this Yeshua, this man who now apparently had the attention of the Vatican, an institution I knew little about other than the veneration in which it was held by the Sisters and many other Catholics I'd come in contact with.

Suddenly, I was swept up by the strangest feeling, strange and familiar, as if I was in the presence of some mystical force, or back in the grip of an accustomed fever. On the island, as I lay in the sand, I often felt that unworldly presence, felt myself separating from myself. I set my teacup in its saucer, placed them both on the table beside me, and fell forward onto my knees, my face against the hard tiles.

"Who *am* I? If you know, Sister, if you truly know, please tell me."

"We believe you are who you are, my son, My Lord. You are Yeshua, The One, the Messiah, The son of God."

"Jesus Christ," Sister Mark added.

"How can that be?" I cried. I held out my left arm and with the fingers of my right hand pinched the flesh above the wrist. "See? I am flesh and blood, not an apparition, not a ghost, not a spirit."

"Our Lord Jesus was a man," Sister Paul said quietly. "He too was flesh and blood."

"But how...."

"That is not for us to say, Gesù. "The Lord works in mysterious ways, and it is not for us to judge them, or to question them. Merely to witness. And to proclaim."

"This can't be," I protested again. "I'm only a man, a simple man, a...a ship's carpenter."

"And was not our Lord a simple carpenter?" Sister Paul asked. "Was he not a fisher of men who cast his net upon the sea? Get up, My Lord, it is we who must kneel to you."

She and Sister Mark both joined me on the courtyard tiles. Despite Sister Paul's admonition, I stayed where I was, and after a moment, the abbess took my hand, then all three of us joined hands. "Let us pray," Sister Paul said, and she began to recite the Lord's Prayer in Latin. Despite myself, I began to laugh at her pronunciation. Sister Paul fell silent, and the two nuns lifted their heads to look at me.

"I confess, sisters, there is much about me I don't know. I have, for the last year, often wondered whether I was Muslim or Jew. Both faiths, the little I know of them, feel familiar to me, comfortable. It never occurred to me I might be Christian. I know next to nothing of that faith, just the little bit I picked up from you, Sister Mark."

"Jesus was a Jew," Sister Paul said. She spoke as a teacher might to a child. "And he lived – *you* lived, My Lord – long before Mohammad, before the Islamic faith was born. And before Christianity – he was the rock on which the church was built."

"You're saying that I'm Jesus Christ, that I'm, what, two thousand years old?" I raised my head to meet Sister Paul's gaze, and laughed again. "In this body, the body of a thirty-five-year-old, I have that on good medical authority."

"That isn't the way it works," Sister Paul said.

"It?"

"Resurrection."

"Magic," Sister Mark said.

"Miracle."

We were silent for a minute. "I've forgotten so much," I said. "More than I realized. You say I'm the son of God. I've...I've forgotten God." I paused. "I know what He is...Who...but only what I've heard or read. I have no memory of God, no knowledge of Him."

"Jesus also resisted accepting who he was," Sister Paul said.

"I have no faith *in* Him."

"We know that," Sister Paul said gently. Did I imagine it, or was she squeezing my hand?

"You know? What do you mean?"

"We know about your loss of memory. We know what you

know and what you don't. It's all part, we believe, of the Divine Plan. You are being tested, just as you were two thousand years ago."

"How do you know, Sister?"

She looked at me with surprise. "It's in the book, as I said. *Your* book. You wrote it yourself."

SISTER PAUL ROSE slowly and excused herself. Sister Mark and I remained kneeling, exchanging furtive glances but no words. My knees began to ache but I stayed where I was. After a few minutes, Sister Paul returned, holding a leather-bound book, I could see it was not my journal.

"Please, Yeshua, sit."

"Only if you will as well."

We sat again in the canvas chairs beneath the olive trees. The tea had grown cold, but I took a sip from my cup to wet my lips.

"Let me read," Sister Paul said.

"The journal's in Aramaic," I protested. "I know you can't read it. Besides, that's not my journal."

"It is and it isn't," she said. "We've had it translated."

"Ah. By who, if I may ask?"

"Someone known to us," Sister Paul said. "Someone we trust."

"Ah." I was speechless, and attempted to say no more. I had come to retrieve my journal, but I hadn't expected anything like this turn of events.

"Let me read," Sister Paul repeated.

"Go ahead."

She flipped through the pages – I could see they were written by hand, in what appeared to be ink, and leaning closer, I could see the script was in Roman alphabet, Italian – until she came to the place she wanted. She cleared her throat.

"The beast that confronted me," she read, "was enormous, larger than a bull, shaped like a centaur, part horse, part lion, with horns from which serpents slithered."

"What? Wait," I interrupted.

"Please." Sister Paul looked up, pursing her lips, like a school teacher at a disobedient child. Later, it occurred to me that for that brief moment, she'd forgotten who she thought I was.

She lowered her head and continued to read. "The beast spoke, 'You are hungry, Yeshua. Allow me to feed you. See this rock? Just tell me you believe in me and I will turn it into bread.'

"'I will not,' I said. 'Get away, beast, you are an abomination.'"

I got to my feet. "That's enough. I'm sorry Sister Paul, Sister Mark, this is a hoax. You're deceiving me, or someone is deceiving you."

I could see the two women were shocked, ashen-faced. "Was there not a beast..." Sister Paul began.

"There was a strange animal on the island, but not a beast, I would never have used that word."

"And did the creature not speak to you, attempt to tempt you?"

"Yes, it spoke – or so I thought, in my delirium. My journal says it spoke, yes, but did it really? I don't think so anymore. And, real or imagined, it certainly didn't say anything like what you've just read."

I reached over and took the book from Sister Paul's hands. Browsing through it quickly, as the two nuns watched me in disbelief, I could see it was filled with exaggerations and fabrication. An entry about fishing had dozens of fish leaping out of the water into my hands, smiles on their rubbery lips. In another, "the beast" lays a trap for me, a hole dug in the sand, lined with sharp sticks, and covered with palm branches.

"Sister Paul, I don't know who did this translation, but whoever it is has duped you. This isn't what I wrote. It's not just poor translation, this is something else. It's fantasy. And where is the original, my journal?"

"It's in a safe place," Sister Paul said. "Don't you worry."

But worry I did. And rue the day I began the journal. What mischief might it still bring?

BOOK 4

Into The Galilee

CHAPTER 18
AN END OF THINGS

I'VE SAID THAT all of my life prior to the mosquito-induced fever is gone, but that I remember clearly everything since. That's not quite right.

For one thing, I remember, if as through fog, the boat ride to the Isle of Flies, the attack of the insects, the hasty paddle back, then the falling into fever and delirium. But do I really remember all that or was the telling of it after I recovered implanted into my mind as a suggested memory? I don't know.

More important, my memory following my recovery does sometimes play tricks on me, especially the events of the ship-wreck, my miraculous survival and my long stay on the second island, events that have come to blur together in my mind. I'd been feverish again, a fever of a different sort, brought on by heat, exposure to the elements, hunger and thirst, during much of that time. I'd faithfully written in my journal, yes, after I'd recovered it. But were those writings based on reality, feverish imaginings, or dreams? And do I remember the reality or the written account of it?

I cannot say.

I was learning that memory is always fallible, mine no less so than any other man's.

And there, in writing, were two versions of the past as recorded by memory: mine, of a creature that spoke of hope; a translator's, of a beast that spoke of temptation. Was one true, the other false? And if, so, which was which?

THE NEXT DAY, I dragged myself back to Beirut, and it must have looked that way.

"What's wrong, Yusef?" Hedberg asked. "You look like you've seen a ghost."

I laughed at that. "Maybe I have. My own ghost, maybe, ghost of my former self."

"You look terrible, no joke. Have you slept? Eaten?"

"Sure."

Sleep, yes. A few fitful hours on the cold, hard sand of the beach below the clinic – a bed that, despite its discomfort, felt remarkably familiar. I couldn't bring myself to sleep inside, under sheets, in such close proximity to those women who wanted nothing less than to devour me whole.

Eat, yes, a few figs and olives gathered in the nearby groves, before slipping away without saying goodbye at first light; and a heel of stale bread an old woman on the bus was kind enough to share with me. She looked at me from beneath thick tangled grey eyebrows, from above the edge of a kerchief that covered the lower part of her face, through eyes of the clearest, most penetrating blue. She seemed to know – but know what?

"You want to talk, my friend?" Hedberg persisted. Then, sensing my reluctance, he answered his own question. "No, get yourself a shower, have some breakfast. My business here is through, we leave soon enough. We'll have plenty of time to talk on the drive back."

But we didn't talk. I waved away Hedberg's occasional feint at an opening, and the drive to Naqoura on the coastal road was marked by either silence or casual chatting. Hedberg didn't even ask me my views on the meeting we'd had the day before, something he invariably did, valuing my take on the individuals we dealt with.

Back in Naqoura, our normal routine resumed as if nothing had happened, yet I remained shaken, and I sensed things would not continue unchanged for long. The Sisters of the Divine Crucifix were unlikely to remain silent, despite the promise I'd wrenched from them.

Sister Paul was certain that the translation was correct, that either my memory was faulty – a reasonable enough surmise – or that my protestations were part of some new Divine Plan. She saw herself as some latter-day Paul – perhaps an actual reincarnation of her namesake – with a mission to spread the word of the Second Coming.

Still, I carried on, accompanying Hedberg on a daily basis, translating as he met with Israelis, Palestinians, Lebanese of all sorts, United Nations soldiers and officials from various countries – most of them spoke some English, but not enough. And I carried on as an occasional surreptitious courier of messages, although I was starting to change my mind about that.

This phase of my life would soon come to an end, though nothing overt happened. For one thing, several months passed and, though I had frequent messages to deliver, I'd heard nothing directly from the sheikh, and his suggestion that he might be able to unearth something about my past was proving to have been a hollow promise. Beyond that, my attitude toward the tasks I'd been given as a messenger changed drastically with a dream one night not long after my return from Jounieh. Since then, I'd been haunted by some of the images I'd come across in the translation of my journal, and in my dream I came face to face with one of them.

I was back on Shipwreck Island, walking along the shore. I came to a pile of palm branches that hadn't been there before. I approached warily, touching a branch with my bare toe, moving it just enough to expose a hole and the brightly pointed tips of sharpened sticks, exactly as it was described in the translated journal. I stepped back from the trap in alarm and became aware that I was being watched. I spun around and there was the Creature who had been my companion on the island, yet not as I had known it. Serpents slithered around this beast's awful head and when it opened its mouth, sharp points of its teeth caught the sun, blinding me for a moment. I looked away and when I turned back, the beast now bore the face of Sheikh Al-Qatar.

A FEW WEEKS LATER, in Beirut again, Hedberg was in a meeting and had no need for me, so I had the afternoon off. I was sitting on the patio of a café on *Rue Wadi Abu Jamile*, not far from the Maghen Abraham Synagogue, having an espresso, lost in my own thoughts, when I was startled by a man who took a chair beside me.

"A fine day."

I mumbled a reply, barely looking up.

"A fine day," he repeated, and I realized then that this was code.

"It is, yes, a fine day." I looked at him, recognizing him as a Lebanese Shia I'd run across before, a thin man who walked with a decided limp, the result, I'd been told, of a bomb, carried by a man he'd been with, that went off prematurely, killing the companion.

"Our friend sends you greetings," he said now.

"And greetings back to him."

The thin man paused, glancing casually around the patio. "He wishes to see you."

For a moment, my heart thumped in my chest. The sheikh wished to see me? Could it be that he had learned something of my past? Then, all of a sudden, and to my own surprise, I grew impatient. Anything the sheikh might tell me, I realized, I would have to view with extreme suspicion. "Well, here I am," I said. "Let him come."

My companion made a face of disgust but he bit his tongue. For a full minute, his silence seemed to vibrate. Then he rose and, without even a nod, turned away. Watching him limp down the street, I wondered idly if I would regret that moment of impatience.

I went into the café and ordered another espresso. I didn't have long to wait. As I sipped the bitter coffee, I considered again the bargain I'd made with the devil. I'd felt all along that what I was doing was harmless – I'd seen no evidence otherwise. Now it struck me that I had no evidence that it wasn't, and again I thought of the trap on the beach, of my dream.

Before long, the man called Abu Niger – whom I'd seen only a few weeks earlier at a meeting with Hedberg – sat down beside me. He was dressed in an ill-fitting suit, with a checkered *kaffiyeh* on his head. The bulge of a pistol was clearly evident under his arm. "A fine day," he said.

"Yes, indeed, a very fine day. A fine day. A very fine day. Wouldn't you say it is a fine day?"

He lit a cigarette and offered me one, which I declined. "Perhaps there's been a misunderstanding," he said.

"No, I don't think so. No misunderstanding. I'm just tired of this game."

"It's hardly a game." He looked at me with shrewd interest.

"It feels that way to me." He continued to gaze at me with narrowed eyes. "Sorry, excuse my poor choice of words."

"Perhaps you would like to see the sheikh?"

"No, I don't want to see him. I'm tired of this. I've had enough."

"It's not that easy," Abu Niger said.

"Yes it is. I didn't sign a contract, didn't swear an oath." I got up. "Give the sheikh my regards and my regrets."

Out on the street, I could feel Niger's eyes burning holes in my back.

I hadn't been with her for several weeks, and suddenly I had a strong urge to see Maryam. It was, I realized, almost a year to the day since I had stood like a child naked before her for the first time. We had become lovers, but in a sense I thought of her as my mother, the first woman to see me naked, to hold me, love me.

I shook my head to rid myself of these conflicting images and feelings, and set off in the direction of the market where she worked.

"I'M GOING AWAY," I said. I had been thinking about what to tell her and decided to be as simple and straight-forward as I could.

"I know," Maryam said.

This response surprised me, but I went on. "To Israel, I think. Or Palestine. I'm not sure where one ends and the other begins.

Or what the difference is, really."

"I know," she repeated.

I frowned. "I don't know for how long. I'm pretty sure we'll see each other again."

"I know that, too." She was smiling now, and my irritation dissolved.

"How do you know these things, Maryam?"

"That I *don't* know."

CHAPTER 19

I SAID GOODBYE to Hedberg. I felt I owed him that much –
much more actually, but that was all I could come up with.

"How will I get along without you?" he asked. "I'm not being
polite, I mean it."

"There are other translators."

"No one like you."

I raised my hands in a gesture of acceptance.

He arranged, at my request, a ride across the border – a white
UN jeep was going into Israel on some sort of business regularly,
so there was nothing unusual about it. When we got to Nahariya,
the first Israeli town on the coastal highway, I asked the driver
to stop and I hopped out. I peeled off my UN armband and
tossed it in the back of the Jeep, gave the driver a casual salute,
and took off on foot. All I had was my almost-empty toolbelt,
slung around my waist, and a backpack crammed with a few
clothes and books, including the translated journal. There were
two copies, Sister Paul admitted, so she couldn't have refused.
It was a travesty, of course, but already I could tell that reading
one of its pages could transport me back to where I'd been when
I wrote the original. It would have to do. And as for the original,

my own journal, Sister Paul wouldn't part with it – she had it under lock and key "in a safe place," she said. "It's a relic."

When I'd protested that it was mine, she replied with a curt, "No, it belongs to the ages." A will of steel, that woman has. My intention was to head south on Highway 2 to Acre – Akko, the locals call it – or, if I didn't like the look of it, on to Haifa, seeking work as a carpenter. I'd had enough of diplomacy, if that's what the work I'd been involved in with Hedberg could legitimately be called, and enough of being a messenger for shadowy men whose purposes were still not clear to me. I wanted a simpler life, at least for a while, and my hands cried out for the feel of tools, for the feel of wood. My hands, at least, had not lost their memory.

I stuck my thumb out, as I'd seen so many people doing, and caught a ride with an Arab farmer, bumping along the rutted coastal highway in the back of his pickup truck. Sitting with my back to the truck's cab, facing the way we'd come, the Mediterranean was on my left, the rugged hills of Galilee on my right. I couldn't see the Sea of Galilee, of course, but I imagined I could smell it. Maryam had grown up in a village along its shores and its waters were the sweetest anywhere, she liked to say. I suggested I visit her village, but she'd turned cross. "No, please don't," she said, and would say no more.

In Acre, I found a room in the old city, in an ancient house with whitewashed walls a street or two away from the citadel. The house was divided into a warren of small cubicles, each rented out to single men. The third floor room I chose had a hard narrow bed and a wooden chair, with a clothes tree to serve as closet. I liked it because its window, which opened with some effort, looked out on the harbour. The landlady was an ancient crone dressed in black, with a hunched posture and wrinkled face, altogether giving the impression of a prune. She merely nodded or shook her head in response to my questions, regardless of which language I used, held up fingers to indicate the price, and gestured and pointed as she showed me the bathroom and kitchen.

I lay down on the bed, meaning just to test its comfort, found it satisfactory and immediately fell asleep. I was on the island again, Shipwreck Island, a place I often went to in dreams, lying in the sand. This time was different, though. The creature who'd so often been my companion in these dreams was gone, replaced by a giant tortoise that taunted me with some of the riddles Mohar conjured up before he drowned, the tortoise's voice a cross between a whisper and a squeak. And, though I couldn't see him, I felt the presence of someone else, another man, sitting behind my right shoulder, in darkness. This presence surprised and disturbed me more than the whispering tortoise did, or the Creature ever had, and I woke with a start.

I went down to the *Ze'ev Frid* marina and spent some time looking at the fishing boats and pleasure boats, lined up on different docks. I asked at the harbourmaster's office about repairs and was sent down to a separate dock where several boats were in dry-dock, suspended in slings above the water. The man who ran the business was a Jew named Begin, heavy-set, with thinning grey hair and beard and wearing a black skullcap. I told him, in Hebrew, my story in the sketchiest way, that I was a ship's carpenter, was shipwrecked and had no desire to go to sea again. I told him my papers were lost in the shipwreck, that my name was Marranos, the name of one of my *Al-Aqba* shipmates. He looked me over with a skeptical eye but asked no questions and told me to come back in the morning.

Begin, like me, had spent some time at sea and was covered with tattoos to prove it. He knew his way around a hammer and saw, and had a good eye, for years he'd been a boss, his hands rarely getting dirty, and he'd grown soft and round. He put me to work patching a hull on a fishing boat but within days assigned me to finishing work in the galleys of yachts and smaller pleasure boats. "You're too good to waste on rough work, Marranos," he said. This pleased me, as I had no real sense of my talent or skills.

I had only the simplest of tools of my own, a few screwdrivers, a pair of pliers, and a hammer, but Begin's shop was well equipped with hand and electric tools and I quickly became adept at their use. The last time I'd used tools, other than for some small repairs at the Sisters of the Divine Crucifix clinic, was when I'd built coffins on board the *Al-Aqba*, but, as then, the knowledge of the tools came back to me as soon as I had them in my hands. "The body has its own memory," the first mate had remarked, and he'd been proven right many times since. I had no conscious memory of beveling or countersinking, yet I knew how to do it, and well, just as, on that first wondrous occasion with Maryam I had known the mechanics of making love, though I possessed no conscious memory of ever having done so before.

The body has its own memory. Yes, I'd observed that many times. My hands remembered wood, the feel of it, both rough and smooth, the grain, its strength and brittleness. With wood and my tools on my workbench, there was never any hesitation. But my brain's memory was not as good and I knew little of wood other than what I had at hand. Begin also had only scant knowledge of finer woods, he suggested I pay a visit to a cabinet maker he knew of in the old city, and there I was introduced to cherrywood, teak and mahogany. He had some pieces sent over to the wharf and I began making use of these fine woods on the yachts I was working on.

Out of Begin's presence, among the handful of other men working for him – all Arabs – I spoke Arabic, and introduced myself only as Yusef. I'd learned, during my time with the UN, that those I spoke Hebrew to took me to be a Jew, those with whom I spoke Arabic assumed I was an Arab. That ambiguity suited exactly the anonymity I was now seeking.

I'd left no forwarding address, even with Hedberg, when I departed from Naqoura, since I'd had no idea where I was going, so I felt reasonably confident the sheikh, should he be seeking me out, would not have an easy time of it. I didn't mention the UN or refer to my time in Lebanon, and I was careful at most times to speak only in Arabic or, if pressed, a rudimentary Hebrew, with no better command than many other workmen possessed. The only person who knew my whereabouts was Maryam, to whom I had written soon after I settled in. That, apparently, was a mistake, although she did nothing overt to betray me. How the sheikh came to know my whereabouts I have no idea.

IT WAS IN ACRE, at around this time, that I met Ahmad Safieh. He'd been working on a fishing boat in dry dock for repairs the crew was doing themselves. I was on the dock planing a cabinet door I'd just removed when he came by, hoping to borrow a bit for his drill. He stood beside me for a moment, watching me work.

"Very nice work," he said in Arabic.

I looked up, suspicious, as always, of a stranger. I saw an ordinary-looking fellow, about my age and of similar build, about the same complexion, same short dark beard, hair a bit shorter, even dressed much the same, in blue jeans, workboots and black T shirt – so it was much like seeing a quick glance in a mirror – except that his shirt was emblazoned with the face of Che Guevara. That was an image I had seen a number of times, on posters hanging on Beirut walls, so I knew who he was.

"Thank you. You're a carpenter too? Or a revolutionary." I lifted my chin in the direction of his chest.

"No, not a carpenter, merely a fisherman. And a farmer. But I appreciate good craftsmanship. And not a revolutionary either. Except in the sense that we all are."

"Oh? What are we in revolt against?"

"Oppression. Injustice. Discrimination. Unfairness. It's a long list."

I put down the plane and wiped my hands on my apron. I'd expected a different sort of answer – the Jews, the Americans, capitalists. "You're a philosopher."

He laughed. "Me? No. My father, he's the philosopher in the family."

"Oh? I'd like to meet him."

We each took a step toward each other and shook hands. "Yusef," I said.

"Ahmad. My father's name is Yusef too."

He told me what he wanted and I fetched my drill and a few bits and walked down the pier with him to a barnacle-encrusted dhow much like the one that had rescued me, this one fitted out with a motor. It crossed my mind that, if the Syrian fishermen had had a motor on their dhow, they never would have drifted within sight of my island, and I might still be there, more likely dead than alive. It took me just a few minutes to drill the holes in the planking that they needed. Ahmad's shipmates, the captain of the fishing vessel and two other fishermen, younger brothers of Ahmad, stood watching. The captain, Nasser Zalloua, was Lebanese, but the Safiehs were Israeli Arabs from a village on Lake Kenneret – the Sea of Galilee – where they fished most of the year in their own small boat, except for the late spring, when large tuna runs in the Mediterranean made the journey to Acre to work for wages worthwhile.

"Come back and join us for supper," Ahmad said when I took my leave. It had been a while since I'd shared a meal with anyone, so I did, and enjoyed it more than any time I could remember in the company of others, with the exception of Maryam. We met on the beach, where a fire was built and two good-sized fish were roasting and a pot of lentils was bubbling. Ahmad proved to be especially good company. Though he had little in the way of formal education, he was well read and seemed unusually worldly. His brothers, Fahd and Isma'il, both younger, were shy at first, but gradually became more vocal as the evening wore on. Isma'il was fond of jokes and told several that seemed to poke fun at the captain, who took it in good spirits. Nasser was a large man with dark wide eyes and a thick black beard who often fished in these waters, he told me. He liked the Acre waters, especially in the spring, when the fishing was usually very good, but the Lebanese crew who'd come with him had grown homesick after only a few days and taken off. He considered himself lucky to have met the Safiehs. He was Shia, they were Sunni, but these differences seemed to disappear aboard ship.

I took a liking to the Safiehs, good-natured men who respected and cared for each other, and Ahmad in particular. After eating, the two of us went for a walk along the harbour. I pointed out some of the boats, surprised by how much I knew about them.

"I was a sailor," I explained. "Or, rather, a ship's carpenter. I spent some time at sea."

"And a woman in every port, I imagine." Ahmad laughed, and so did I.

"Now why would you imagine something like that?"

"A good-looking fellow like you? You must have broken a lot of hearts. Anyway, isn't that what they say about sailors?"

"I don't know, is it?"

At this point, I told him a bit about my history, leaving out the shipwreck and everything that followed.

"And you remember nothing, truly?"

"Nothing. I had to relearn how to read, how to hold a fork, how to brush my teeth and wipe my ass. You're laughing, yet it's true. Funny, though, when I held a hammer and a screwdriver in my hands for the first time, I knew exactly what to do with them. But my parents, childhood, everything else, all gone."

"Even your name?"

"Especially my name. Made up – there are a lot of Yusefs, I could as easily really be one as not. But who I am…I don't know."

Ahmad was silent, thinking. "That strikes me as a wonderful thing, Yusef," he said finally.

"Really? Why?"

"You don't remember the bad things you did, the stupid things, all the times you felt like a fool."

"Or the good things, I don't remember them either."

"But it's the bad things, the sins and errors and false steps that haunt you, don't you think? You keep playing them over in your mind, 'if only I hadn't done that, if only I'd said such and such…' Regrets and disappointments, we all have them, but not you. You don't have regrets, Yusef, not for the major part of your life, anyway. It's a new beginning, a second life."

"And you said it's your father who's the philosopher in the family."

On the walk back to their boat, Ahmad invited me to visit him and his family on their farm, near Tiberias, on the Sea of Galilee.

"I'd love to. I like it here in Akko, and this job is good, my boss is good to me. But I've been wanting to take a look at the lake."

"There's always work for a carpenter with your skills, Yusef. Come and stay with us for as long as you want. I'm sure my father can put you to work fixing one building or another."

Just before we parted, Ahmad touched my shoulder. "Yusef...if that's your name, mystery man without a past, do you know...are you Arab or Jew?" He laughed abruptly, out of embarrassment.

I smiled. "You're not the first to ask, believe me. Arab...I think."

He laughed again, more assured this time. "Again, this is maybe not such a bad thing, you know."

"Not knowing?"

"Yes, not knowing."

"We're all the same, you know."

He paused, thinking. "In the eyes of Allah, yes, I'm sure that's true."

"If there's a difference – *if* there is one – it's of our own making."

Ahmad laughed. "Now who's the philosopher, Yusef Marranos?"

We said good night, Ahmad walking down the dock to the boat where he and his brothers had bunks. I turned to walk back to the old city. It was late and the night was dark, the sky brilliant with stars and a slim slice of a new moon. The rich salt smell of the Mediterranean was pungent in my nostrils. I replayed our conversation – what he'd said about being without sin or regret, about being reborn, had struck a chord. I was reminded again that it was over a year since my rescue from the island. I'd said those words that had prompted Ahmad's comments – "I don't know who I am" – to the Syrian fishermen, to the nuns, to Maryam, to Hedberg, now to him – and each time it hurt again, as much as the first time. Would I ever know?

Memory is a curse, I thought.

But if you remember, you're bound to have regrets, as Ahmad pointed out.

And if you forget, you're haunted – by the possibilities of what you might have done that you shouldn't have and of what you didn't do that that you should have.

Either way, you are somehow incomplete.

Memory, I came to realize, is a part of who you are. Should it be taken away, you have lost part of yourself as much as if you'd lost an arm or a leg. You are diminished.

I had known and reconciled myself to the fact that the better part of my life was simply gone. If I was, as the Canadian doctor I'd met estimated, somewhere around thirty-five, then thirty-four years of my life had disappeared, about half of what I might reasonably expect to live, barring a violent or illness-ravaged premature end.

But I'd come to have faith in my *present* memory, my memory of that stage of my life that started after my recovery on board the *Al-Aqba*, my memory of the remarkable events of the last year or so. I reasoned that because the period my memory covered was so short, it was bound to be so much better than the average person's, I had so much less to remember, I could remember it all the better.

Lying in bed in my narrow room, listening to the waves splash up against the pilings in the harbour and the thick stone seawalls to the north and south, I thought that now I had a new list of regrets, if not necessarily sins, not yet. I was sorry that I hadn't said to Ahmad, "Oh, I have sins, I have disappointments, I have regrets, I just don't remember them. They haven't been washed away, though, they're still there. Some day they may catch up with me."

Just before I fell asleep, I thought again of my irritated conversations with the sheikh's emissaries at the café near the Maghen Abraham Synagogue. I'd angrily rebuffed the idea of meeting again with the sheikh. Why had I done that, I wondered now. Was I perhaps afraid to hear news of my past life he might have unearthed? Why would I be afraid of that?

The sea was in my dreams that night. A large ship, no fishing *dhow* or freighter, but a steamship, a cruise ship, in waters that seemed familiar, the clear blue-green of the Mediterranean. Shouting on a passenger deck, an old man in a wheelchair, shots fired, the splash of blood in my eyes. More shouting, and then a splash, as if a gull had crashed into the sea.

A FEW DAYS LATER, I had a second visitor at the work site, this one not nearly as welcome as Ahmad Safieh had been.

Another of Begin's crew, a plumber named Rasil, came up to where I was sitting on the dock in the sun eating a pita stuffed with falafel. "Fine day," he said.

I looked up, alert. I'd seen him around the shop and on the pier, working on a large yacht, but we hadn't talked before. "Yes." I went no further.

He was a heavyset man with a close-cropped beard and piercing black eyes, through which he gave me a calculating look. "The sheikh sends his regards, translator."

I waited a beat before replying. "You have me confused with someone else, perhaps?"

"I don't think so."

I finished my sandwich and the cool tea from my thermos cup, wiped the crumbs from my shirt and went back on board the ship I was working on, and down the stairs to the cabin. When I glanced outside a few minutes later, the plumber was gone.

Later in the day, Ahmad stopped by, to say goodbye. "Our repairs are done. There's still another week to the season so we're heading out to catch as much as we can."

"And after that?"

"We'll be going back home. I have my truck. It's mostly a piece of junk, but got us here, it should get us home. Come see us sometime, Yusef."

"I will. Good fishing. *As-salam alaykum, shalom aleikhem.*"

We both laughed, and embraced.

That night, sleep stayed away. I dressed and went for a walk through the old city, winding up at a spot that overlooked the harbour, the bay beyond and the open sweep of the Mediterranean. The scent of salt and fish was strong in my nostrils. Far out, I could see lights of fishing boats, and hear the music of the waves. To the south, the distant lights of Haifa cast an undifferentiated glow on the water. Behind me, the Citadel and the Crusaders' fortress loomed out of the darkness, remnants of long-gone civilizations that had come to Akko, left their mark, and moved on.

The plumber Rasil – yet another of the sheikh's men – came into my mind and I shivered. To get him out of my mind, I directed my thought to Ahmad, the conversations I'd had with him, and of his invitation. And of what a good man I took him to be, he and his brothers. I thought about his father, "the philosopher in the family," as Ahmad described him, wondered what he was like.

Dawn was almost in the sky behind me when I found my way back to my room and bed. I was asleep instantly and woke not long after, judging by the faint light pressing against my window. It was not a sound that startled me, but a scent, a pungent, musky odour that was familiar. Beside the bed, sitting on his haunches, was the Creature, half bull, half lion, that had visited me on the island.

It had been several months since I'd seen it, and I'd come to believe it had only been a figment of my imagination, a hallucination.

"I told you, Jesu, there is nothing to fear," the Creature said.

"I'm not afraid," I said.

"Then what is it that keeps you? This is not where you are meant to be. It is time."

"Time for what?" I asked, aware that I had asked the exact same question of the Creature on the island.

The Creature also repeated itself: "You will see."

There was so much more I wanted to ask the Creature, but somehow I was not able.

I slept fitfully for another hour or two, then rose, gathered my things together and slipped out of the house, leaving a few shekels and a note on the kitchen table for the landlady. Begin was already in his office on the dock. "I must be going," I told him. "I've put all the tools back in their places. Thank you for your kindnesses."

"I didn't expect you'd be here long," he said good-naturedly.

"Oh? Why was that?"

He paused to consider. "Something in your eyes."

CHAPTER 20
INTO THE HILLS

TIBERIAS, THE CITY on the shore of Lake Kinneret, was no more than an hour's drive west, I'd been told, but I chose to make the journey on foot. Ahmad had said it would be at least a week before he and his brothers would be home, so I was in no hurry; seven days to walk across country through the Galilee hills suited me fine.

I caught a ride in a truck carrying iced fish north on Highway 4 to the small Arab town of Mazra'a and was let off at the southern outskirts. I stood there on the side of the dusty road for a minute, getting my bearings. I was about midway between Highways 85 to the south and 89 to the north, two well-traveled roads that wound their way through the hills from the Mediterranean to the Sea of Galilee. There were no other vehicles on the coastal highway and no buildings within sight. When I was satisfied there was no one about observing me, I turned my back to the Mediterranean and took a small gravel road heading east, inland. The road soon deteriorated to a lane leading to a ramshackle farm. I skirted around it and plunged through uncultivated land toward the forest-clad hills, which rose through a hazy sky in the distance, perhaps an hour or two's walk away. As I walked, I was trailed by a black bird, circling high above me. I knew that bird, or thought I did.

I soon entered woods that grew increasingly thick and the bird disappeared. The outer fringe of pine quickly gave way to stands of oak and eucalyptus, the dense canopy of their leaves shuttering out the sun, and I stumbled on protruding roots and mushrooms thrusting their heads up through the forest floor, profusely carpeted in needles, leaves and underbrush. Just as I was beginning to think I might be lost, the woods tapered out again to pine, then abruptly ended and I found myself in what appeared to be a narrow valley, with the woods behind me and a platoon of low-rising hills up ahead. I reckoned that it would take me no more than half an hour to walk from one side of the valley to the other, and sure enough, after about fifteen minutes, I reached the valley bottom, where I came upon a stream, bubbling and sweet-tasting. It was too small to be a river, but had most likely played a hand in carving out the valley.

Again, I paused to check my surroundings. Once out of the woods, I was able to satisfy myself that no one was following. I'd lost sight of the black bird while under the trees, but now I could see it was still with me. It swooped down, as if to check on me, and I could see the sharp point of its beak, the glint of its eye.

I crossed the stream by hopping from one large dry-topped stone to another, and almost as soon as I was on the other side I began to hear the jingle of bells and the bleating of sheep. Then I heard a sharp whistle, and almost immediately became conscious of several sets of eyes on me. I stopped and stood still, waiting.

"Who goes there?" a voice asked, in a lisping off-kilter Hebrew. The question was not shouted but I heard it clearly enough, and I realized the voice was coming from behind an olive sapling only a few metres away.

"My name is Yusef Marranos," I replied. "I'm a carpenter far from home, seeking work. I'm on my way to Kenneret. I mean you no harm."

There was silence, but gradually, a small form emerged from behind the tree I was looking at. It was a child, a little boy, no more than ten years old. Other small forms materialized then, from behind trees or shrubs or piles of rocks, and I was surrounded by half a dozen boys, all half my size or smaller. They were dressed almost identically in brown shorts made of a sturdy cotton and sleeveless pullover shirts of various colours, and wearing sandals.

"What brings you here, Yusef Marranos?" one of them asked, in a tone so aggressive it made me laugh, so out of synch it was with his child-like face.

"Just chance." I put down my pack and toolbelt, the easier for them to see they were nothing to be alarmed at. "I was heading toward Acre but took off across country on a whim. I've heard of the Sea of Galilee and was hoping to bathe in it."

The boys laughed. "Kinneret is a long way off, many days of walking," one of them said. Again that oddly slanted Hebrew.

I felt foolish admitting that I meant to take a week or more getting there. "I didn't really know. I'm a stranger here, just had a whim and started to walk. I was walking for a couple of hours, I think, going east by sight of the sun. Then I was in a deep woods, the sun hard to see, and I may have gotten turned around. Then I came out here." I turned my head to indicate the direction from which I'd come. "I don't really know where I am."

The boys laughed again. "Yes, Yusef Marranos," the first boy said, "you are truly lost." This time, his tone was sarcastic.

"Where am I, then?" I asked. "What is this place?"

The boys looked at me with curiosity. "This place is...this place," one of them said. "It's here. Home."

"Well, what I mean is, what is it called?"

"Called?" another boy asked. "As he said, Home."

"Does it not have a name?"

Now the boys looked at me with suspicion, as if I had violated some unspoken code, or tripped some warning they'd learned.

But one boy, probably just six or seven, said "I think I've heard my father use a name. I don't remember it. We just call it Home, or This Place, as you called it."

We stood silent for a minute, all of us, I think, absorbing this information in different ways. "You can speak to my father," the last boy who'd spoken said at last. He turned and began to walk away, glancing over his shoulder once to indicate that I should follow, which I did. The other boys fell into step behind us.

We were on a path, just a well-worn indentation in the grass. It took a slight turn and suddenly there were flocks of sheep, whose bleats I continued to hear during my interrogation by the boys, and more boys, none more than ten years old by my reckoning. Soon a shack with a thatched roof came into view, and beyond it I could see more dwellings. First, though, we passed through numerous plots of cultivated land, in which many vegetables were growing, lettuce, tomatoes, asparagus, zucchini, radishes; a mixed orchard of olive, date, fig and apricot, and a vineyard, all tended by older boys, and girls too. They looked up as we passed, and one boy, perhaps seventeen or even older, called to us: "Who's that you have with you, boys?"

"A visitor, lost. We're taking him to see my father," the boy leading the way said.

The older boy held his hand flat against his forehead to shield his eyes and squinted. "And to the rabbi, Mordecai, take him to the rabbi."

Just past the gardens, the path widened and was paved with flat stones. As soon as we entered the village, I began to see people, adults as well as children but in a strange configuration. Every adult was accompanied by a child, men by boys, women by girls, and often these pairs were holding hands. These children were older than the shepherds, in their teens. I noticed too that many of the adults carried what appeared to be walking sticks. None of the adults took any notice of me as the boys who were my guides led me through the narrow streets, though some of the older children looked up with apparent interest. All the buildings, houses and a few shops, were built of stone and covered with vines. There was no painted trim, no splashes of colour anywhere, nothing, really, to distinguish one cottage from another.

Nonetheless, the boys brought me to a cottage, and the boy who had led the way knocked on the door, then immediately opened it and went in. I followed, and the two of the other boys also entered, while the rest stayed outside.

"Father," the boy said, "I've brought a visitor."

It took a moment for my eyes to adjust to the dimness. There were no curtains on the windows, but the light that poured in was meagre, and there were no electric lights or burning candles. Gradually, the form of a man, sitting alone in an upholstered armchair, came into focus. I saw too that a girl somewhat older than the boys I was with sat by one window, a book open on her lap. She had, apparently, been reading to the man when we interrupted them.

"Who goes there?" the man asked, in that same peculiar dialect the boys spoke. "Mordecai, who have you brought? Esther, bring a chair for our visitor."

I drew closer and sat across from the man on a rickety wooden chair. There was just enough light for me to see clearly that he was blind, and, though my first impression was that he was an old man, I could see he was no more than forty. I couldn't help but think of my two encounters with Sheikh Al-Qatar, who also had not been as he first appeared.

"My name is Yusef Marranos," I began, and I repeated what I'd told the shepherd boys. "I seek no more than some food and a place to spend the night. Perhaps you can direct me?"

The man listened intently, allowing his glazed eyes to close.

"Welcome, Yusef Marranos," he said when I'd finished. "I must apologize for the behaviour of my son and the other boys if they were rude or seemed suspicious. We have very few visitors here."

"As I said, I'm here by chance. I became lost in the woods. But, no, your son and the other boys were not rude. Just...cautious. I don't blame them. We live in dangerous times."

"Woods?" the man asked.

"Yes, the woods just, west, I guess it is, of town, just before the meadow where I came upon the shepherds and their flocks."

Again, he listened intently, opening his eyes this time.

"Ah. Yes, dangerous times." He paused and nodded his head. "For people like us, outcast Jews, the times are always dangerous."

The blind man fell silent and I could see he was thinking deeply. When he spoke again, it was not in the odd Hebrew dialect but in Aramaic. I recognized it and understood it but was surprised – although I'd read it and written it myself, I'd never heard it spoken. "Esther, take our visitor to the rabbi," he said, speaking to the girl, who I took to be his daughter. "Stop for no one, let him speak to no one else."

"Are we in danger?" the girl asked, also in Aramaic.

"I don't think so," her father said slowly, turning his face in my direction. I was reminded again of the sheikh, how, in my interview with him, many months earlier, I had the feeling that he was studying me, though I knew that was impossible.

"My father wishes me to take you to meet our rabbi," the girl said to me in Hebrew. I knew that any hint that I'd understood their conversation would cause an upset, so I merely nodded.

The boys were waiting outside and fell into step behind us as the girl led the way through the narrow streets. The sun was sinking in what I thought was the east – could that be? I was thoroughly confused about directions. There was still enough daylight for me to see that the village's stone buildings were not only all much the same, but they seemed exceedingly old. We passed several pairs of adults, men and women, and children, boys and girls, and it came to me with a start that they too were blind, that the children were their guides.

"Is everyone in this place blind?" I asked Esther. "The adults, I mean."

She was slightly ahead of me and she glanced at me over her shoulder, giving me a penetrating look with eyes that were a startling blue. "Yes, we begin to lose our sight here at...puberty," she said, hesitating before that word. "My sight is going already. It'll be gone before my next birthday."

"How old are you, Esther?"

"Fifteen."

The *shul* was a building much like all the others in the village, small, one storey, built of stone, covered with ivy. We waited outside while one of the boys went in to summon the rabbi. Esther covered her head with a shawl she'd had around her shoulders. I could hear a tap-tapping on the floor approaching from within. The door opened and the boy emerged, followed by a man no larger than a boy, feeling the way ahead of him with a stick. He seemed quite old, dressed entirely in black, with a large black hat covering a seemingly bald head and a grey beard that came down to his waist and was tucked into the front of his baggy trousers. His eyes were completely opaque.

"Well, well," he began slowly. "This is a surprise. A pleasant one. We don't often have visitors. I don't remember the last time." He didn't introduce himself.

I smiled. "You are, this place, that is, a little off the beaten path. What is this place, what is it called?"

The rabbi ignored my question. "And I'm the oldest man in the community."

As with the first old man I'd met in the village, the rabbi faced me squarely, his head tilted up, and seemed to be examining me with his lifeless eyes. "What is your name, traveler?"

"Yusef Marranos. I was born in Gaza. I've been living in Lebanon, working for the UN. I'm a carpenter. I'm on my way to Kenneret." I hadn't meant to mention either Lebanon or the UN, but there was something about the rabbi's thoughtful gaze that didn't permit obfuscation.

The rabbi's face remained expressionless until I mentioned Kenneret. "Ah, I've heard of this great sea. Its waters are said to have healing powers."

"That's what I've heard," I replied, though I had heard no such thing, just, from Maryam, that the water was sweet.

"Yusef Marranos," the rabbi said. "That's not your name."

I was taken aback and tried not to show it, so strong was the feeling that he could see me. "You're right, my name is Masoud. I call myself Marranos sometimes."

"Masoud. That's not your name either."

"I have papers. In my pack. I can show you."

"Papers?"

"Identification papers."

The rabbi took a step closer and placed his right hand on my chest. I could feel the heat of his hand through my shirt, and my heart beating strongly against the light pressure. "No, *Yehoshuah*, some call you that, am I not right?"

I took a deep breath and became conscious of a slowing of my heart. A calmness came over me like a breeze. "Some, yes," I stammered.

"I see."

I couldn't help but laugh.

"What is amusing, *Yehoshuah*?"

"I'm sorry, Rabbi, I mean no disrespect. It's just a funny thing for a blind man to say."

"Ah. Yes. But though I am blind, I can see some things clearly."

The rabbi turned to Esther and gave her instructions in Aramaic.

"Is he the one, *rebbe*?" she asked.

"I don't know," the rabbi said. "Perhaps."

I was led to a cottage a few streets away and put in the care of a widow, an old woman named Rebecca. She resembled the old Palestinian women I'd seen so often in the refugee camps, small, bent over, wrinkled, dressed in black shapeless dresses, heads covered with scarves from which wisps of grey hair wriggled free. She was silent at first, heating a meal of mutton stew and lentils on the top of a wood stove, and making me a bed of straw matting near the fireplace, which she lit as a chill descended after the sun's setting. She was assisted in all this by a solemn young girl who also said not a word, but the old woman managed very well for someone without sight.

In the morning, after a restless sleep in which my dreams led me unwillingly back to my islands, my hostess was in a better mood, almost jocular. She bustled about, preparing a porridge of oats and milk sweetened with honey, commenting on the weather – "a fine day for your walk, traveler" – and her neighbours, and making jokes with the child, who was called Rashi.

"Guess my age, traveler," Rebecca said as we sat at her table, and she winked at the little girl, who giggled. Esther had not given the old woman my name and she hadn't asked for it. And I, after my experience with the rabbi, was reluctant to offer it.

"Sixty," I offered, thinking to flatter her.

"Sixty! Are you dreaming, traveler? What world do you come from? One in which the dead walk among us?"

"I'm sorry, I didn't mean to offend. "Fifty...?"

"Fifty! I'm the oldest woman in the village, but certainly not that old. I'll be dead soon enough, thank you, no need for you to begin to dig my grave."

"I give up, how old then? I'm not good at guessing games."

Rebecca stood up and began to clear the table, obviously tired of me. "Forty-two years old," she said, lightly, and then, with added weight, "ancient."

Before the sun was up much higher, I'd been escorted – by a different troop of boys, older than the shepherds, grave and silent – to the eastern edge of the village. One boy pointed out a path that led across a meadow and into trees, the Galilean hills rising brown and furred with green beyond. I set off with the feel of their eyes on the back of my neck and, after a hundred metres or so, when I turned to look back, the boys were gone. The black bird, though, had materialized above me. It cried out once, as if in greeting.

CHAPTER 21
A VILLAGE OF WOMEN

I SOON REACHED the edge of the valley and the path began
to climb, taking me deep into hills covered with rockrose and
thorny gorse brush, a riot of bright pinks and yellows, and
stately oak. The path grew fainter and fainter, then died out
entirely, and I kept my bearings by the sun whenever I could see
it through the canopy of trees as I passed occasionally through
dense woods, ahead of me in the morning, then behind me.
I stopped by a brook and drank deeply, found fruit to eat, dates
and, to my surprise, bananas, then walked on. When the sun
set, I built a fire against the side of a rocky outcrop, ate the dried
lamb and oatcake Rebecca packed for me, boiled water in a tin
cup I'd brought along and brewed leaves and berries I gathered
nearby, letting my hand and eyes decide which to pick. On the
back page of the translated journal, using my stubby carpenter's
pencil, I made two vertical marks, one for each of the days I'd
been in the hills. I slept soundly on a bed of moss and boughs.

On the morning of the third day, I rose with the sun and
headed off again, climbing higher and higher into the Galilean
hills. By afternoon, I was tromping through a woods of towering Lebanon cedars and eucalyptus, following the path of least

resistance when, just as I spied daylight ahead, a form appeared in front of me, someone, a large man dressed in a black robe. I stopped, then took another step forward. No, not a man, a woman, standing at least three metres tall, and holding a sturdy staff. She stood perfectly still, blocking my way, but I drew closer and as I did her face and other details of her appearance came into sharper focus: she was a handsome woman, preternaturally tall, as I said, with rivulets of curly yellow hair flowing from under her headscarf. What I had taken to be a cloak was merely a voluminous dress that enveloped her body. Her eyes were as blue as the Mediterranean.

"What manner of beast are you?" she asked, first in Hebrew, then repeated in Arabic.

I answered in Hebrew. "I'm a man, as you see."

"A man?" She sounded incredulous.

I took another step closer so she could see me better, then another. We were four or five metres apart.

"Yes. I'm a traveler, a stranger here."

"A stranger indeed. And yes, I can see you are a man. Forgive me. I've never seen a grown man. You're the first man I've seen with a beard."

I was nonplussed but decided not to inquire. Still, my right hand, of its own accord, went to my chin and stroked my beard.

"I've seen paintings, of course, of men with beards – our Lord and his disciples."

I was surprised but chose not to respond to that, instead repeating, "I'm a traveler," and then went on, "on my way from the shore of the Mediterranean to the shore of the Kenneret, from one sea to another."

"A pilgrim?"

"Yes, you could call me that. Yes, I am a pilgrim. My name is Yusef."

I heard the crack of a branch snapping behind and looked over my shoulder to see another woman taking up position. She too was exceedingly tall and carried a staff. She peered at me with intense curiosity.

The first woman cast her eyes over me in an appraising way. "How long have you been traveling, Yusef?"

"Three days, I think, since I left Akko. Two days since I was in a village...I never did learn what it was called. All the adults there were blind."

The woman nodded her head. "Ah. A long way to come from there. You must be hungry and tired."

"I've eaten some on the way, fruit mostly, and slept on the ground, comfortably enough. But yes, tired and hungry."

As we talked, I was conscious of other women taking up position on either side of me – in all, I was surrounded by half a dozen women, all as unnaturally tall as the first, with grave expressions on handsome faces, dressed almost identically in black, flowing dresses, all carrying staffs. Like the first woman, thick strands of hair flowed carelessly from under the scarves they wore, but their hair was dark. All of them kept their eyes fixed on me – I felt like I was being devoured by them. Unlike the dead eyes of the adults in the village I'd left behind, these eyes seemed to see everything.

"Come with me, then," the yellow-haired woman said. She turned and led the way out of the woods into a meadow. I followed, and the other women fell into line behind me until we were clear of the trees and again they took up positions around me in a military formation I'd see UN troops use to accompany detainees. Just as had happened when I'd entered the valley of the blind people, I heard the jingling of bells and the bleating of sheep. Several large flocks soon came into sight; they were tended by children, boys and girls, and small black and white dogs which set up a clamour of barking as they caught my scent.

The women led me through the meadow and down a hill toward a set of buildings. A group of children fell in behind us, a few of them running ahead and walking backwards the better to examine me. One young boy reached out and touched me, pulling back his hand quickly as if from a hot stove. The women talked quietly among themselves in Latin, reminding me of the Sisters of the Divine Crucifix. I gave no sign that I could understand.

"A man, an actual man," two or three of them kept repeating, as if saying a mantra.

"Can it be, truly?" another asked.

"We've heard of such things," another replied.

"And a goodly man," one of them, who appeared to be the youngest, said, her voice filled with wonder.

Only the yellow-haired woman, who led the way, remained silent.

The village we entered was much like the one I'd been in a few days earlier. The houses were tall and square, built of logs though, not stone, and covered with ivy, all very much the same, one to another. What was unusual about them was their height, just one storey but walls four metres high to accommodate these women. In the centre of the village stood a building imposing by comparison, easily three storeys high, with a steeple and topped with a cross.

"You're Christians," I said.

The blonde woman looked at me sharply. "Of course. Melkite."

"Ah. I've met some Melkites, in Lebanon."

"Lebanon?"

"From the Greek Orthodox tradition, but allied with Rome."

Again, an incredulous look. "Rome?"

"I'm sorry. This is none of my business. I didn't mean to intrude, disrupt. I'll just be on my way."

"No," the blonde woman said harshly, and the others began to murmur to themselves, shaking their heads in distress. "Wait here." She pushed open the church's heavy door and went inside. In less than a minute she returned, accompanied by a priest in a black hassock and white collar. At first glance, I thought him unusually short, as small as the rabbi in the village of the blind, whose stature was due in part to his stooped posture – then I realized that he was a boy of no more than thirteen, with a wispy shadow of a mustache.

"Well, well," the boy said, "what have we here?"

"A man, Father Demetrius," the blonde woman said, echoed by a chorus from the other women, "a man, a man."

"Yes, so I see." The boy priest stepped outside and the women surrounding me stepped back to give him room. He circled me, tilting his head to the side. Standing in front of me again, looking up, he reached out and touched my beard. "Ah, just like the beard of Our Saviour." He paused, peering at me. "Could he....?" He mumbled. He shook his head, then answered his own question, "No, of course not."

The women murmured, nodding their heads, and the boy priest, emboldened, reached out again, this time yanking at my beard, which was just long enough for him to grip.

"Ow. What are you doing?"

The boy stepped back. "Just making sure you're alive." He paused. "Why *are* you alive?"

"I don't understand. Why shouldn't I be?"

The boy and the women exchanged glances. The blonde woman bent close to him and whispered in his ear. "Because boys die before they become men," he said. "Everyone knows that." He gave me a soulful look, sad and resigned. "I have less than a year to live myself."

I SLEPT THAT NIGHT on a hard pew in the church. Father Demetrius, the boy priest, and a dozen other boys, husky fellows but, like the priest, in their early teens, kept guard. "This is for your own good," the priest said. Earlier, they'd led me to a house where an elderly woman, not quite as tall as the other women I'd met, with eyes big as platters, fed me a stew of lamb and roots and bread, with a glass of sweet wine to wash it down. Then I was trooped back to the church. By this time, the streets were filled with young women, all as tall as young trees, jostling to get a look at me. They called out to me, reached out. My platoon of boys and a few older women, led by the blonde who'd first greeted me, kept them at a distance.

"This is all very upsetting," Demetrius told me. "They've never seen a grown man before."

"I mean them no harm," I protested.

"That's not the upset," the priest said, but he would go no further.

Among the dozen guards who kept me company through the night was a younger boy, not yet in his teens, whom I learned was the priest in training. "There's another one, even younger, behind him," Demetrius said. "He needs his sleep."

With a natural life span of no more than fifteen years, the boys of Golgotha, as the village was called, were resigned to what life had dealt them and content to fulfill their duties, chief of which was to ensure the reproduction and survival of their community. And, at any given time, one of them was the designated spiritual leader, assigned to a life of study.

As I relaxed in this company of youths, I let down my guard and spoke to Demetrius in Latin, telling him I was on my way to Kenneret. He was surprised at first, giving me a long look before sighing, as if having come to some understanding, and relaxed himself. Then, as much as one can in a language like Latin, we chatted. His command of the language was impressive, and, indeed, I was impressed by Demetrius's learning.

"I guess your priestly duties preclude you from the other duties of manhood here," I said, choosing my words carefully.

"Of course," Demetrius said, shocked. "I take a vow of celibacy, like any priest."

My sleep was fitful, and I was awoken before light. Father Demetrius wished me godspeed and blessed me, and again I was taken, this time through empty streets and escorted by the troop of boys, to the old woman's home, where I was given a breakfast of porridge and tea. As she'd been the previous evening, she was silent but her enormous eyes devoured me. Then, as dawn was breaking, I was escorted to the east side of the valley. As we walked, one by one my guards broke away, and by the time we were into woods, a couple of kilometres from the village, only three, the sturdiest of the boys, remained.

I heard a commotion above me and I looked up, saw, to my surprise, a quartet of monkeys swinging from branches high above in the forest canopy. There were a few monkeys on my island, but I hadn't seen any since. I stopped to watch them. I turned to the boy behind me, gesturing upward, but he and the others were gone.

As I continued east through the woods, the monkeys followed me, chattering and never falling out of sight; I was, in effect, handed off from one group of guards to another. I had asked Demetrius how far he thought it might be to Tiberias but, though he had heard of the city and the lake, he had no idea. The village he presided over, like the village of the blind I'd stopped in earlier, was self-sufficient and had very little knowledge of the outside world.

I walked on, stopping only to rest from time to time, to drink water from streams I passed and to eat fruit and nuts I picked from trees, to the accompaniment of scolding from the monkeys. "Don't worry, my friends, there's plenty for all of us, I won't take that much," I told them, but they were unconvinced.

By the time darkness fell, I'd walked, by my reckoning, fifteen kilometres or more, through woods and meadows, across a narrow valley and climbing higher into hills. My escort of monkeys stayed with me throughout the day, running ahead on grass when we were out of the trees, where one time I surprised a small herd of gazelle, and scurrying quickly back to higher elevations when the opportunity arose. For a while, a red fox followed us, curious but keeping a respectful distance.

The smell of fresh water was enticingly ahead, growing stronger.

I was in a deep woods – junipers, pine and oaks – when I made camp, gathering a bed of feathery pine boughs in the hollow created by the unearthed roots of a large chestnut tree.

I made a small fire to heat tea and prepared a simple meal of sausage and dried fruit.

There was just enough light from the fire to read a few pages from the journal translation I pulled from my backpack. I opened it to the beginning and read a few entries from the lifeboat. In this version, there were twelve on board along with me, and their names, predictably, were Simon, Peter, James, John and so on. Judas was the last to go, playing the role of Mohan the riddle-maker. The curious whale I'd made passing mention of turned into a sea monster that devoured some of the drowning seamen and hurled curses at me.

I thought about the trap in the sand that appeared several pages later in this hoax of a journal. The sheikh had laid a trap for me, I realized, a trap as soft and slippery as sand, and I couldn't be certain that I'd completely escaped it yet. By this time, though, I'd lost my feelings of anxiety about being followed. If the sheikh's men were pursing me, it was more likely that they'd already be in Tiberias, waiting for me.

I put the book away, shaking my head in some combination of disbelief, amusement and anger. As I waited for sleep to come, I attempted to count the sprinkling of stars visible through the overlay of leaves, and when that proved fruitless, I counted on my fingers the days since I'd left Acre. There were now four vertical marks on the journal's back page. Providing I hadn't miscalculated, or gotten lost somehow, I should arrive at Kenneret soon, perhaps the next day, earlier than I'd expected.

Somewhere in the woods I heard a growl and a shuffling through the underbrush. One of the monkeys swung down from the tree beside me, and approached. It was no bigger than a terrier, brown, and, by the flickering light of my fire, I could see its face, comical, almost human, its eyes brown, liquid, luminous. It squatted on its haunches beside me and examined me, tipping its head one way, then the other. It reached out a paw and I took it in my hand, remarkably soft in my palm.

"*Mox*," the monkey said, speaking in Latin. "Soon."

CHAPTER 22
BABEL

DURING THE NIGHT, it began to rain but my nest remained relatively dry. My morning attempts to relight my fire, though, were in vain and I was content to munch on a heel of dark bread the old woman who'd fed me the day before pressed into my hand as I left. The rain soon dwindled, but the heavy fog that accompanied it persisted. So thick a fog, almost as heavy as ones I'd encountered at sea, was surprising so far from a body of water, making me think I was perhaps within easy reach of Kenneret. There was no sign or sound of my monkey friends.

I gathered my belongings and set off, although with no sun to guide me I was unsure of the proper direction. I blundered forward in more or less the way I'd been going the previous day, but it was impossible to see more than a few metres ahead of me and I soon became disoriented. I walked for an hour, tripping on roots and brushing against low-hanging branches, until I came to a spot that was instantly familiar, the place where I'd slept. I sat down on a sodden tree stump and shook my head. After a minute, my reverie was broken by the unmistakable sound of a foghorn.

I leapt to my feet and followed my ears. The foghorn grew louder and was joined in a syncopation of bells and bleating.

Within minutes, I'd come to the edge of the woods and entered a meadow sloping down into a deep valley. As I emerged, the fog began to thin and quickly dissipated under the heat of a brazen sun, directly overhead, revealing herds of sheep, goats and even cattle in the distance, and a brilliant blanket of wildflowers, purple anemones, blue lupins, yellow marigolds. There was no sign of the lake, though, or any body of water other than a winding stream that defined the valley floor.

I walked in the direction of the closest of these herds, which were goats, and, after passing fields of tobacco, cotton, artichokes and corn, came upon an old man sitting on a tree stump, wearing a prayer robe, *tellefin* and a *yarmulke*, and smoking a corncob pipe. Beside him sat a boy with long curly sideburns growing like ferns beneath his *yarmulke*. A small black and white dog lay between them, its head erect and alert, a low growl coming from its throat. The man and boy both looked up as I approached and, rather than showing alarm, as I expected, the old man broke into a wide, toothless grin. "Hallo, stranger," he called out in Hebrew. "*Shabbat shalom*."

"Hello and *shabbat shalom* to you too. I hope I'm not disturbing you."

"Disturbing me? Certainly not. I'm delighted to see you. I'm Rabbi Menachem. *Shabbat shalom*." He gestured toward the boy, who grinned at me shyly. "This is my grandson, Abraham."

As I came abreast of them, I could see, from the thick lines on the man's weathered face, and the white grizzled hair that stuck out of his head around the *yarmulke*, that he was truly old, and that his eyes, a faded brown, were studying me with as much interest as I was him.

"And I you, Rabbi," I said. "I daresay you don't see many strangers here. This village is a bit out of the way."

The old man laughed. "Out of the way, oh yes, we are that. As for strangers, no, I can't remember the last stranger I've seen, if ever I have, and I'm four score years and then some."

"But my presence doesn't alarm you – I'm glad of that."

"Alarm me? Why should it do that? We're all children of God, are we not? You're my brother, long lost, happily found. Lucky for you, though, that you came upon me. Not everyone who lives around here feels the same."

"That's too bad, I approve of your way of thinking." I introduced myself and briefly explained my journey. The old man listened intently, his eyes growing wide when I mentioned the lake.

"I've heard of this great sea," the rabbi said. He sighed deeply. "I'd like to see such a wonder before I die." He turned to the boy. "Perhaps, Abela, you'll get the chance."

I didn't immediately reply, and before I could he pushed himself slowly to his feet, using a stout oak staff for leverage. "Come, you must be tired and hungry. You will be my guest. Tonight is the third *shabbos* of the month and there will be a special service at *shul*. Did you hear the *shofar*?"

"Ah, that's what it was. I thought I heard a foghorn, but I knew that couldn't be."

The old man looked at me blankly, and just then, we heard the *shofar*'s call again. At the same time, bells began to ring out, and a wailing much like what I'd often heard coming from mosques as the faithful are called to prayer.

"This must be a special day indeed," I said. The expression on the old man's face turned quizzical. "I thought the *shofar* was blown only on the high holy days."

"Ah, that. I admit, my son gets carried away. He loves to blow the horn. And what harm is there?"

He nodded to the boy, who remained silent throughout our brief encounter, and set off with me in tow, leaving the boy behind. The dog leapt up and began to follow but a whistle from the boy returned him to his place.

The old man walked with a surprisingly sprightly gait. We passed a number of small flocks of sheep and goats, each one minded by an old man, a boy and a dog, sometimes two dogs. As we passed, the old men called out greetings, some in Hebrew, others in Arabic. Some of them were dressed much like Rabbi Menachem, in patched trousers and flannel shirts beneath their prayer robes, and sporting *tellefin* and *yarmulke*; others in the long white robes of Muslim *imams*; and, much to my surprise, one dignified-looking old man was turned out in the black shirt and white collar of a Maronite priest. "Bless you, my friends," he called out in Aramaic. All appeared friendly, though none of the men rose, and Rabbi Menachem showed no sign of wishing to pause and engage in conversation.

The village we approached was set against the side of a steep chalklike cliff, the small houses clad in stucco painted in various pastel shades of blue, pink and yellow. I could see people walking about, and as we drew closer, the din of the bells and *shofar*'s cry and the chanting of the *muezzins* grew louder. By the time we set foot on the village's crowded cobblestone streets, it was only just possible for the old man and I to hear each other.

"What is going on, Rabbi?" I asked, leaning toward his ear.

"What do you mean?" he shouted.

"All this hubbub."

The old man looked perplexed. Then the expression on his face melted into a lopsided grin. "I told you, it's the third *Shabbos*. There'll be a feast tonight."

"And the mosques and churches? They're having celebrations too?"

Even as I spoke, I became aware that everywhere I looked, there was a mosque, a synagogue or a church, all with crowds of people gathering in front of them. Indeed, every block on the streets of the village contained one house of worship or another. Men and women called out greetings as we passed, in Hebrew, Arabic, Aramaic and Greek, and to my surprise I also heard snatches of words in Akkadian and Sumerian, languages I recognized though I'd never heard them before and knew to be extinct. And I noticed too that the pleasingly coloured houses were matched to these houses of worship, blue houses clustered near cross-topped churches, yellow ones next to mosques with their minarets, pink houses surrounding synagogues. By the time we'd reached Rabbi Menachem's *shul*, we'd passed half a dozen synagogues or more, each one sending out a call for prayer.

The synagogue before which we now stood was just slightly larger than the houses around it, a stuccoed stone building with only a Star of David above its wooden door as ornament.

"So many *shuls*, rabbi," I said, "so many mosques and churches. This village doesn't look big enough for them all."

The old man laughed. "Yes, we suffer from an abundance of worship, though some would say we *enjoy* an abundance." We were in front of his synagogue, yet he made no move to enter. Instead, he sat down on a wooden bench to the left of the door and relit his pipe. He gestured toward the seat beside him, which I took, stretching out my legs. "You know, friend Yusef, it wasn't always this way. There's a story here." He chuckled. "Perhaps you'd like to hear it?"

"I would, Rabbi. Yes, please."

The old man puffed on his pipe and nodded to a young couple dressed in black approaching the synagogue, the bearded man tall and erect and seeming even taller in his black felt hat, the woman, clearly pregnant, puffing with the exertion of keeping up with him. They paused and each, in turn, bowed down before the rabbi to kiss his hand. He introduced me to them, "This is my son, Avram, and his wife, Ruth."

"Glad to meet you," I said. They looked at me with shy curiosity, then nodded again and entered.

"Avram is my third son," the rabbi said.

"Ah. Do you have many?"

"I do, eight sons and four daughters, as the Torah prescribes. We suffer too from an abundance of children." He laughed again. "God told us, go forth and multiply, so we do."

"Very commendable, Rabbi."

The expression on the rabbi's face turned sad. "Of course, my poor wife, Rose – may her name be a blessing – she *really* suffered from the abundance of children. Dead three years now."

"I'm sorry to hear that, Rabbi."

The old man sighed. "What can you do? It's the cycle of life, as God ordains it."

He gestured, first to his right, then to his left, taking in the rows of pink houses. "As you can see, many children, many, many grandchildren."

"Ah, I see. Your family is your congregation."

"Of course. I also have brothers, and many nieces and nephews. Making a minion is never a problem."

"I see." I thought back to the number of houses of worship I'd counted, and did some quick calculations. "So...there is a synagogue for every Jewish family? Am I right?"

"You've figured out our secret." He grinned at me from around the stem of is pipe.

"And the same for the mosques, and the churches."

"Certainly."

"So...I'm guessing, there are half a dozen Jewish families here, maybe eight, the same number of Muslim families, more or less, and two or three Christian."

The old man closed his eyes and his lips moved as he did his own calculations. "That's about right."

"And tell me this, Rabbi. The Jewish families...couldn't they get together and have one synagogue?"

"That's the way it once was. As I told you."

"Yes, so you did. And you promised me a story."

"You've told it yourself, friend."

Now it was my turn to laugh. "So I did. Tell me this, though, when did this happen, this falling apart into separate congregations?"

"Oh, that was a long time ago, Yusef. Long before me, before my father, may he rest in peace, before my grandfather, blessed be his name. Long, long ago, beyond human memory."

"I see."

We sat in companionable silence for several minutes, enjoying the sunshine, greeting worshippers as they arrived and entered the synagogue.

"And tell me this, Rabbi," I said finally, "has there ever been thought given to rejoining, getting back together?"

The old man bent over and knocked the bowl of his pipe against his boot. Ashes and embers spilled onto the cobblestones. "Yes, most assuredly." He stood up, stretching his arms, and I stood too. "But that would involve giving up our differences, or letting them fester, don't you see? No, no, this is a better way. We all live in peace here."

The rabbi pushed open the synagogue's heavy wooden door and we were about to enter when, above the surrounding din, we heard a woman's voice calling, "Yeshua, Yeshua."

The woman rushing toward us was dressed in the unmistakable manner of the Sisters of the Divine Crucifix, in a loose white robe open at the sides. At first, I took her to be Sister Mark, though I knew that couldn't be, this woman was older, and her eyebrows, the only hair on her head, were dark.

She came to a halt in front of me and immediately dropped to her knees. "Yeshua," she gasped, breathless, "it's you. I couldn't believe my eyes." She spoke in a halting Latin.

"Sister, get up, please," I said. I could feel Rabbi Menachem's inquiring eyes on me.

"Sister Thomas, what is this?" he asked.

The nun ignored him. "We knew you were coming," she said, reverting now to a jumbled mixture of Latin and Italian, "but we had no idea it would be so soon."

"What do you mean? How...?"

I was interrupted by the rabbi, "Good *shabbos*, Sister, can I help you?"

"Please, sister, get up. My name is Yusef. You've got me mixed up with someone else, I assure you."

"No, no, it's you, you are the one. We were told, and here you are. Praise be to God, halleluiah."

The rabbi looked at the nun, then at me, with a perplexed expression on his wrinkled face, and it became clear to me that he had no idea what she was saying, any more than she could understand him.

"What is this place?" I asked the rabbi, in Hebrew, and repeated my question to the nun, in Latin.

"What is it?" the rabbi echoed.

"What is your village called?" I repeated the question for the nun.

"Ah," the rabbi said, "Babylon."

At the sound of the word, a light of recognition came into the nun's eyes and she nodded her head. "Yes, Babylon."

THE NEXT MORNING, I set out early, before the village had begun to stir. The bells of the two churches were silent, the *muezzins* and the *shofar* blowers still asleep in their beds, as were all the good people of Babylon, except Rabbi Menachem, who wiped sleep from his eyes, made me a cup of strong tea and carefully wrapped a lunch for me in a square of softened parchment as I washed and dressed.

The evening before, I had asked him numerous questions he could not answer, shaking his head in response with a rueful smile. I asked the nun questions too, but no sooner than I'd begun than she bowed and took her leave. I asked the rabbi about her but he could tell me little. "They have a tiny church, those Sisters," he said. "There are only a few of them. No men, don't you see, so no children. They keep to themselves."

We were sitting comfortably in the living room of his modest house that sat squarely behind his synagogue, sipping from glasses of homemade plum brandy. I took a deep breath and asked him the question that was forefront in my mind since entering this odd village. "Your secret, as you put it, the secret of this place, is that each group speaks its own language. You don't understand each other yet you live in peace, or seem to."

"Oh, we do," the rabbi insisted.

"Perhaps you noticed that I understand and speak multiple languages."

"I did."

"All languages, of fact – or all I've been exposed to."

"That is indeed remarkable."

"And I *don't* live in peace, rabbi. Why am I this way?"

Rabbi Menachem puffed on his pipe before replying. "Language is a gift from God," he said finally. "But a curse too. A test God set for us."

"Yes, a gift and a curse. *And* a test. One I don't always meet properly."

The old man gazed thoughtfully around the unadorned walls of his living room. "There are many directions to this life God has given us, young Yusef. North and south and east and west, and all the points in between."

"I don't understand."

"God gives us the directions, but we choose the direction we go."

In morning light, the rabbi's words were no clearer than when he'd spoken them.

"There is so much I don't understand," he told me as I stepped out of his house. "As it should be. The ways of *Yahweh* are not for us to know."

"Perhaps He wouldn't object if you inquired," I said with a smile.

The old man smiled too, showing me his tobacco-stained teeth. "Ah, perhaps. But I'm too old, set in my ways."

"We are never too old in the eyes of God," I replied on impulse.

I still knew so little about God, or if there even was such a thing, but it seemed appropriate. Then, not wanting to become engaged in conversation, added quickly, "Thank you for your hospitality, Rabbi."

"Are you off to find the Sea of Kenneret?"

"Yes. I hope to be there soon."

"I can only dream of such things." He smiled again. "Perhaps I'll go back to sleep for a while."

Dull grey light lay on the fields as I passed by sleeping herds and their slumbering shepherds. Only the dogs, ever alert but silent, lifted their heads to watch my departure. There were, as the rabbi said, many directions, but mine, eastward toward the great inland sea, was set, at least for the moment. Beyond that, I had no idea which direction I might go, where I might wind up. By the time I'd reached the next ripple of hills to the east, the sun was just starting to be visible ahead of me. I was completely alone on the trail. Soon, though, the familiar black bird joined me.

"Lead me home, bird," I called to it.

The bird did not reply.

CHAPTER 23
THE SCENT OF WATER

WITHIN AN HOUR, I was in thick woods, plane and pine and eucalyptus, with only occasional flashes of sun, visible through rents in the blanket of leaves, to guide me. Even better was the scent of fresh water, seemingly growing stronger with every step I took. I came upon a clearing with a bubbling spring when the sun was at its highest and I stopped to drink, fill my canteen and eat the lunch the rabbi prepared for me, goat cheese on thick dark bread with slices of ripe tomato and a few falafals. Tracks of various animals in the soft ground surrounded the spring, including one I recognized immediately, larger than my hand, an oval central pad with four claws. I listened, but heard no sign of the Creature, or any other animal. When I set out again, I heard rustling in the leaves above and was surprised to find that my escort of monkeys had returned.

They were still with me, keeping a reserved distance, when I camped for the night, in an open area that would afford me a brilliant view of the starry sky. I ate the last of the falafels and cheese, even though that meant I'd have no breakfast, and saved only a little of the water left in my canteen. I felt that I was close to my destination, would surely arrive at the lake some time the following day.

I sat up beside a crackling fire until well after darkness fell, thinking over the events of the last several days, smiling at the memory of some of them, frowning at others, and contemplating the taste of fried fish I expected to be eating soon. The plumber Rasil came into my mind yet again – that man, whose path had crossed with mine for no more than a minute or two – was continuing to haunt me. The travesty of the journal translation was also in my thoughts, but when I dug the book out of my pack to make a mark for the day, six of them now in a row, I resisted the temptation to read more – I knew it would just upset me.

The darkness around me was alive with sounds – the chattering of the monkeys overhead, the hum of insects and the love songs of tree frogs, a sure sign that water was nearby. I thought I might hear the familiar growl of the Creature who visited me so many times before, or that one of the monkeys would draw close. I yearned for a sign of some sort, but there was nothing.

AGAIN, I ROSE EARLY, as soon as light began to filter through the trees, anxious to get going – this was, by my calculation, the seventh day of my journey. The forest was silent as I picked my way around fallen trees, their roots like tombstones before their decaying bodies. There was no sign of the monkeys but when the forest thinned and opened out onto a ravine with a tumultuous stream at its bottom, I heard their chattering over the rush of water and saw them leaping from stone to stone in the spray at the stream's edge like children.

I stood on the bluff overlooking the rapids for several minutes considering. From my vantage point, the water seemed wild, the rocks over which it poured treacherous. I couldn't cross it, not at this spot, and I wasn't sure whether I even needed to.

Surely this mountain cataract was not the Jordan. More likely, it was a tributary that would run into the great river directly, or via the Sea of Galilee.

There didn't seem to be any compelling reason to cross the stream, but I was drawn to the notion. I gazed at the other side, feeling certain that I should find some way of crossing.

"What should I do?" I called to the monkeys. Immediately, the smallest of the quartet, the one that had spoken to me, looked up, though just for a moment. Then he turned to the others, chattering, and they began to lope downstream, pausing after a hundred metres or so to see what I was doing. The slope was steep, but it was punctuated with rocks to provide footing and I began to cautiously make my way down.

It took me fifteen minutes or more to reach the bottom, the monkeys, all the while, patiently waiting. Up close, the rushing water, hissing and writhing like a serpent, seemed even more forbidding. The bank on which I stood was no more than a foot above the water, and was strewn with rocks, making walking difficult. It took another several minutes to reach the sandbar where the monkeys waited. As I approached, they set off again.

I followed and, after a while, I came to a place where the flowing water turned sharply to the right. A dry gravel bed lay straight ahead in a path the river must once have followed. I began to follow the gravel bed, which gradually narrowed into a track barely wide enough for me to walk. The terrain became more rugged, studded with rocks of various sizes and shapes, which made walking difficult, but I pressed on. My monkey companions were nowhere to be seen.

In a few more minutes I came to a stone arch that must have at one time in the distant past been carved by the incessant flow of water. I hesitated for a moment, then stooped my head and stepped through. Instantly, I felt a change, a stillness, the air noticeably cooler, as if a cloud rolled over the sun, but the sky remained clear and blue. The ceaseless birdsong that followed me as I walked along the river suddenly stopped.

Curious, I stepped back though the arch. The sound of birds, sweet singing, filled my ears, and the air grew warmer again. I stood there for a minute, looking around me, my senses alert, then again bent through the arch. Cooler air, silence, except for what I first took to be the buzzing of bees, a faintly familiar sound. Close to the arch stood a pistachio tree, heavy with nuts. I picked a handful, shelled and ate them, picked and ate some more until my hunger was sated. As I ate, the faint buzzing continued. I looked down and saw a gleaming white stone, looked closer and realized it was a skull, much like the one I'd encountered on the beach of my island, broad at the back, narrow at the front, with curved horns. The buzzing was coming from the skull and, just as had happened over a year earlier, I realized the skull was whispering to me. I squatted down beside it and listened, but the whispering was indecipherable. Gradually, though, I began to make out one word, first its vague shape than its distinct sound: *"Jesu."*

I MADE MY WAY back to the stream, where I found the monkeys waiting for me. The smallest one gave me a quizzical look but didn't speak. Then they set off again, leading the way. Less than an hour passed as we carefully made our way downstream, my companions patient and attentive. The sun was more than halfway through its ascending course from the eastern horizon to its mid-point in the sky, and, despite the nuts I'd eaten, I felt hungry.

Finally, we entered a narrow valley where the stream widened and slowed. Bushes laden with purple berries grew along the banks, and I ate my fill, leaving my mouth and hands covered with rusty stains. I sat down in the shade of an olive tree to rest while, once again, I considered the possibilities. The monkeys sat quietly beside me, like obedient children.

From where I sat, I could see the water moving almost serenely downstream, the roar of the rapids behind it. I still had no idea whether crossing to the other side was necessary, but I yearned to. The water was wide here and appeared to be deep, more like a river than a stream, surely one could swim across. What I didn't know was whether I could swim. I had a faint memory of swimming ashore to my island on the night of the shipwreck. But had I really swum, or was I washed ashore by the tide? I looked to the monkeys, but they had fallen asleep, the warm rumble of their snoring circling comfortably above their heads.

If I was going to attempt to swim, I should do it soon, while the sun was still high. I stood up and the monkeys roused themselves, stretching and snorting, then scampered into the trees, where they set up a clatter. I followed them into the woods to investigate and found them at the water's edge. The stream had taken a turn and narrowed as it approached another sandbar. Narrow enough, perhaps. I took off my pack, swung it once above my head and let it fly – safely into sand on the other side.

The monkeys took this as a signal and the leader jumped in, the others following. I stood at the water's edge for only a moment, watching their progress. The first monkey was already halfway across. I dove in and began to swim.

I was in the sea again.

Struggling, lungs heaving, my mouth filled with surf, my eyes stinging, blind. Gradually, though, as my arms and legs developed a rhythm, a calm came over me. I lifted my head and opened my eyes, saw that I was in the river, halfway across, not much further to go. I heard the chattering of the monkeys and realized that they were around me, one ahead, one behind, one on either side. Their chattering was like laughter. I rolled over on my back and saw a rainbow through the film of moisture on my eyes, a deep blue cloudless sky, a brilliant sun, a flock of white birds and one black one, wheeling above me, calling out what sounded like my name, *Yeshua*.

Water streamed off my clothes as I walked onto the sandbar on the opposite bank. I stripped everything off and hung my clothes from branches of olive trees and sprawled on my back on the sandbar and let the sun dry me. I was on my island again, back in my kingdom of sand, sand, my friend and comfort. The sun, now at its highest point of the day, poured its heat down on me. To my surprise, the monkeys brought me gifts: bananas, dates, figs, a coconut.

The calm that came to me in the river lingered and I dozed for more than an hour, untroubled by dreams for the first time in as long as I could remember. I awoke to the sound of songbirds and the gentle motion of water lapping at my feet. I felt, somehow, as if I were home.

The sand I lay in was comforting somehow, as if *it* was my home. And why not? Had I not, in some mysterious way, been born – or *reborn* – in the comforting arms of sand?

I remembered my notion while on the island that, like a grain of sand, I was unique. Along with that memory came its companion, that I had no idea who this unique person was. All these months later, I was still no closer to an answer.

Home. I sat up and looked around, but nothing was familiar other than my immediate memory of the scene from before I'd fallen asleep. If I had ever been here before, here or anywhere in these hills I'd been traipsing through for days, I had no recollection at all. Over a year after those events that ended my career as a sailor, I still had not a glimmer of who I might be, where I might be from. I'd heard people – sailors, fishermen, the nuns at Jounieh, Hedberg and my other UN colleagues, Maryam, Jews and Arabs alike – speaking of home, often fondly, sometimes longingly, occasionally with displeasure. Always, when I heard such talk, I experienced a hollow feeling, as if something was missing from inside me, something more tangible than mere memory, like an organ cut out by surgeons and leaving a void within my body. Now, I felt a flush of warmth coursing through me, filling me, as if I had ingested a piece of home with the fruit I'd eaten earlier.

My clothes were dry and I redressed quickly, eager to be on my way. I set off with the monkeys in the lead, racing through the grass, swinging from trees when we entered woods. The gulls that called to me in the river flew above. We followed the course of the stream as it swung to the east and grew wild again, narrow, rock-strewn, frothed with white, as we descended from the hills toward a wide valley. We came to a vantage point, a place where a large rock jutted out of the earth like the prow of a ship, affording a sweeping vista to the east. Far in the distance, I could see an expanse of blue, the lake I had come so far to see.

A dream I'd had on the island came back to me immediately, sharp and clear as a photograph. I was standing on a cliff or a bluff high above a sea, its waters blue and serene, seagulls whirling above me in a cacophonous cloud, calling a sound I couldn't decipher. Was it my name? I could see small triangles of white in the distance, the sails of fishing *dhows* and smell the fresh scent of sweet water. The dream puzzled me when

I awakened, because there was no cliff on the island, no high ground at all, and certainly no sails in the distance during my tireless gazing out to sea. Nor, of course, was the scent that rose from the ocean, *that* sea, sweet. Now here, a year later and many miles away, I saw the same sight, smelled the same scents, heard the same calling of gulls. Again, they seemed to be calling out my name, but I couldn't make it out.

CHAPTER 24
THE SEA OF GALILEE

A TRAIL LED FROM the lookout rock down the mountain in a torturous, winding path. It was late afternoon when the monkeys and I reached the valley floor, which was in full bloom with wildflowers of every colour and description. The trail became a road, first just dirt and gravel, then paved, over which the occasional automobile or truck passed by, the drivers waving to me cheerfully. We passed orchards of olives, dates and grapes, fields of cotton and maize, and meadows with herds of sheep and goats tended by young boys and old men who nodded greetings and showed no surprise or alarm. I'd lost my escort of monkeys by now – suddenly, they were no longer with me, and all but one of the gulls had flown away too. I came to an intersection and a signpost with arrows pointing south to Tiberias, six kilometers, and north to Ginosar and Migdal, where I believed the kibbutz Maryam had grown up in, was situated.

I could see the blue water of the lake, the sun, low in the sky now, shining brightly above it. My nostrils filled with the sweet scent of it.

There was more traffic on the road south, and I easily got a ride, with a group of young soldiers in fatigues already crammed into an old Volkswagon Beetle convertible, yet they managed to make room for me. "Where are you headed, old man?" the driver, a blond boy with a neatly trimmed moustache, asked.

I laughed. "Do I really seem that old?" But I was suddenly conscious of how disheveled I must be, my clothes dirty and wrinkled, my hair and beard wild.

The soldiers laughed too. One was a young woman with long black hair in a braid. "Not so much old, maybe, but old world. We meant no offence."

"Oh, I'm not offended, just curious."

"Well…" The woman paused, choosing her words carefully. "You look a bit like a biblical prophet. Elijah, maybe."

They dropped me at the Tiberias fishermen's quay. The sun was lying on the horizon like the yolk of an egg and fishing boats were pulling into their berths as I walked down to the old stone jetty. It was only a minute or two, nodding greetings to various crewmen, before, as if Providence was guiding my footsteps, I found Ahmad tying his boat up. "*Salam*, Ahmad," I called to him, "*masaa el kheer*, good evening."

He looked up and I thought I saw a dark hesitation cross his face, but perhaps it was merely puzzlement. Then his face lit up. "*Najjar*, you're here."

"I told you, I had a yearning to see this lake."

Two men followed him as he jumped from the deck of his boat, one I recognized as his brother Isma'il. Ahmad embraced me in a bear hug. "You came," he said, pulling back to better look at me, holding my elbows in his hands.

"I did."

"You remember Isma'il? And this is our cousin, Anwar." He turned to the cousin, a curly-haired man with broad shoulders. "Anwar, this is our friend Yusef, from Akko. "Yusef…."

"Najjar," I said on impulse.

"Ah, yes. Carpenter. But it was something else in Acre, was it not?"

"Yes, but that was Acre. This is Galilee. Is it not?"

"Ah, I see." Ahmad's smile slid for just a moment into a frown, then returned. "Yes." He turned to his cousin: "Yes, this is our friend Yusef, from Akko. Yusef Najjar."

Anwar and Isma'il were amused by this exchange. "And are you one?" Anwar asked. "A *najjar*?"

"I am, a ship's carpenter by trade, but I can do anything with wood."

"Maybe then, since you're here, you could do us a favour and mend a few things on our boat," Ahmad asked. He turned sideways and gestured toward the boat. "What do you think of her, Najjar?"

The boat was not much different from the *dhow* that rescued me from my island, but on a smaller scale. It was shaped like an arrow, with oarlocks and a single mast for a sail not much larger than a bedsheet, with no motor. Its deep belly, I could see, was perhaps a third full of squirming fish.

"Nothing like your Lebanese friend's fine motor boat at Acre," I said, "but this has classic lines."

"Classic indeed, Yusef," Ahmad said. "This sort of boat has been working this sea for hundreds of years, maybe thousands. They say Jesus's fishermen friends used a boat like this, that he preached from one. We see no need to change it."

"I'll be happy to do some work on it."

"Plenty of time for that," Ahmad said. "In the morning, first thing, we head out. Come fishing with us."

"I will."

"THE FISHING HASN'T been very good this year," Ahmad said.

We'd unloaded the fish from their *dhow*, eaten and slept on the beach, and were out on the water before the sun showed its face, Ahmad, Isma'il and me. Anwar was spending the day with his family. There was no wind at all, so Ahmad didn't bother with the sail, the two brothers falling into an easy, practiced rhythm with the oars.

I dipped my hand in the clear blue water and brought it to my lips. Maryam was right, the water did taste sweet.

As light began to seep into the sky, we reached a spot that suited Ahmad. It seemed unremarkable to me, just a place on the still, dark water, with no discernible landmark in view, except that the solitary black gull that so often was my companion circled high above, calling its familiar cry. No other boats were visible, but Ahmad told me there soon would be more than we could count within sight. "We sleep a little less, but catch a little more," he said with a grin.

He lowered a concrete block on a rope that served as anchor. Then the nets were cast over the side. I watched from the stern as they gradually sank, the red and blue buoys gently bobbing. Ahmad and Isma'il were on either side of the boat. They lit cigarettes and leaned against the gunnels. As the first glints of sun skimmered over the lake, the buoys began to dance, the water to boil just beneath the surface. "Allah be praised," Ahmad shouted, "what is this?"

The nets were so heavy it took all three of us to pull them up, and the boat was soon filled with thrashing fish, banging against our sandaled feet, their eyes wild. "What are they?" I asked.

"Tilapia. Some people call them St. Peter's fish."

The boat was so full there was no point casting the nets again. A breeze sprang up, so Isma'il hoisted the sail and we sped across the water. We passed several boats heading out as we approached the pier, their sails down and their oarsmen straining against the wind, and the brothers hailed them; "Great fishing today," Ahmad called.

We unloaded but the fishmongers had yet to arrive. Ahmad walked to the harbor office to make a phone call to let his parents and wife know we were coming. Then we brewed a pot of tea and sat down on the pier to wait.

"Never been back in this early before," Ahmad said.

"Never had a morning like this," Isma'il agreed.

"No sense going out again," Ahmad said. He and his brother exchanged glances. "There's only so much they'll buy."

"And the others are sure to have good catches too," I said.

The brothers looked at me, their eyes filled with expectation, and again exchanged a glance between themselves, but they said no more.

BOOK 5

A Fisher of Men

CHAPTER 25

THE CLOCKMAKER

WE TOOK OFF from Tiberias in Ahmad's ancient truck, heading west first, on Highway 77, then south on 65 toward Afula, just Ahmad and me, Isma'il having chosen to stay at the lake and keep fishing with Anwar. When we passed the looming dome of Mount Tabor on our right, the white walls of the Catholic church at its apex shining in the sun, Ahmad nudged me. "This is the place of the light, that's what they say." I nodded to signify I understood, though I didn't.

Ahmad's truck was blue once, but every flake of paint had long since chipped off and its colour was now almost a uniform rusty reddish brown. Its springs and shock absorbers had all-but disintegrated, the muffler was gone, the exhaust fractured. It left a trail of oil spots like animal droppings in the dusty gravel lining the road. In the back, we piled my few tools along with some new ones and lumber I'd bought.

I'd had the impression the Safieh brothers lived in Tiberias, an ancient town that developed into a fairly modern small city, but no, their homes were on the family farm near the mostly Arab village of Gan Ner, some fifty kilometres away. During fishing season, though, they spent most of their time on Lake

Kenneret, sleeping either on their boat or at the Tiberias house of their cousin Anwar, who fished full-time.

The truck rattled like a handful of castanets as it bounced over the corrugated road. The countryside was mostly deserted, but now and then we passed a gravel track leading to a village and once a paved road, signs pointing to Nazareth. In the distance, we could see fortified buildings on a hill, an Israeli settlement. At Afula, a good-sized town, we stopped at a building supply store Ahmad knew and bought more lumber, including several fine teak boards I was surprised to find, and a few power tools.

Back in the truck, Ahmad left the highway for a gravel road going south and east. A few minutes after that, he slowed and steered off the road and across a shallow ditch into a field. "Checkpoint up ahead," he shouted over the truck's roar. "The Territories are just to the south." I hadn't seen anything.

He drove slowly to keep the dust to a minimum but still we raised a noticeable cloud. The field inclined up slightly until we reached the top of a stony ridge. The hard sandy plain opened suddenly into a deep *wadi* and the truck plunged over the edge and down, veering sharply to avoid erratic rocks and scattering sheep grazing on the sparse grass. Ahmad pointed out buildings on the opposite ridge, part of a neighbouring kibbutz. Deeper in the valley, I could see an oasis of trees and one rectangle of darker green, where a few horses raised their heads to observe us dispassionately, and a cluster of small buildings. As we drew closer, the raised arms of a surrealistic windmill in the centre of the compound came sharper into focus and when we pulled up and Ahmad turned off the engine, I could hear the mill creaking and complaining. "This is where I live," he said.

An old man was coming from the largest building to greet us. He was dressed in the loose white pants and shirt of the

Palestinian peasants, a colourful cap on his head, a *kaffiyeh* around his shoulders. He looked to be about sixty, white-haired and with a white mustache above his broad mouth, a mat of white hair protruding from the v of his shirt that exposed his barrel chest. He and Ahmad embraced, then the old man turned to me. "This is my father," Ahmad said. The old man was powerfully built and when he took my hand in his, his grip was firm and I could tell he could easily crush my hand if he wanted to. His eyes, beneath shaggy brows, were dark, and tufts of white hair grew like spikes from his nostrils.

"I've been looking forward to meeting you, Abu Ahmad," I said.

He snorted a deep-bellied laugh. "Call me Yusef."

"That's *my* name," I said with a laugh. "Yusef Najjar."

"They call you Yeshu'a too," the old man said. "And Jesu."

"That's right." I was surprised. "Some do."

"We've all heard of you here," he said. He gave his son a glance. "Is it true you are the one?"

Ahmad put his hand on his father's broad shoulder. "Papa!"

"That's all right," I said. And to Yusef: "I'm not *the* one or even *any* one. I'm just who I am, a simple man, a carpenter eager to do some work, someone grateful for your hospitality."

"The hospitality is a pleasure, and no more than anyone else would do."

"Your son tells me we're just inside Israel."

The old man grinned, displaying an irregular array of crooked teeth, some of them blackened. "The Jews don't like to admit it. We're citizens, same as them." He pointed to the ridge we'd come over, marked by a few straggly pine trees. "That's the Green Line. You *were* in Israel, but you had to drive through the Territories to get here – for about a minute. Then you're back in Israel. And all unofficially, very hush-hush." He laughed. "If you were to climb one of those trees, you could piss on this side in Israel or the other side in the West Bank. It's all Palestine, but tell that to them." He made a rude gesture, but his tone was remarkably free of bitterness or rancour.

Ahmad led me on a quick tour, pointing out the house he and his wife Muna and their five children lived in, on the other side of the yard, and the houses of three of his brothers and their families, a bit further away. At the edge of the yard stood a power pole with wires stretching from the power plant at the kibbutz just over the hill. Shorter wires connected the pole to each of the houses in the compound.

"The Jews are happy to oblige us," Ahmad said simply. "We do things for them in return. We're all good neighbours here."

He showed me the hut he had in mind for me. It was built for animals and over the years was used for various forms of storage. It had a stone foundation and a rough frame of weathered boards of various sizes and types, over which scraps of tarp and rags were stretched. The roof was straw. One whole side, facing east, was open, and I could see the light would be good there early in the day, although it was dim now, late in the afternoon. It was empty except for some gardening tools scattered about on the floor.

"We can get this stuff out of here, my mother will sweep it out good, we'll bring in some tables, a bench. And over there a bed. It's not much. Will it do for you?"

"Perfect. This is exactly what I want." Ahmad started to turn, but I put my hand on his arm. "Really. Thank you."

Ahmad backed the truck up to the hut and we began to unload my cargo of wood. The old man appeared at the doorway of his house, interrupting us. "Come to eat," he called.

The house I followed him into was as nice as any I'd visited in

Beirut or the countryside around it. It was built entirely of stone, the inside dry-walled and painted throughout. Indeed, inside, it looked much like a city house, with rugs and many cushions covering the floor, photos and paintings and other objects on the walls, a sofa, an easy chair that reclined, a television set in one corner, a crammed bookcase, with the Koran open on the top shelf, numerous electric lamps and several unlit kerosene lanterns, a fireplace made of stone with a broad black mantle. There was a clock on each wall as well, two cuckoo clocks, a small grandfather-style clock, and a clock fashioned from a dinner plate. The ticking from these clocks was incessant, a sea of mild white noise over which our voices easily sailed as we talked.

"You have a fine eye for clocks, Yusef," I said.

"A fine eye and a fine hand," he replied. He stood a bit straighter, and his chest expanded with pride. "I make these myself. Later, I'll show you more."

The common area took up half of the total space of the house, with perhaps a third of that devoted to a kitchen, with a sink, electric refrigerator, a wood stove. In the rear of the house, two closed doors led, I presumed, to bedrooms. At the near side of the kitchen stood a rickety-legged table laden with food that Ahmad's mother and wife prepared: roast lamb, bulgar, pita, figs, dates and oranges. I was led to understand that the children – Ahmad's and his wife's – were eating with cousins at another house in the compound. "We're all one big family," Muna said. "Nobody ever bothers to count how many children are at their table, or whose they are."

As we filled our plates, the clocks chimed six o'clock, not all at once, but first one, then, barely had it ceased, the second, and so on, the grandfather clock particularly melodious, the cuckoo clocks noisy and comical. We sat on cushions on the floor and ate.

Ahmad's mother, Hayfa, was a petite woman with quick movements, wearing a black dress and colourful head scarf. Her slim face was handsome once and even now it shone. She'd welcomed me as if I were a relative when we entered the house, and now she made sure I had the choicest pieces of meat and plenty of everything. Ahmad's wife was exactly the opposite of his mother, a slim woman as tall as Ahmad, dressed in blue maternity dress, under which her swollen belly was prominent, with a yellow flowered vest and a red kerchief around her neck. Her lustrous black hair was uncovered, in the manner of the women of Beirut but not those in the refugee camps. She smiled constantly, showing good teeth and healthy gums, as if she were flirting, but she sat beside Ahmad and, whenever she could, let her hands rest for a moment on his arm or shoulder, even his neck.

"This is a fine meal," I said, wiping my mouth and addressing the two women. "Thank you, Hayfa and Muna. And a fine house, Yusef Safieh."

Ahmad's father raised his head from his plate with a grin. "I was born in this house," he said. "Four brothers and six sisters, all born right here." He gestured with his thumb over his shoulder, to the closed doors. "All my children born here. And my father too, born in this house, and his sisters and brothers. My grandfather built it, my father added to it, I've added to it. No one can say that we're squatters."

This last, I knew, was a reference to trouble the family had a year or two earlier when they built a second floor on Ahmad's house. The Israelis, Ahmad told me, fined them for building it without a permit. Yusef refused to pay and instead spent three months in jail.

"This land has been in my family for four hundred years,"

Yusef said, "from the days of the Turk." He nodded, chewing reflectively on a piece of lamb. "One of my grandfathers, great great great *great*, was a soldier in the Turk army, in numerous campaigns. He helped put the boots to the Egyptians. For his bravery and service he was given this land, the whole *wadi*, from ridge to ridge, presented to him by the Sultan himself. There was no deed, no paper, just the word of one man of honour to another. For four hundred years, my family raised horses here, fine horses for the Turk army, later for the British. Sheep. Grew oranges, figs. The best olives in the Galilee." He turned to his wife, smiling. "Isn't that right, *Ummu*? he asked, using the Arabic word for mother. "Now the Jews say they made a garden out of the desert!" He pursed his lips and blew, as if he were spitting, but his tone was more of exasperation than anger.

The women cleared the dishes and brought out tea and sticky *kanafeh*. Yusef got up and retrieved a hookah from its place on the mantlepiece. With great ceremony, he loaded the tobacco and lit it. He offered the mouthpiece to me first. The smoke was strong, pungent.

Yusef watched me carefully, his eyes narrowed and shrewd. "Where is your home, young Yusef, Yeshua?" he asked quietly.

"My papers say I was born in Jarara, in Gaza," I said. "But I can't really say. I was ill, Ahmad may have told you, and lost my memory. My world began barely a year ago when I awoke from a deep fever. Before that, just a blank page."

The old man nodded his head reflectively. "Not such a terrible ailment to have, perhaps. Compared to some others."

"Yes," I agreed. "I'm not haunted by my sins and my errors, as some men are. Your fine son here pointed that out to me." I shook my head. "Well, sins and errors, yes, but only recent ones."

"We're all of us haunted in this way," Yusef said, "but that too is not such a bad thing. Better to remember our errors, even our sins, than to keep repeating them." He and Ahmad exchanged a glance.

The old man took another puff on the hookah and passed it to me.

"Jarara," he said. "A fine village to be from."

"You've been there?"

"No, but they're all good, these villages, good places to be, to be from. Even if you're not."

"I think you're right. I've been in many fine places. I've been a traveler."

"Ah. A fine thing to be." He laughed. "I was a traveler too, when I was a young man. I was in Cairo in 1947 and 1948, when the Troubles occurred." He puffed on the hookah, sucked on his teeth. Then he told this story:

"I was to be an engineer. The first in my family to attend university, to be a professional. That was the plan my father had, from when we were little. My brother Ahmad was the eldest, it was he who would inherit the horses. I was quick with my hands and clever" – he gestured toward one of his clocks – "so they said, so I was to go to school. The British were here then. There had always been Jews here but now more and more were coming, and there was talk there would soon be a flood of them. That was all right, we all lived in peace then, good neighbours. No one believed the British would give the country to them, that was unthinkable. So life went on. I went to Cairo to study at the university."

I was reminded of something Hedberg told me once about British guarantees.

"News came of fighting that winter," Yusef went on, "but my father sent word I should not think of it, it was just scuffles in the street with Jewish ruffians. I was to attend to my studies. At the university, I belonged to a group of students, all from Palestine, and we all had the same word from our fathers. Don't worry, stay, study. Yasser Arafat was among us, one of our leaders even then. He too was studying to be an engineer, a year or two older than me but just a boy too.

"But then, in spring, April, we learned of the death of Abdel Kader al-Husseini, our great general, in a battle at Jerusalem, and then, later that same day, the massacre at the village of Deir Yassin, a hundred dead, maybe more, a black day for all of Palestine. We Palestinian students were electrified, galvanized.

"Some of us had had military training. They called a meeting together and we all vowed to fight to the death." He paused, looking at me. "You're surprised, perhaps, at our passion, Yusef? It is a symptom of youth. Some might say a weakness of youth, some might say a strength."

"Perhaps both," I replied.

The old man nodded and resumed his story. "We went outside and lit a great bonfire and burned our schoolbooks and notebooks and student cards to show there was no going back.

"We set out on foot, a hundred strong. We had old British rifles, Lee Enfields, stolen from an armoury, ammunition, bread and dried meat for two or three days, the clothes on our back. Egyptians fed us as we passed through their villages, as if we were their own, and when we crossed the border we were home and we had no concern for food or a place to sleep or hide.

"We broke into two groups, one group, under a man named Abu Sitta, a fine man, moved on to Beersheba, where a rebellion had broken out, but I and some of my friends went with some men from the Muslim Brotherhood, devout Egyptians who volunteered to join our fight, and we attacked a kibbutz near

Khan Yunis in the Gaza Strip – not too far from your home village, young Yusef." The old man grinned at me. "Arafat was with us. The Jews were ready for us, though, and they were too strong and pushed us back and pursued and we had to make a run for it. In one hour I had used all my ammunition and my Lee Enfield was no more than a club. A fancy useless club. We hid where we could."

"Then a great thing happened and a terrible thing happened. The great thing was that the combined armies of the Arab nations invaded and drove the Jews back. The terrible thing was that they forbade us from fighting, we Palestinian boys and men who were ready to defend our homeland, the officers of the armies said no, this is soldier work, not for civilians. Work for we wiser Egyptians and Syrians and Jordanians, Iraqis and Lebanese, not for mere Palestinians. They didn't know I was descended from a man who kicked Egyptian ass!" He grinned again. "Work for men, not boys – they didn't say that but that's what they meant. They took away our guns – even my empty Lee Enfield – and sent us away, like fathers sending their young sons to the house to help the women while they go into the fields.

"Then, of course, another terrible thing happened. These so-called men, these professional soldiers, were sent packing by the Jews, some of them just boys like us." Yusef's eyes glistened with tears. "This was a great loss, a great humiliation. But the way we Palestinians were treated by our so-called brothers, that was the even greater humiliation. *Al Nakba*, they call it – the catastrophe! Our own country and they drove us away! Everything that's happened since then, it comes from that moment, I believe. Allah saw and he was unhappy. He punishes us, that's what I believe. He punishes the Syrians and Egyptians and Jordanians, all the Arab states, for treating us that way, punishes us, we Palestinians, for allowing it to happen, for obediently doing as we were told, like children." He shrugged. "Ah, but that is Allah's will, and what can we do? We can't even understand it."

We sat in silence following Yusef's story and, as if on cue, the clocks began to chime seven o'clock, first the sonorous tones of the grandfather, then the comical squawk of a cuckoo, then the simple *ding, ding, ding* of the plate clock, then the second cuckoo, even gaudier than the first. I was transported by Yusef's story, and now, when the ringing of the clocks ceased, I asked, "So you bear no bitterness?"

He thought for a minute, puffing smoke. "Yes and no. Toward the Jews, no. They've done terrible things to us, but maybe they had reason. I'm not one to say they must go, I've never thought that. I would share this country if our leaders would let us, our leaders on both sides. So toward them, no, they are what they are and do what they must, as their own god commands them, just as we do what Allah commands. Allah and their God, their Yehowah, they're cousins, you know.

"I'm not one of those who deny the Holocaust or the other terrible things the Jews endured in Europe. I'm an educated man, I've read much, and I'm a fair man who asks only that people are fair to me. The Jews have a saying, 'Never again.' You've heard that? That could be our saying too, it should be. *Never again.* But we should say it together, in unison."

Again, he paused to pass the hookah.

"But you asked about bitterness. Toward the British, yes. The world told them to look after Palestine and instead they gave it away. The Jews had a fair claim, yes, but so did my people. They could have done things better, more fairly.

"And towards the other Arabs, their leaders, Nasser and

Hussein and the other backstabbers, yes, for what they did. But also no because they too are only what they are. Do you feel bitter toward the serpent when it bites you? No, because that is its nature, as Allah made it. If you allow the serpent to bite you, are you not the one at fault for getting in its way?"

"You're a wise man, Yusef Safieh," I said.

"I am as wise as Allah allows me to be, no more, no less. But would I have done any better, had I been in charge? Who can say? Probably not."

I was reminded of Sheikh Al-Qatar and his assertion that Allah gives us choices, but allows us to decide which ones to make.

Ahmad's father took a puff from the hookah and seemed for a moment to be studying the trail of smoke that rose from it. "You know, there's not much trust in this world. The Jews, they don't trust us, not even me personally, who has been such a good neighbour to them. But who can blame them? And we, not even I, don't trust them. And again, who can blame us? Somewhere in the *Qu'ran* – forgive me Yusef, I'm not so religious a man as some others, that I can quote the holy book by verse or page – somewhere it says 'trust in Allah,' that Allah asks for our trust. Well, that's easy enough to do. Trusting our neighbours, that's hard. But wouldn't it be a better world if we could?"

There was silence for a minute as all at the table contemplated this thought. I broke the silence with a question: "Did you return to Cairo, to your studies?"

The old man smiled ruefully. "No, no. After all that happened, I had no stomach to return to Cairo, to see the self-satisfied smug faces of the Egyptians. And the truth was, I had no head for studies. I was clever with my hands, yes – see my clocks! – but not with books. I came back here and worked with my father and brothers. I married this good woman" – he nodded toward Hayfa, who sat silent throughout his story, her eyes fixed on her husband's face – "and I had no desire to go anywhere else. My father died, my eldest brother died, killed in 1967 during that little war, another humiliation. So much changed then, but not for us, really. The Israeli soldiers come and go, they hustle and bustle at their checkpoints, Jewish settlers come, but our little *wadi* goes mostly unnoticed and life goes on here, as it does in our village, Gan Ner. We're Israeli citizens, but – what's the expression? Second class? – yes, perhaps a bit second class. But even second class is good, better than in a lot of the Arab countries where we Palestinians are third and fourth class. Eleven children Hayfa gave me, eight who lived, still live, good boys and girls all of them." He gazed fondly at Ahmad, then at Muna. "Now grandchildren, fourteen so far with my children here and in the village, and soon another one." He gestured toward Muna, who smiled broadly in response. "Allah punishes Palestine, He makes the Palestinian people suffer. But He gives us pleasures too, satisfactions." He paused to relight the hookah and the ticking of the clocks rushed in to fill the silence. "Perhaps that is Allah's lesson to us, that is what life is."

"You mean," I asked, "that the suffering is not punishment?"

"I'm not saying it isn't – haven't we sinned? Aren't we deserving of punishment? But maybe not. Maybe suffering is to remind us that we are flesh, the pleasures and satisfactions to make it bearable."

CHAPTER 26
A PARTNERSHIP

I WALKED UNDER moon and starlight with Ahmad and Muna to their house on the other side of the *wadi*, listening to the groan and thump of the windmill's blades as they turned in the light breeze, and feeling as peaceful as I could ever recall.

Their house was like others I'd seen in the West Bank, but more comfortable. The outside seemed like the rudest of dwellings, a rough wooden frame, much like that of the hut I'd been given but on a wooden platform, and covered entirely with a green plastic tarpaulin, actually a series of such tarps expertly sewn together, the seams then sealed with beeswax. Two clear plastic windows were fitted into the tarp on either side of the house, east and west. There was both a solid wooden door and a second one with a screen. An addition with several children's bedrooms occupied the house's rear, built to replace the second storey they'd been forced to dismantle.

"Why the addition is acceptable and the second floor wasn't, Allah only knows," Ahmad said, shaking his head.

Muna made up a bed for me of cushions on the living room floor, privacy provided by a blanket hung from the rafters. Two of Ahmad's father's clocks hung in the room, but their ticking and chiming didn't disturb my sleep, which was without dreams.

In the morning, after a fine breakfast of stewed figs and dates and strong tea, I walked back to Ahmad's father's house, meaning to clean out the hut, and was surprised to find it already emptied and swept clean, and an extension cord was strung from the house to the shed's window, providing electricity. I started to set up workbenches and my tools. Sun streamed in and I liked the way the light fell on the bench I would do my work on. Standing behind it, arranging my tools just so, the adze and the rasps and the vice, I could see dust motes dancing in the rays of sun and I felt something move through me. I thought I heard someone call my name but when I looked there was no one, nothing there.

A moment later, Yusef appeared in the door of the hut.

"Come see my clocks, Yusef Najjar."

"With pleasure, Yusef Safieh."

He led me to another hut, on the other side of the house. It was about the same size as the one I'd been given, but newer, the tarpaulin as snugly fitted as on Ahmad's house. A large window faced east and, with the door open, provided as much light inside as in my workshop. A workbench cluttered with tools, gears and springs took up most of one wall, but mostly the hut was filled with clocks, dozens of them in all manner of repair and disrepair, their ticking a delirious dissonance of sound. I stood in the doorway, dumbfounded. There were square clocks, rectangular ones, round ones, clocks hanging on the walls, clocks on tables, tall standing clocks. A few were in metal cases but most were in wooden chests, simple boxes made of plywood and painted with bright enamel in various colours, with round or square openings in the front to expose the clock face. A few were made from old picture or mirror frames. There were also several cuckoo clocks with crudely carved birds.

Yusef laughed. "I know, I know, Yusef Najjar, you thought I was merely a simple farmer, making a simple living from his sheep and his horses, the few figs and olives we manage to harvest. I am, all that is true – and smuggling as well, though there is less and less the Israelis need these days. Before the short war, you know, they had nothing, the Jews around here, they relied on us. If there was a wedding, oh, the mother of the bride would come to us with a shopping list. The bride's dress, this big in the bust, this in the hips" – he mimed a woman's hourglass shape with his hands. "And the food, the decorations, everything, everything you could want was to be had in Jordan. The Jews couldn't go there, but I could, and I was glad to oblige, I was a good neighbour. I made a good living then, with my truck and my donkey cart. We could buy whatever we wanted on the other side of the river, and coming home, there was the occasional Jordanian border guard, that's all. A *dinar* in such a fellow's hand made him your friend for life." He laughed again at the memory and wiped his eyes.

"Not so much anymore. But Allah has instructed me never to be idle, and who am I to go against Allah's wishes?"

The old man led me into the workshop and we sat on two stools at his bench. "My clocks are all over this district, Jews buy them, Arabs, and in the West Bank too. Some have gone as far away as Egypt and Saudi Arabia, or so I'm told. I'm always tinkering with a clock, and I sell many. They tell good time."

"This is wonderful."

He picked up what seemed to be a tangle of machinery from the bench. "This one's almost done. All it needs is a case of some sort. That's the part I don't like. Give me gears and springs and I'm in bliss. With wood, I'm all thumbs. I usually just bang a few boards together."

If he was hinting at something, I didn't understand him, not then. It was true, the wooden cases of the clocks on display were simple, but not crude. I didn't know what to say, so I merely repeated my last words, "This is wonderful, Yusef Safieh, really wonderful."

The old man put the clock down. "They say you too are clever with your hands."

"Nothing like this. I'm a simple carpenter. I cut and join and polish, but nothing like this intricate machinery."

"That isn't what I've heard, Yusef Najjar."

He showed me several clocks, how he fitted the gears and other pieces together, but I am not mechanically inclined and I could barely follow him. "All I require of a clock is that it tell the time," I said. "If it's beautiful, and if it sings, as yours do, so much the better. How it works doesn't concern me."

"You talk like a *mullah*," the old man said, a small smile playing around his lips. "Allah works his wonders and don't question them."

"And if you did?"

"Maybe you would understand better."

I laughed. "Last night you said we can't understand Allah's will."

"His will, yes. I mean, no, we can't understand that. His wonders, that's something else."

"But does Allah wish us to understand?"

"Why would He not? Does He have secrets? Does He fear we might go into competition with Him?"

I laughed. "I'll say it again, Yusef Safieh, you're a wise man."

He beamed with pleasure.

"I don't suppose, Yusef, you know your father's name?" he asked.

"I don't know, Yusef Safieh. I don't know my father."

"Yes, you mentioned your loss of memory. No memory of your mother either, then?

"No, I don't know her either, I'm very sorry to say."

"This is very distressing, very sad. A son who knows neither father nor mother. For all purposes, an orphan."

"No, nothing as tragic as that, Yusef Safieh." I laughed quietly. "True, I became an orphan, but without troubling my parents to die. As I told you, I...I was sick, a terrible fever. When I regained consciousness, my memory was gone. All memory, wiped clean. I pray that my parents are indeed alive, both mother and father, but I have no idea who they might be, where they might be, or how I might find them. I don't even know what country I was born in."

The old man's distress seemed to deepen with this. "That is a tragedy. It means you don't know who *you* are, Yeshu'a."

I noted the change in the name he called me but made no comment. "I used to think that too, Yusef Safieh. When the fullness of my situation hit me, when it sunk in, I was devastated. Yet that was over a year ago, and here I am. I've re-invented myself, and I continue to do so. I'm what they call a work in progress."

Yusef Safieh's face gradually relaxed as he considered my words. "Yes, I can see that." He put his hand, hard with callouses, on my shoulder, his touch surprisingly gentle. "Let's just see how we can help reinvent you yet again."

Back in what I was quickly starting to think of as my workshop, I felt invigorated. I set up the jigsaw I'd bought the previous day. Then brought in the wood from Ahmad's truck and selected several pieces. Already I had something in mind. I set to work and I felt happier than I had in several weeks, since I last saw Maryam. The hours sped by. Hayfa brought me a lunch of cheese and pita and figs and a thermos of hot tea but I barely paused to eat. I did pause, when I thought the old man was probably in the house having his lunch, to take my tape measure and steal from my hut to his. By evening, the chest I was making was assembled and I was sanding it, preparing it for the first coat of stain, when Yusef Safieh came to fetch me to supper. I heard his footsteps and expected to hear his voice calling out my name, but the footsteps ceased and I felt him standing silently behind me.

"This is for you, Yusef Safieh."

"For me?" He came around and stood beside me.

"A case for the clock you're working on."

He took the case from my hands and examined it from all angles, his eyes growing big.

"It's not done yet," I said.

"It's beautiful already."

"It needs more smoothing, a stain, varnish." I rubbed my thumb along the grain. "This will be smooth as glass."

"And will it fit, do you think?"

"Oh, I've measured, Yusef Safieh. It will fit." I opened the door so he could see inside and his face lit up the hut.

And so I became not the carpenter I'd meant to be, building houses and barns and, perhaps, boats, *dhows* like the one Ahmad and his brothers sailed on the Galilee, but a cabinetmaker, a maker of wooden housings for clocks, beautiful polished wooden chests of oak or olive or cypress within which beat the hearts of Yusef Safieh's intricate time-pieces. We became partners, Yusef and Yusef, our signatures burnt with a hot nail into the bottom of my cases. Yusef Safieh's boast that his clocks were to be found all about was true, he already had many satisfied customers. But it was also true that the cases in which he placed most of his clocks were crude affairs. When word spread of the clocks we now had for sale – wall-mounted cuckoos, shelf clocks and grandfather clocks – demand increased manyfold, as did the prices we could command. Yusef Safieh arranged with Ahmad and one of his other sons, Fahd, whom I'd met fishing in Akko, to take on more of the chores of the farm, and he devoted himself exclusively to the making of clocks, while I applied all of my working time to the design and construction of their cases.

"Who would have thought, when I was a student in Cairo, doing poorly on my exams, that one day I would make my living, and not a bad one, with mechanical things?" the old man asked.

"And that Jews would be your best customers," Ahmad added wryly.

"Allah does indeed work in mysterious ways."

"And with a sense of humour," I said.

Another of Yusef Safieh's sons, Dawad, came to apprentice with him, and another, Bashir, and a young grandson, Majid, came to assist me – I presented the boy with a broom and gave him the task of keeping the floor and bench free of sawdust and wood chips. And yet another son, Juda, who had a shop in the village selling clothing and dry goods and was clever with business, became our agent, bringing our wares and news of them to a wider market. Soon our clocks were available not only in Juda's shop but in the finest jewelry stores in Tel Aviv and Haifa, Beirut and Amman, Cairo and Baghdad.

And so it was that, once again, my life was changing, in ways I could not have imagined earlier. Maryam would soon return to my life as well, but not soon enough; I knew only that I missed her badly.

CHAPTER 27
MARYAM

ONCE AGAIN I WAS a worker with wood, the feel of the wood comfortable in my hands, the smell of sawdust and resin familiar in my nostrils.

I worked primarily in my shed, at a workbench, with fine hand tools, constructing intricate cases for clocks. But I also found time, with Bashir's help, to improve the workshop, and to build a small house attached to it, and furniture for it. I was thinking of Maryam and wanted to invite her to join me, but I couldn't ask her to sleep on a cot in a carpenter's shed. Instead, we talked weekly on the phone – I in Juda's shop on one of the few phones in the village, she at her cousin's sweet shop in Beirut, me calling her on certain days at particular times – and we exchanged letters.

My connection with Maryam, my work with wood and the success of the clocks business, kept me satisfied.

But after each of our telephone conversations, it came to me how much I missed her – I felt her absence viscerally.

In our first such conversation after I'd arrived at the Safieh farm, I told her something of my trek across the Galilee Hills. She'd laughed at my brief description of the old men, the blind men, the tall women.

"Sounds like the village of old men near where I grew up," she said.

"Old men? Just men?"

"*Ancient* men. Maybe I'll take you there, Reuel. Some day."

"I thought your parents were dead."

"They are. I have a larger family, though, aunts and uncles, cousins. It's been a long time since I've seen them. Reuel, I think you'd be interested in the grandfathers."

"Your grandfathers?"

"Not exactly."

But in the calls that followed, whenever I mentioned progress on the house I was building, or suggested she come for a visit, even a short one, she grew cool. "Where you are is too close to where I don't want to be," she'd say, and quickly change the subject.

DAYS PASSED, and weeks and months, and I was content. I felt more at home living in the Safieh compound than any place I could remember, and the family made me feel like I belonged there, that I was one of them. Often, during the rains of winter, I would spend the whole day at my workbench, pausing only to stop and eat the lunch Majid would fetch me, or to share a joke with Bashir, who was proving a quick student of the woodworking art, working at a bench across the room. Every day was essentially the same – taking my meals with Yusef and Hayfa or Ahmad and Muna, talking with the old man, playing with the children – but different enough that I could distinguish between them, and I became aware that my memory, once entirely blank, was, slowly, like grains of sand in an hourglass, filling up with the minutia of days.

The wars in Lebanon and along the Israeli border, which we were constantly reminded of on the radio news Yusef listened to faithfully in the evening, seemed far away. And I rarely thought of the sheikh and his sinister minions.

The only interruption in that sweet routine, save for the birth of Ahmad and Muna's fifth child, a girl, soon after I moved into the compound, was the occasional arrival of a supplicant seeking a miracle. "Miracle" was the term they used, sometimes speaking Arabic, sometimes Hebrew, sometimes English, for these people were as likely to be Orthodox Jews or Christians as Muslims. They were mostly women, bringing with them a sick child, but also men and women with afflictions of their own, from blindness to cancer. I always greeted them cordially and treated them with respect, and assured them I was not a miracle-worker.

"But Jesu," they would say, "we have heard..."

"I know," I replied, "but you are mistaken, whoever told you this was mistaken. I am just a man, a simple carpenter."

To appease them, I would always place my hands on the child, or on the eyes of a blind person or on the part of the body where there was pain. And afterwards, I would sometimes get a note of thanks or hear in the village that there was a cure, a "miraculous" cure, or even that, without me, the outcome might have been worse.

"No, no thanks to me," I would say.

And often the reply would be "But, Isa, you are too modest."

AFTER DINNER, depending on where I'd eaten, there would often be a game: with Ahmad, it was chess; with his father, backgammon or as he called it, using the Turkish word, *tavla*..

Both are games of strategy and took some time for me to learn the basics, but I soon took to them both, more so *tavla*, perhaps because Yusef was less competitive than his son and would often point out errors I'd made or was about to, rather than gleefully take advantage of them as Ahmad would.

"They still play this game at the Turkish military academy," Yusef told me, "to teach the officer cadets strategy. There's a family story that my great-great-great-great grandfather – do I have enough *'greats'*? – was taught to play by the Sultan himself, that they played every night in the Sultan's tent during the Egyptian campaign. Is the story true? Probably not, but I like it." The old man looked up from the *tavla* board, his face lit up.

During these evenings, I'd often daydream about the childhood I might have had. I pictured myself as a child in pajamas lying on the floor in front of a fire, playing backgammon or cards with my father – in these fantasies, the man always had the face of Yusef Safieh, and the woman who brought us cocoa and pastries, the woman I imagined as my mother, had the face of Hayfa.

"I wish I had a family story," I replied, "one to either believe in or not."

I recognized the tone of bitterness that crept into my voice. Yusef and I exchanged rueful glances.

"Ahmad once told me I was lucky not to have a history – no regrets or disappointments," I said. "Smart fellow, that son of yours. Still, it would be nice to know where I came from, what sort of person I was... I don't know who I am, *what* I am."

Again, I didn't like the tone of my voice and I stopped.

We were sitting at the kitchen table, across from each other. Yusef reached across the table now and placed his hand on mine, surprising me with the lightness of his touch. "True, we don't know who you were," he said, "but we know who you are. That's good enough for us. More than good enough, Yeshu'a." He paused. "Or Yusef Najjar. No matter your name."

ANOTHER DAY, I came into the house in mid-morning to make a cup of tea and found Hayfa at work in the kitchen. I stood for a moment in the doorway watching her at the sink. She'd taken off her customary headscarf and placed it on a chair, and I could see the streaks of grey in her loose hair. I must have taken a step inadvertently and she spun around at the sound.

"I'm sorry, *Ummu*, I didn't mean to startle you." Then, embarrassed, I added: "And I didn't mean to call you mother, forgive me. I presumed too much."

"No, Yusef, don't apologize. It's only natural." She dried her hands on a dish towel. "But call me *Ummi*."

The distinction, I knew, was a fine one, the latter term more familiar. "I will," I said, feeling grateful. "Thank you, *Ummi*."

Hayfa's face lit up. "I've had seven sons. One more will hardly be noticed."

I went back to my work feeling, for the first time I could remember, that I was part of something larger than myself.

SOMETIME THAT WINTER, in one of our weekly telephone calls, Maryam surprised me by mentioning that my former employer, Mohammad the carpet merchant, had asked about me.

"I told him you were in the Galilee," she said. "I hope that's all right."

I didn't see why it wouldn't be and said so.

But a few weeks later, she told me she thought someone had been following her. "I'm frightened, Yusef."

I thought immediately of the sheikh and his shadowy men and asked her to describe the man, but he didn't sound like anyone I knew. Still, it made me feel her absence all the more.

"Why don't you come join me," I said. "The little house I've been building is almost ready."

She usually said no to this suggestion or diverted the question. This time, to my surprise, she hesitated. "Maybe," she said after a moment.

A few days later, Juda's son Ghazi came on his bicycle to say there was a call for me, from Maryam. This was the first time she'd phoned me and I was anxious as I walked to the village and waited for her to call again.

"Guess where I am," she said when I answered the phone. She sounded breathless, excited. "In Tiberias."

I was alarmed. "Did something..." I began.

"No, nothing, Reuel. I haven't seen that man again, if that's what you're thinking. I just couldn't wait. I woke up yesterday morning and I felt strange, I didn't know what it was, I walked around in a daze for an hour. Then it came to me – you were calling to me. I don't mean on the phone."

"I was thinking about you," I said.

"It was such a strange feeling. I couldn't resist it. I packed a few things and left. I couldn't remember the name of the village you're near but I knew it wasn't far from Tiberias."

I thought of my own week-long hike from Acre. "But how..."

Maryam laughed. "I took the bus, like normal people."

"Ah, and how did you..."

"I went to the harbour, as you said you'd done. I knew you wouldn't be there but I thought I might find someone who knew your friends...and I did. Isma'il, is that his name? It wasn't hard. He gave me this number to call. And here you are. No miracles, Yusef, just wanting something bad enough."

"I'll come to get you," I said.

"Okay, don't rush. Yusef, it is so good to be here on the lake. Much better than I thought it would. I'm home!"

Hearing her say that was another surprise. "I thought you didn't want to be there," I said.

"That's what I thought too. But everything is changing, Reuel. And so is my thinking about...well, some things."

Ahmad was good enough to offer to drive me – he was dividing his time those days between the farm and the fishing boat, so the drive was nothing to him. We dropped everything and were on the harbour in not much more than an hour. Maryam was sitting on the dock where the Safieh boat was tied up, wearing a skirt and blouse, her chestnut hair hanging free and her face to the sun. The scent of water and fish was in our nostrils as we embraced.

That night was the first we'd slept together in a bed other than hers. "I'm so glad to be here with you," she said.

I started to say I was glad too, but was choked with emotion and words wouldn't come.

"Do you believe in forgiveness, Reuel?" she asked.

"Are you talking about me? Did I do something..."

"No, no," she replied quickly. "Not you, dear man. I just mean, I don't know, in general. There's something I thought I could never forgive. And now I'm thinking that maybe I can."

"Why is that?" I asked. I knew she wouldn't answer if I asked what there was to forgive. I was certain it was something connected to her family, and just as certain that she didn't want to talk about it.

"It's because of you, dear silly man. Don't you know that? I feel I can do anything when I'm with you."

"You know, in my brief life since I lost my memory, no real harm has been done to me," I said. "I'm fortunate, perhaps, but I have nothing to forgive." I paused to laugh. "And as for my life before that, there too there's no need for forgiveness. I have no knowledge of whatever harm that may have been done to me then."

Maryam surprised me then by taking my right hand in hers, raising her left and looking deep into my eyes. Her own eyes, wide and misted with tears, were an even brighter shade of blue than usual. "Under the deep night sky above this humble roof, and in the eyes of God, I vow to take you as my husband."

"I too," I said, nodding my head. "Under the eyes of God, vow to take you as my wife." And to myself I thought, "Dear God, if you really exist, please hear us."

Maryam gave me a quizzical look. "And to which God did you vow?"

"The one whose eyes are on me."

"And which one is that?" Her smile grew mischievous. "Yahway or Allah? Some other God?"

"Aren't they all the same?"

"I don't know...are they? I don't think Yahway thinks too well of some of the things people do in Allah's name."

"And vice versa, I'm sure."

"Yes, probably."

"So, maybe *not* the same. Maybe two faces of the same God. Two sides."

"Working against each other?"

"God is mysterious – isn't that what they say? He works his wonders in mysterious ways?"

"Yusef," Maryam said, dropping my hand and frowning. "I believe we are talking theology."

CHAPTER 28
THE ANCIENTS

FROM WHERE I STOOD, at the edge of the meadow, the lay of the landscape changed dramatically. On my side of the narrow ravine, sheep grazed peacefully on lush grass. On the other, fire or drought or some other natural disaster had blighted everything, leaving twisted tree trunks, charred ground, a thick coating of alkali in the shallow bowl of an empty pond. No fence or shepherd was necessary to keep the sheep in their meadow.

I'd left Maryam with her aunts - two women in their sixties with grey hair tucked into buns – while I went off in search of the men called "the ancients." As the aunts had shown us around the kibbutz compound, I noticed smoke rising from beyond a hill and was told "that's where the old people live."

"You mean, a retirement home?"

"No, we have one here for our old folks," Aunt Tilda said. "These are the really old people, the ancients. Some claim they're hundreds of years old. *Meshuganah*. No one really knows their story. They keep to themselves."

A hundred metres or so beyond the far side of the pond, a thin trail could be seen winding its way up a steep embankment leading to a plateau. I scrambled down into the ravine, then up the other side. There was no sign of life, the bird songs that accompanied me across the meadow now silenced.

I walked across the pond, rather than around it, my sandals raising clouds of alkali dust. The trail was completely bare of vegetation, no sign even of lichen on the rocks. As I began the climb to the top of the plateau, I was surprised to be joined by a monkey. It resembled the monkeys that accompanied me through the Galilee Hills but its fur was darker. It drew close to me, peered at my face, then turned and scampered ahead, pausing now and then to look behind and make sure I was following. The climb took a good ten minutes. Once on the flat top, my monkey companion disappeared into the branches of a giant, gnarled sycamore clinging precipitously to the lip of the cliff – a solitary sentinel, whether to keep people out or in, I couldn't say.

I stood for a moment looking around me. To the west and below, I could see the blue waters of Kenneret, sparkling in the sun, the flat top of Mount Arbel looming behind it. To the east and north, endless hills leading up to the towering bulk of Mount Hermon.

I began to walk along a well-used path and began to see signs of habitation – a fallen-down fence, a wooden shed abandoned to the elements. I passed no cultivated field, no sheep or goats, no fruit trees, just a scattering of stunted pines. After a few minutes' walk, a cluster of stone dwellings, little more than huts, with crude chimneys from which thin wisps of smoke emerged. As I drew closer, I saw several people sitting outside huts, alone or in pairs, all men, wearing earth-coloured robes and *yarmulkes*, and, as Maryam warned me, all seemingly very old. Most of them were oblivious to my presence or ignored me – some appeared to be deep in prayer. I walked on, pausing to say hello to each old man I passed, but none replied. Shortly I came to what appeared to be a village square of sorts, an open area with a gravel path that led to a building larger and taller than any of the others, its windows embellished with stained glass *mogen davids*. Two old men sat on crude wooden chairs across from each other at a small table which, as I drew closer, I could see was a chess board. The pieces on both sides were carved wood, seemingly identical. The men raised their heads and turned toward me. Within their wrinkled faces, their twinkling blue eyes seemed surprisingly young.

"Welcome, Yusef Najjir," one said.

"Jesu, is it you?" the other asked.

I was taken by surprise. "You know me?"

"Of course," the first man said. "We've been expecting you." It took me a moment to realize he was speaking in Latin.

"But, how..."

Both men shrugged, crooked grins appearing on their weathered faces. The man who'd spoken to me was completely bald except for bushy *peyes* that merged into a dirty white beard that flowed down his chest. The second man was beardless, except for a few days of stubble on his rounded cheeks and long braided *peyes*, and had a full head of meringue-white hair. Both wore *yarmulkes*.

"We know things," the bearded man said. "Something we *don't* know is *how* we know."

"But you know who I am?"

"Not exactly," the white-haired man said. "We know who people say you are. And we know you say no. Who you are, *what* you are, that we *don't* know. Only time will tell that."

"Two thousand years, and we still don't know if the first guy was what he said *he* was," the bearded man said with another shrug. My face must have registered shock; he gestured to a third chair, and I gratefully sat.

After a moment, I was able to smile. "The first guy," I repeated. "Two thousand years."

"Jesus," the white-haired man said impatiently. "He said he was the son of God, he made promises – promises *we* believed." He waved a hand to indicate himself, his companion and the larger community. "Now, I ask you, has sin been eradicated? Suffering?"

"My friend here is impatient," the bearded man said. "I'm an optimist. I like to keep an open mind. There's a phrase I like, 'the jury's still out,'" he said in English. Then he abruptly switched to Yiddish: "Was he a *mensch* or a *schmuck*? Like I say, the jury's still out. It is for Jesus, and for you too."

"You could be the One," the white-haired man said, speaking in Aramaic.

Again, I was taken aback. "Could be," I repeated slowly. "How will you know?"

"Like my friend said, time will tell," the bearded man said. "It's not what you say but what you do. We've got our eyes on you. And God will let us know. Well, maybe."

"Maybe?"

The bearded man laughed. "Last time, He was a little ambiguous."

The two men introduced themselves, switching to English: the white-haired man was Whitey; the bald man was Pinky – he pointed to his pink bald dome. This they told me with straight face, then broke into laughter. "Once upon a time, I was called

Matthew," Pinky said, "but after so many years, one gets tired of the same old thing."

Whitey nodded. "I was John. We're all here, you know, the original twelve – Thaddeus, Simon, Andrew, Peter... all but Judas. Mark and Luke too, some of the others, Paul...."

It took me a minute to absorb what they were telling me. "Disciples of Jesus," I finally said. "His followers. But that *was* two thousand years ago."

"Exactly," Whitey said. "A man gets tired...bored. Too old and infirm to do much but sit around and wait."

"Wait to die," Pinky said. "Some of us *longing* to die. But as you can see, it isn't happening."

"God won't let us die – that's what we've figured," Whitey said, "but even God can't stop us getting old, our bodies from falling apart."

"Why would God do this to you?" I asked.

"*Oy gevalt*, that's the sixty-four dollar question, isn't it," Pinky said in Yiddish. "We don't know, but we have theories. We're being punished. That was Thomas's bright idea. We all thought he was a genius. Then he died – one of the few of us who have. We figure God rewarded him for his brilliance."

"Or is punishing him in a different way," Whitey said. "For his impertinence." Again, a big smile.

"Punishing. Why would God be punishing you? I thought you were the chosen."

"Exactly," Pinky said. "*Chosen* is right! Unless we win God's favour, as a few have, we'll live until the true Messiah comes. That's our punishment for believing that nonsense about Jesus, for putting ourselves above God. Jesus was punished too, but then redeemed because of his forgiveness."

"So Jesus was not God's son?"

"Oh, maybe he was," Pinky said. "Maybe not. Who can tell? He was punished for believing he was. What son gets along with his father anyway?"

"We're not so sure about Jesus," Whitey said. "We believed in him, but he abandoned us. He doesn't speak to us, nor does God."

"We call ourselves born-again Jews," Pinky said, again in English.

Whitey ignored him. "For centuries, we've debated the pros and cons, held mock trials, taken turns as prosecutor and defenders, and we're still not sure if he was the true messiah or a false messiah, an illusion."

I took a minute to absorb all this. "And Judas...you said Judas isn't here?"

"Ah, yes, Judas, that back-stabber," Pinky said. "He was beloved above all, he was redeemed." He saw the look of doubt on my face. "He was the hero of the story, after all. No Judas, no betrayal, if that's what it was. No betrayal, no crucifixion, no death, no resurrection."

"This was part of Thomas's theory too," Whitey said.

"Doubting Thomas," Pinky said, and both men broke into laughter.

"But isn't there a contradiction here?"

"Ha ha, of course. This is all part of God's maddening plan. You live as long as we have, you get used to it."

Pinky got up, stretched, smacked his lips. He was shorter than I'd expected, no more than five feet tall, his robe wrinkled and threadbare. "A cup of tea maybe?" He tottered off in the direction of a nearby hut.

In his absence, Whitey explained that the village had a

gasoline-powered generator that allowed for limited electricity. "They take good care of us down in the kibbutz," he said. "We're a pretty healthy bunch – over the years, we've built up immunity to almost every germ – but sometimes one of us gets sick or has a fall and hurts himself. A doctor or a nurse comes up. We used to grow all our own food, were pretty much self-reliant. Age takes its toll. Now, they bring us food, books and magazines from the library. We read a lot. There's even a TV set in the synagogue. Reception's not so good, some days the picture is clear."

After the crucifixion, the disciples were driven out of Jerusalem as heretics, he explained. "We scattered, preached the gospel – oh, yes, we continued to believe. Had lives. All of a sudden, we were well over a hundred years old, our wives, even our children gone. Gradually it dawned on us, this isn't a fluke. We sought each other out. Strength in numbers, you know." He winked. "Over the years, a few of us died, no rhyme or reason that we could tell. Most of us survive."

They wandered for quite a few years, Whitey went on, his discourse smoothly changing from Latin to ancient Greek to Aramaic to Hebrew. They eventually settled near Tiberias toward the end of the Roman period. "Saw the Arabs come and go, the Crusaders, the Maluks, the Turks. We weren't so popular with any of them. Eventually, we got tired of it all and went across the sea and up into these hills. After centuries, the Jews forgot about us. The Christians too. The *world* forgot about us. God too, maybe."

"And you've been here all that time, then?"

"Most of us, yes," Whitey said. "I have." He extended one leg and pointed to it. "Bad legs. I don't get around as well as I once did. Our friend Pinky, though, he's a wanderer. Has good legs.

He's been all over the world. But he always comes back here. This is home."

"You know, the people in the kibbutz think you're all crazy up here," I said. "Some of them do, anyway."

Whitey laughed. "Maybe we are." He twirled a finger beside his head. "Group psychosis. *Meshuganah*."

We both laughed. "For your age, you're very up on modern ideas," I said.

"I told you, we read a lot. What else is there to do? Pinky and me, we play chess, endless games. The others...well, you saw some of them. But those *kibbutzniks*, they're all our descendants, great-great-great-infinitum-grandkids. Who doesn't think the older generation is a little nuts? But we're family, they look after us."

Pinky came back with a thermos, three mugs and a bottle of brandy in a basket. He placed the mugs on the edge of the chess table and carefully poured. "A little *schnapps*?" He took the cork out of the bottle and poured a bit into each mug of tea without waiting for a reply.

"I don't know what sort of lies my friend has been telling you," Pinky said, switching again to English. "Take what we say with a handful of salt, Yusef Najjir." He presented me with a dead-pan face.

"Have you heard this one? A nice Jewish girl brings home a suitor. He calls on the girl's father to ask for her hand. The father asks the young man the usual questions, to all of which he replies he's a Torah scholar devoted to study, and God will provide. Afterwards, the man's wife asks him about the young man. "Well," the father says, "he has no skills, no money, no ambition, no prospects. On the bright side, though, he thinks I'm God.""

"I've heard that one a thousand times," Whitey said. "Get some new material."

Pinky stuck his tongue out at his friend.

"You know," he said, turning back to me, "seriously, Christians are just impatient Jews. They feel guilty for their sins, are anxious for salvation. They *kvetch* a lot. They can't wait for the true Messiah, so they invent and embrace a false one."

"He's right," Whitey said. "We are born innocent. As infants, we remain innocent – shitting our diapers, even pissing the sheets is not sin, but a child's nature, as the poisonous bite is a scorpion's nature. As the child grows, sin begins to develop in the form of greed, impatience, envy, temper and so on. Sin evolves – we have choice, yes, God gives that to us, but we make bad choices. We sin and God punishes us, like a master pulling sharply on the leash of a dog. So these are the stages of life: innocence, then sin, then punishment, and finally, perhaps, redemption. We can't really know – redemption can only be our hope."

There was silence after he finished this speech. We sipped hot tea.

"Thank you for the lecture, professor," Pinky said, grinning at me. "Maybe our guest has an opinion in the matter?"

"Me? No – except yes, I believe in forgiveness." I thought of the conversation Maryam and I had on the subject not long before.

"Ah, forgiveness, yes, that's good, forgiveness is an antidote to sin," Pinky said. "But forgiveness is a human thing, I forgive you, you forgive me. God doesn't forgive, He redeems. Forgiveness is as close to God as we can ever become, as it was made in the image of redemption as we were made in the image of God. A little forgiveness goes a long way with God."

We sat in silence for a few minutes. The sun was hanging low in the west, and I imagined that Maryam was getting impatient.

Ahmad would arrive soon at the kibbutz's gates to pick us up.

I rose from my chair and offered my hand to the two men, who also got up. There was a wet spot on the chest of Whitey's robe from where he'd spilled a bit of tea.

"Why have you told me all this?"

They exchanged glances. "We're gamblers," Pinky said, gesturing toward the chess board.

"Maybe you are who some people think," Whitey said. "It's always good to have friends in high places." He grinned.

"If you get a chance, put in a good word for us," Pinky said. "*Enough already.*"

I turned to go then stopped. "Wait a second. You know so much about me – you knew my name, knew I was coming – you know so much, period. Can you tell me something about my past? Anything. Where I come from, my parents...anything. I need to know who I am."

The two old men exchanged glances. "Sorry, *boychick*," Pinky said in Yiddish. "Like we said, we know some things, but certainly not everything. And we don't know how we know the things we do."

"We don't know any more about you than you do," Whitey said in his stiff, formal Latin. "Time will tell."

I stood there gazing at them, feeling as miserable as I could remember. "Why would your God do this to me?" I asked finally.

"Oh boy," Pinky said. "*Vot a qvestion!*"

Again I turned to go. "One more thing," Whitey said. "Something is coming, that much we know. What it is, we don't."

"Something is coming?"

"For you, Yusef Najjar," Pinky said. "Be careful."

CHAPTER 29
TWO COMMISSIONS

ONE BEAUTIFUL SPRING morning a few days later, on my way to my workshop after breakfast with Maryam, I caught a rustling in the branches of an olive tree through the corner of my eye and thought I saw the black bird that had followed me that I hadn't seen in months. It made me realize that I'd been here at the Safieh farm for almost a year.

I stopped and let my eyes scan the tree, but there was no further motion, just the gentle breathing of the leaves in the slight breeze blowing in from the east, smelling of water. There were many olive trees on Yusef's property, most were in two groves, one on the south side, the other to the north. This tree was the only olive in the courtyard, by the houses, beside the ever-turning windmill, and seemed special somehow. I was reminded of the story of the apple tree in the Garden of Eden. When I was in Lebanon, I'd read the Torah – Sister Mark introduced me to it, in English, and Hedberg gave me a beautiful leather-bound Hebrew edition I'd carried with me to Acre and across the Galilean Hills – and I'd found many of the fables of Genesis charming. A few of them, Eve and the serpent and the apple tree among them, lingered especially in my mind. Now it occurred to me that, since apples aren't native to this part of the world, the tree in the story was more likely to have been an olive.

I plucked a ripe olive from the tree and put it in my mouth, and was startled by the bitter taste. I recalled that, as Yusef explained to me, a lengthy curing process was required to turn this fruit edible. I shook my head, thinking that just a moment before, I'd been content – as content as ever I'd been – and that the olive I quickly spat out was a bracing reminder that I hadn't always been. Things can change, I thought, as quickly as I could pop an olive into my mouth.

Then, as if the olive was a warning, in a matter of only a few days several surprising things happened.

YUSEF SAFIEH WAS out of breath and his hand shook as he held the letter out to me to inspect. It was on stationary from the British embassy in Tel Aviv, handwritten in Arabic, addressed to us both.

"I have the honour to inform you of the embassy's desire to purchase a clock from you for her Majesty, Queen Elizabeth," the letter began. "The fame of your clocks, your cuckoo clocks in particular, and word of the quality of your craftsmanship have spread far and wide, even to the shores of Great Britain and to the attention of Her Majesty. On the occasion of her birthday this spring, the Ambassador would like to present her with one of your cuckoo clocks as a gift.

"May I request an appointment at a time convenient to you for me to visit your studio and select a design? We can discuss cost and other details at that time. Please reply to me directly."

It was signed "Reginald Hastings, cultural attaché."

"This is wonderful," I said.

"More than wonderful," Yusef Safieh said. "Imagine, the Queen herself, with one of our clocks." He laughed out loud. "Should we have the cuckoo speak Arabic or English?"

"Why not Hebrew?" I relied. "Or all three?"

We set about writing a reply – yes, of course, we'd be delighted – and suggesting a time around lunch a week later, which would allow enough time for our letter to reach the embassy and any reply to reach us. Usually, mail was sent or retrieved from the post office only once or twice a week when someone from the compound went into the village, but a grandchild on a bike was dispatched that afternoon to post our letter.

The very next day, another letter came, this one addressed to me, care of Yusef Safieh. He had gone to the village himself that morning and, he told me, was the subject of the postmistress's joke that he had become so popular that he had to check his mail daily. He brought the letter to me in my workshop with a small smile. "How on earth..." I began, but he'd already discreetly disappeared.

The envelope was postmarked London. It and the letter within were written in English, neatly typed, on letterhead from The Proust Gallery, 100 Carnaby Street, London. "My dear Yusef Najjar," it began. "I hope you won't object to my writing directly to you. I'm an art dealer, with my own successful Soho gallery, and a private collector. I'm always on the lookout for new talent. I've heard wonderful things about your paintings from an associate in Tel Aviv. As it happens that I will be in Tel Aviv next week on business, I wonder if we could arrange to meet and for me to see some of your work, with an eye toward representing you in London, and possible purchase." It went on with contact information, a closing "looking forward" sentence and was signed, in an elegant flowing script, in lilac-coloured ink, "Francine Proust."

I shook my head, amused and puzzled, and read the letter a second time. I thought of the ancient man Whitey's warning, "Something is coming." The coincidence of receiving this letter immediately on the heels of the one from the embassy struck me as more than peculiar, and the woman's misunderstanding – believing me to be a painter – ridiculous.

I read the letter to Maryam – she knew a little English, but not nearly enough to read. "Your paintings are known the world over, Reuel," she teased.

It pleased me to see how relaxed Maryam was. Since her arrival at the Safieh compound, she'd become a part of the extended family. Hayfa and Muna and the other daughters-in-law embraced her and she was glowing in a way I hadn't seen before. She'd been tense from the moment she announced she'd like to visit her family through the several days leading up to our visit to the kibbutz, but afterwards was calm, even serene.

Her aunts had been friendly and appeared to be genuinely happy to see her, but there was no sign of uncles – they were "in the field," we were told. And I learned from the aunts something about Maryam she'd never told me, that her father and mother had been killed fighting in the Six-Day War in 1967. The aunts – one was her mother's sister, the other her father's – had raised her.

Maryam had little to say about the visit. When I asked her about her parents, she brushed the question aside. "It's history," she said. As for the aunts, "It was terrific seeing them again" was all she'd say. And of the uncles, nothing. Still, I had the feeling that an old wound had finally healed.

Now, she was delighted by the letter from London. At dinner that evening, she had everyone in laughter when she introduced me as "the esteemed painter."

"Esteemed, yes," Hayfa said, joining the joke. "A painter, maybe not." It was one of the few times I'd heard her speak at the table.

"Why not?" I replied. "Maybe in my former life I was a painter. And an esteemed one to be sure."

THE COINCIDENCES CONTINUED. The following afternoon, Ghazi, Juda's eldest son, rode his bicycle from the village to summon me to his father's shop for a telephone call. Ghazi, who was twelve, made the bicycle trip to his grandparents' many time bearing messages. This time he was particularly excited.

"A lady, a British lady, calling from London." He was breathless, barely getting the words out. "She'll call again at four sharp." He tugged at my sleeve, as if to emphasize the urgency.

I glanced up at the cuckoo clock hanging on the wall above my workbench – just the works, still awaiting its case but telling time perfectly nonetheless. "That's two hours away, Ghazi," I laughed. "There's plenty of time. But tell me, when did she call, and what did she say exactly? Did she say her name?"

The words came stumbling out of him, bumping up against each other. He hadn't spoken to the lady himself, of course, and was only conveying a message from his father. But from what his father said, and what Ghazi overheard of the conversation, it soon became clear that the caller was my correspondent, the British gallery owner Francine Proust. And I was curious enough, that after putting away my tools, I set out for the village.

It was only a couple of kilometres away, half an hour's brisk walk, an hour at the leisurely pace I preferred. Ghazi set out to accompany me, quickly grew bored and sped off, peddling furiously.

I arrived at Gan Ner with plenty of time to spare and stopped at the café for a cup of coffee. The Safiehs were tea drinkers and I missed the coffee I'd grown addicted to during my time with the UN – Hedberg drank a dozen cups a day, and I'd often join him.

I was at Juda Safieh's shop five minutes before the hour.

Juda, Ahmad's eldest brother, had the right of inheritance to the farm, but he had no taste for that life and he'd become a shopkeeper while still a young man. Now he was in his forties and by all appearances prosperous. His shop sold traditional Arab clothing, much of it made locally, and imports from Europe, as well as crafts and, of course, an array of clocks built by his father and me. He also did bookkeeping for some of the other village businesses, helped people with taxes, and had one of Gan Ner's few telephones, usually available to anyone who needed to make or receive a call. It was he who had come up with the name for our clock-making business: *Two Yusefs*.

"You two are going to make a fortune," he'd told us when he saw the first of his father's clocks transformed by my cases, almost a year earlier. "You, Najjar, I'm going to make you a star."

Despite his affable nature, I was always slightly uncomfortable in Juda's presence. Physically, he was entirely unlike Ahmad: portly, with a round belly, usually dressed in a western-style suit, though always with a checkered *kaffiyeh* on his balding head, and immaculately clean, with polished fingernails. When we'd met for the first time, there was something immediately familiar about him, as if I'd met or seen him somewhere before.

"Do we know each other?" I asked.

"I don't think so, I don't know how we could, yet you do look familiar to me."

"I look a lot like your brother Ahmad," I said, and we both laughed.

"Yes, you do, but that's not it."

We each rattled off a string of places where we might have met – he travels to Tel Aviv and Jerusalem often on business – but no, there was nothing in common. Yet the feeling that we did know each other, at some other time, stayed with me and was always present when we were together, faintly disquieting.

Now, he greeted me with a joke: "See? I told you. A star. Already London is calling. Soon, Paris, Berlin, New York. And the women...."

He ushered me into his small office at the back of the shop. A black telephone sat in its place of honour on his desk. We both glanced up at the clock, one of his father's simple designs, in a round teak frame. It was exactly four o'clock. We watched the second hand sweep once around the circle, pass twelve and begin a second pass. The phone rang.

I picked up the receiver and said hello, first in Arabic, then English. "Oh, Monsieur Najjar, how lovely to hear your voice," I heard in reply, a woman's voice, soft, cultured, the accent very British. I had heard accents like that many times while working with the UN. "I'm so glad to reach you. I can't tell you how embarrassed I am about the confusion."

"Oh?" I said. "And what confusion is that?"

There was a pause, then: "I'm afraid I didn't do my homework. I heard your name, more than once, as someone with great talent, great potential, and I apparently misunderstood, I thought you were a painter."

"No, I am a simple carpenter. And I noticed you called me Monsieur – I'm not French, if that's what you think."

"Oh, dear, my goodness, I *am* in a muddle. I'm terribly embarrassed. This serves me right for relying on information from others and not finding things out for myself. Oh, I *am* mortified. You must think I'm a complete fool. Perhaps I should excuse myself and hang up."

"That's not necessary." I laughed. "A harmless mix-up. Don't give it another thought."

"You *are* kind."

"Not at all. As I said, I'm not a painter, just a simple carpenter, so you probably don't want to talk to me anyway."

"No, no, not simple at all. I've now had the opportunity to see some of your work, your exquisite clocks. There is nothing simple about them."

"Well, thank you."

"And though I misunderstood, I was certainly not misinformed about the quality of your work. I would be honoured to show your clocks in my gallery – they are indeed fine art."

We talked for a full five minutes more. She explained her gallery represented several Israeli artists and a couple from the Territories, that she would be in Israel in a few days and hoped to meet with me. I made clear to her that I only built the cabinets, the clockworks themselves were made by Yusef Safieh. That didn't deter her and we agreed that she would pay a visit five days later, on Tuesday. I gave her directions to the village and to Juda's shop, where she would be met at noon.

THE BRITISH CULTURAl attaché arrived at Juda's shop promptly at noon on the following Monday in a Black Range Rover with diplomatic plates driven by an Arab man named Bakr. Ghazi met them there, as arranged, and served as navigator as they drove the final way to the Safieh farm.

Reginald Hastings was a tall, sallow-faced man with deep-set blue eyes, a narrow nose and impeccable manners, much in the manner of other British diplomats and bureaucrats I'd met while working with the UN. His Arabic was good but not up to all the nuances and figures of speech of the language. His companion, introduced to us by Hastings as a Tunisian, was short and swarthy but clean-shaven and, like Hastings, neatly dressed in shirt, tie and a seersucker jacket. He seemed to be driver, assistant, translator combined. He spoke to us in rapid-fire Arabic and slowed down considerably when he shifted to English to address his superior.

We sat down to a lunch of lamb and fig stew, as fine a meal as Hayfa, Muna and Maryam could concoct. We spoke in Arabic, with Bakr only occasionally interjecting a few words in English for Hastings' benefit. It didn't matter – no business was discussed at the table, only pleasantries and compliments to the food and its cooks, the incessant ticking of the house's clocks barely noticeable. At one o'clock, they began to sound, the grandfather clock pitting its deep bass against the squeaky soprano of the cuckoos.

The Englishman ate slowly, smiling and clearly enjoying himself. He appeared relaxed, confident. He explained the peculiar circumstances of the Queen's two birthdays: the actual anniversary of her birth, April 21, and the traditional public celebration later in spring, this year scheduled for June 12.

Afterwards, with tea and a few ceremonial puffs of Yusef Safieh's hookah behind us, our host led us outside and into his workshop. The Englishman had already made appreciative noises over the clocks on display in the house but now his eyes widened. He and Bakr conferred, both in English and Arabic, and Bakr inquired about the wood used for the cabinets of several clocks. Hastings finally settled on a cuckoo mechanism with one of Yusef's brilliantly feathered birds. We then walked across the courtyard to my workshop, where I had arranged a few different cases in my workbench as examples, alongside a sheaf of drawings. Quite a few finished clocks also hung on the walls, as well as several empty cabinets of various designs and woods. Stacks of boards of different wood stood in a corner.

"I can make a case to your specifications," I told them. "If you have a design in mind..."

"No, no," Hastings protested, "we'd like something entirely original."

The attaché finally settled on a highly varnished cherrywood case with considerable scrollwork. It was agreed that the royal insignia should be embossed on one side and the initials ER for Elizabeth Regina on the other. We'd already agreed the cuckoo would be mechanical, with a movable beak.

We then agreed on a price satisfactory to all of us.

As they were preparing to leave, Bakr took me aside. "And perhaps, since it is for the Queen, after all, the case housing the cuckoo could be a bit larger than the one we were looking at." He spoke slowly and plainly now, in strangely accented Arabic. And as he spoke, he seemed to be winking at me – perhaps it was no more than a nervous tic. At any rate, the request seemed reasonable enough. I nodded agreement and thought nothing more of it.

The following day was Francine Proust's turn to visit us. Again, Ghazi met her at his father's shop and drove with her to the farm, in a rented Peugeot. The woman was surprising in every way. From her voice on the telephone, I'd expected her to be young, no more than in her thirties, but Francine – she insisted I call her that – was well into her fifties, her blonde hair streaked with grey, her handsome face lined with wrinkles. During lunch – something more casual than the day before, pita and falafel – she chattered away in English and wooden Arabic, occasionally lapsing into French – and once, when Yusef told a joke, she replied with a phrase in Hebrew. She observed that I followed her conversation closely and remarked, in English, "You have a wonderful facility with language, Yusef."

"As do you, Francine."

"Oh..." Her voice trailed off and the ever-present smile faded. "German was my first language, what we spoke at home. And Hebrew in the synagogue, of course. But I heard numerous languages in the camp. For some reason, they stuck with me."

I didn't understand her reference immediately. "Camp?"

"Oh..." Instead of replying, she extended her left hand, turning it palm up, to display the tattoo on her wrist, faded but still visible. I'd noticed similar faded tattoos on one of Maryam's aunts during our visit to their kibbutz, and on Pinky's wrist, but hadn't given them a second thought.

I'd heard of the concentration camps, of course – Hedberg made them and the Holocaust in general part of my Mideast education – but this sight of smudged blue numbers etched into skin was chilling. "Ah, I see."

"Ancient history," she said brightly, waving her hand. "Yes, Polish, Ukrainian, Russian, Czech, Hungarian...I heard them all in the camp and somehow made them my own. I don't know how."

"I had a similar experience," I said. "Not in a camp. I was a sailor – a ship's carpenter. Several of us were sick, with a high fever. When I recovered, I'd lost my memory but developed, as you say, a wonderful facility with language."

"No memory at all?"

"Nothing."

"So you have no knowledge of your parents, your childhood, anything like that?"

"No, nothing."

"And no knowledge of what you'd done, where you'd been before you lost your memory?"

"No, just that I was a carpenter on board a ship. And that is not a memory, just what I was told when I awoke from my fever."

"So maybe you were a painter after all," she said.

"Maybe. We joked about that very thing after your letter arrived."

"And perhaps you are French. Maybe I was correct in my assumptions, not wrong, after all. Maybe I know more about you than you do yourself, Yusef Najjar." She was laughing now and the others at the table were looking at us with curiosity, making me realize we'd been talking in English for several minutes, excluding them.

"Perhaps."

"You're a self-made man, Yusef Najjar," Francine Proust said. "You've re-invented yourself."

At this point, I switched back to Arabic and changed the subject, and our pleasant lunch continued through a dessert of fresh figs and oranges and tea.

Before we'd sat down, Yusef took Francine on a tour around the house and she'd *ooh*'d and *ahh*'d over the clocks on display and also over Hayfa's weavings on the living room walls. And she'd been enchanted by the pealing of the bells and squawks of the cuckoos at one o'clock. Now, the Safiehs and Maryam excused themselves and I led our guest to my workshop. The cabinets I'd laid out on my bench the previous day were still there, and she examined them closely, as well as the ones on the walls. She stood in rapt silence, as if in an art gallery, before one piece, then another and another.

"This is very fine work, indeed, Yusef."

I couldn't help smiling. "Even though they aren't paintings?

She reddened with embarrassment. "Oh, I am a silly girl."

"And not French?"

"A very silly girl indeed. I know you're just teasing. Thank you for being so gracious."

She smiled, flirtatiously, I thought, and I was reminded of Sister Mark, the way she appeared drawn to me. I thought too of Maryam, whose attentions to me seemed somehow different, as if she, though knowing so little of my life, could see me for who I really was, really am.

Francine took a notebook from her shoulder bag and made a few notes. "I love your work, Yusef. Not just the workmanship, which is considerable. There's real artistry here. Art, not just craft. And Yusef's clocks are wonderful, some of them just darling. I'd be proud to have some of these clocks hanging in my gallery. Would you be willing to have me represent you in London?"

And so it was agreed. We called Yusef out and came to a financial agreement. Our clocks would sell in London for a great deal more than we were charging. We walked slowly through my workshop again as she singled out this clock and that. She would take them with her today, and arrange to have them shipped from Tel Aviv.

And then, one last surprise. "One of your clocks in Buckingham Palace, that will surely be a boost to interest in your work," she told us.

Yusef and I looked at each other. Neither of us said a word about the cultural attaché's visit the day before. "How do you know about that?" I asked.

"Oh, the art world's a small place." Francine's smile seemed innocent enough, and I nodded, taking her at her word.

She went back into the house to talk to Hayfa while we loaded her car. Before she drove away, she'd added three weavings.

Afterwards, I felt restless. I went for a walk through the meadow, deep into the *wadi*, where a trio of Yusef's older grandsons watched over the flocks. I kept going over in my mind the events of the last week: the letter, the phone call, the two visits. The ancient men's warning echoed in my ears again and a feeling of disquiet came over me such as I hadn't felt in several months, not since my last night in Akko. I looked around, half expecting the appearance of the Creature that had come to me that night, but no, I was alone, and the air through which I walked was warm and still, as if I were moving through a pool of sun-lit water.

The path I was following took a turn around a small copse of fig trees and on the other side a flock of sheep and goats, half a dozen or so of each, quietly grazed beside the dry riverbed, which was banked on either side by thin strips of sand. I was sweating from the heat and I took off my shirt and lay down, shifting my back to press my shoulder blades into the welcome gritty itch of the sand's embrace, and I was immediately transported back to the island which, despite the brief prelude on board ship and lifeboat, I had come to think of as the place of my birth. The sun which hangs indiscriminately over Israel and Palestine beat down on me, but it was a different sun I felt, the relentless sun of my desert island.

I closed my eyes. Images and sounds flashed through my mind, a splinter of what might be memory. A face, a woman, hair grey, features blurred – was that my mother? Or a distorted image of Francine Proust? A tall man, the scent of wood shavings on his hands, again his face blank, except for a sharp, narrow nose – my father? Or was that Reginald Hastings my mind had conjured up?

Through the discordance of sounds jangling in my ears, a voice tiptoed closer, a man's voice speaking a language both familiar and indistinct – my father? No, just the first mate, summoning me back to life: *"Come on, Carpenter, hold on."* And then memories flooded in: the ship, my shipmates, my bewildered return to the living, the storm, its terrible aftermath, the agony on the lifeboat, Mohan's last words to me, "'I must be master of my own fate,'" my long sojourn alone on the island. Once again, I remembered the Creature that had visited me, there and several times since. A familiar smell inundated my nostrils and I opened my eyes.

"Oh, it's you."

"Of course," the Creature said. It sat beside me on its haunches, as it had once before, gazing at me impassively. It seemed even larger than before, its barrel-shaped body far broader than a man could entirely engulf in his arms, the massive head, with its flaring nostrils, bared teeth and curving horns, frightening to look at. "Didn't you call me?"

"Did I?"

Implacable silence.

"Yes, yes, I guess I did."

The Creature gazed at me. Again, I was struck how much like a lion it appeared, and I wondered if it was contemplating eating me. I shook that thought from my mind.

"I've told you before, Isa, you have nothing to fear from me."

"I don't fear you. It was just a thought."

"You have *nothing* to fear. You must act accordingly."

"Act? I don't understand."

"Think, Isa, think."

I closed my eyes, the better to concentrate, to do as the Creature bade me, but no thoughts came, and when my eyes opened, I was alone. Now thoughts *did* come – I thought again of the peculiar coincidences of the calls from the British embassy and Francine Proust, the sudden interest in Yusef's and my clocks. Now this new visit from the Creature, the first in a year or more. So not a figment of my imagination after all.

I remembered the discussions I'd had with Sister Mark about God, his mysterious nature.

Was the Creature God? Or an angel sent from God, a messenger? Or perhaps a demon, sent to tempt me – but no, the Creature had never done me any harm or suggested anything that led to harm. Not yet. My thoughts shifted to my own brief career as a messenger, on behalf of the blind sheikh. Then back again to Sister Mark, what she'd said about the fisherman, that I was The One. "What one?" I'd asked, but she only turned away. And then to my return to the clinic, the way Sister Paul and the others had fallen to their knees. The travesty of the translated journal.

It was said that I was The One, the Son of God. Yusef Safieh heard rumours, he half believed them. Ahmad too heard talk;

he was more skeptical than his father but not entirely. And the ancient men I'd met recently met – skeptical, to be sure, yet curious, perhaps even hopeful. I thought Maryam believed it to be true. The Sisters of the Divine Crucifix were certain of it. Was I the only disbeliever?

It was preposterous, of course...but could it be true, even possible? Or was I perhaps – and more likely – a fallen angel of some sort, if there were such things as angels, and if they could fall? Was I not – and this the most likely of all – merely a man, like any other man? A son of God, if one insists there is such a thing, but a son like any other?

I thought again of the Creature and the other animals I'd encountered, the monkeys that followed me through the forest, the fish that filled the boats of my companions.

Who was I? *What* was I?

"Am I the One?" I asked aloud. "Creature, am I the One?"

But the Creature was gone, and there was no reply.

CHAPTER 30
AN END OF DAYS

I THOUGHT THAT I might sleep better with Maryam beside me, and some nights I did. Other nights, as before, were disturbed by dreams. I awoke one night from an especially troubling dream, one I'd had many times before, going back to my days on Shipwreck Island, but never in such sharp detail.

I dreamt of an explosion. In many ways, this dream was similar to the earlier ones: the explosion itself, an earth-quaking deluge of noise, though not loud enough, apparently, to waken me; a quickly growing cloud of dark smoke; the clatter of falling debris, like hard rain; a sharp acid smell filling my nostrils, the banshee wail of sirens – all of this was familiar. There were differences in the details, quickly apparent. Though I had never been there, to my knowledge, nor know much of the place, I knew this was London – perhaps the oddly shaped caps worn by the crowds of policemen who quickly assembled was the clue. And the bright red jackets and black bearskin hats of soldiers, some lying sprawled in the street, others staggering away from the scene of destruction.

There was one other significant difference. In this dream, I seemed not to be an observer from afar, or above, as I usually was, but actually present, on a street just a short distance from the epicentre of the explosion close enough that the blast's force almost knocked me off my feet, close enough that I felt the heat, choked on the smoke.

I heard, slicing through the other hubbub, the clear sounding of a bell, then another, a third, a fourth and with measured grace on through the twelves of a clock's circuit, and I knew with certainty, though I'm sure I'd never seen or heard it or even *of* it, that it was Big Ben. By the time of the final tolling, all other sound ceased, and when the last echo of the bell's final clap evaporated into the rancid air, there was a full, deep silence, an other-worldly silence.

It's this silence to which I awoke, my ears filled with it. And, as usual when waking from such dreams, I too was filled, with a sense of foreboding and helplessness, different this time only in that this foreboding was deeper than I've felt before. Once again, I heard the crackly voice of the ancient disciple Whitey, "Something is coming," and Pinky's addendum: "Be careful."

Maryam had her arms around me, her lips on my cheek. "Just a dream," she whispered, "a bad dream."

"No, more than that," I said. "It means something."

She looked at me with wide eyes. "What does it mean, Reuel?"

"I don't know what."

AFTER SOME HESITATION, I began to work on the commission for the Queen.

What I had in mind was a fairly conventional cuckoo cabinet, rectangular, forty centimetres high by thirty wide, and thirty deep, a bit larger than the mechanism Yusef was working on would require, as Bakr suggested, with an inverted V roof, in the style of an alpine chalet. In the front panel, I cut a circular hole for the clock face and a smaller hole above it for the cuckoo to make its entrances and exits. I built that first, out of cherrywood boards, pegs and holes, leaving the back panel off to provide access to the cabinet, and gave it a good sanding, making it as seamless as possible. Then I set to work with the scroll saw and chisels making leaves and flowers and a carved bird, with wings spread, an olive leaf in its beak, and facing left rather than the traditional right. Finally, for the sides, using an image I'd traced, I cut the lion and horse from the royal coat of arms. This took the better part of a day, with Majid, recently turned ten, standing beside me much of the time, passing me tools as I called for them.

At dinner, Yusef and I compared notes. His work, all mechanical, was more complex and painstaking. We were planning something really special: the cuckoo, of course, but some other things as well. Yusef is very clever, yet some of this was beyond him, and he'd sent away to a manufacturer in Switzerland for a miniature music box. Still, it would fall to him to put all of this together. "All I have to do," I told him, "is provide the giftwrap."

To be making a clock for the Queen! I was excited, and exhilarated by the intricacy of Yusef's clock and the beauty of my cabinet. Still, I was troubled.

The next morning, I devoted myself to sanding the cabinet until it was smooth as glass, painting it and adding other embellishments. After lunch, escaping from the heat, I walked down into the southern olive grove, into the cool of the shade. I lay down on a soft bed of grass beneath one of the larger trees. My mind was busy with the intricacies of the clock – the case turned out to be as complex as the clock itself. Gradually, my mind emptied itself and I lay still. I felt its presence before

I heard anything, even before the smell, and when I opened my eyes the Creature sat beside me, looking at me. I sat up, my back against the smooth bark of the olive tree.

"You hesitate, Isa," it said.

"Do I?"

"You do."

"I did," I agreed. "But I'm doing what you asked."

"I? I asked you nothing."

"Suggested then."

"I suggested nothing. I merely told you not to be afraid."

"And to act accordingly."

"Yes."

"If I hesitate, perhaps that's why."

The Creature turned its head away from me and gazed down the *wadi* toward the dry creek bed.

It took me a while before I could say what I was thinking, but finally I did: "What you ask of me is wrong."

The Creature turned its gaze back to me. "I asked you nothing, Isa."

Then, for the first time, the Creature touched me, lowering its massive head and dropping the end of its snout gently against the back of my right hand where it lay on my knee. I could feel the Creature's breath on my skin.

"You have nothing to fear, *najjar*. Ply your trade. Do what you think right. All will be revealed in good time."

Then it was gone.

I sat under the olive tree for a while longer, thinking, my head filled with echoes. *Do what you think right*, the Creature had said. All right, I thought, I would. Then I got up, went back to my workshop and back to work, turning my attention to the inside of the cabinet. I lined the sides of the box with strips of lindenwood shaved almost paper thin, and placed a shelf five centimetres above the bottom upon which the clock mechanism could rest. I placed an old clockworks of Yusef's on this false bottom and screwed the back panel into place. Then I unscrewed it and, as gently as I could, pried it off. I could see that the strips on the side were starting to come loose. I closed the panel again, and, as I'd anticipated, the shelf on which the clock mechanism sat collapsed.

"You're looking awfully pleased with yourself," Maryam said at lunch. "What were you doing this morning?"

"Making a mousetrap," I said.

THE ROYAL CUCKOO CLOCK was a work of art. I'd been skeptical when Francine Proust said all our clocks were art, but this one really was. I'd gone all out with the scrollwork and entwined leaves, using subtly striped zebrawood, and the robin on the top. I'd spent the better part of a day fashioning a gull, like the one that followed me at sea, painted jet black, with a herring, painted red, in its beak. On reflection I decided a robin would be better. This one had blue wings, spread wide, and was rich in detail, down to the tiny insect in its beak. The latter – an inspiration! – was as close a reproduction of the horrible biting flies that laid waste to my memory as I could produce. As requested, the royal insignia was embossed on one side and the initials ER on the other, beneath carvings of the lion and horse from the royal coat of arms.

If the case was magnificent to see, the clock itself was a mechanical miracle. Driven by both weights and springs, it combined a bird, a *muezzin* and a music box. On the half hour, the bright yellow cuckoo would appear and whistle one note, then retire to its nest. Then, exactly one minute before the hour, music would begin, "Rule, Brittania" playing on the even hours, "God Save the Queen" on the odd ones. Then, at the stroke of the hour, the cuckoo would appear, flapping its wings, opening and closing its beak and chirping the required number. The bird would then retire, the door would close, then re-open and out would come the tiny *meuzzin*, dressed in white robe and headscarf, and chant the call to prayer.

On the clock's bottom, I'd inscribed our label, *Two Yusefs*.

Between the labour and the expense of the equipment, the clock was probably worth twice the price we'd negotiated. "But that's only money," Yusef said, philosophically. "What an honour, and what great advertisement for our clocks."

"Yes, but let's not ever make another like it," I said.

"Agreed. This is one of a kind."

Maryam was full of praise for the clock. "It's a masterpiece, Reuel. This should be in a museum, where everyone can see it, not in a palace."

I said nothing in reply. It was likely, I knew, that except by Hastings and his assistant, and perhaps a few others, the clock would never be seen again.

ON THE APPOINTED DAY, June 3, a little more than a week before the Queen's official birthday, Hastings' assistant Bakr drove out to get the clock. He bypassed Juda's shop in the village, finding his way to the Safieh farm on his own, driving the same black Range Rover, but this time, I noticed, with different license plates, not the diplomatic ones it had before.

He inspected the clock, looking it over from all angles and

paying particular attention to the back, upon which I had pasted a small note in English: "Remove with Care." The screws attaching the rear panel were not easily detectible but I pointed them out to him. "In the event mechanical adjustments are required," I said. He nodded in approval.

Bakr politely declined tea or anything to eat. We placed the clock in a wooden crate I'd built for it, put it in the trunk of the Range Rover. His visit occupied no more than half an hour and he had neither commented on the clock nor said thank you. As he closed the lid of the trunk, he leaned close to me and whispered, "The sheikh sends his regards." Then he drove away.

THAT NIGHT, I couldn't sleep. The following day, I had no appetite. All day, I sat at my workbench sanding one piece of wood after another. I had it in my mind to build a pretty jewelry box for Maryam, had taken measurements and carefully cut the pieces, but by the day's end, all of them were sanded down beyond use.

Again, I didn't sleep, again, I didn't eat. Again, I spent the day in my workshop and accomplished nothing. Maryam asked me what was wrong, but I couldn't say. She put her hand on my arm and I felt the current of heat that bound us, but I was unable to reply. My tongue, my body, my mind, all were mute.

On the third day, Maryam convinced me to drink a half a cup of tea. The radio was on in our kitchen and the music was interrupted by a news bulletin: after PLO rocket attacks across the border for the previous two days, Israeli forces launched an invasion of southern Lebanon. I thought sadly of Hedberg and my other UN colleagues and could listen no more.

I took the teacup with me to my workshop. Standing at my bench, I picked up my tools one by one, examining them as if seeing them for the first time – jigsaw, hand saw, adze, small hammer, drill, rasps, screwdrivers – and recalling that day on the *Al-Aqba*, after my recovery, when I'd held tools like these in my hands for what might as well have been the very first time. I'd used them then to make coffins.

I stood by the open window, gazing down the *wadi* to the dry stream. I cocked my head – I thought I heard the chattering of monkeys.

I walked down the incline to the olive grove, where I'd often gone to think in the cool of the shade. The creek bed was almost always dry and today, though there'd been no rain for some time, a trickle made its musical way down the sandy channel. I knelt beside it, cupped my hand and wet my parched mouth with water as cool and sweet as I remembered from the stream on my island. I lay down under my favourite tree, the oldest and tallest, my back against its smooth bark. My eyes may have closed for a moment. I felt the Creature move beside me, smelled it, and when I opened my eyes it was there, as I was certain it would be. Its massive lion head was held erect, the mouth open wide enough to see the black gums and the large, sharp teeth, but as always I had no fear. The Creature's eyes, deep black pools, gazed at me with what I took to be a mixture of sympathy and admiration.

"You have done well, Isa," it said.

"Done?" I was surprised.

"Everything that was required."

"But...."

"You did what was required, Isa, no more."

I nodded my head, not in understanding – not *complete* understanding, at any rate – but acceptance.

"It is not for you to know," the Creature said. "But to do. That is the way."

The Creature turned his head and gazed along the water channel, then up the slope. "This is a good place, *najjar.* You have chosen well."

We sat in silence. I might have dozed off, and the Creature too may have slept. Finally it spoke again: "There are many choices, *najjar.* It is for you to choose. Things happen, with you or without you. You can choose to be part or to stand aside. Be a prophet, be a carpenter, be both, it's up to you."

I let my eyes follow the Creature's gaze up the slope, toward the buildings where the Safiehs live, where I live, Maryam and I. When I turned back, the Creature was gone, even its scent dissipated in the gently moving air. I had a feeling I would not see it again.

I closed my eyes again and within minutes I felt the earth trembling. I opened my eyes in alarm, half expecting to see a fissure in the earth and swarms of blood-sucking flies, as was described to me after I'd awoken from my fever on the *Al-Aqba,* all those many months ago. But there was no fissure, no flies, and the trembling ceased and all was as it was, the sun shining down on me through a clear and cloudless sky, a soft breeze ruffling the leaves of the olive tree above me, the music of the trickling creek in my ears. I walked slowly back up the hill, pausing beside the windmill to listen to the whirr and thud of its blades, then on to my little house, to our bed, Maryam's and mine. She was nowhere in sight, at Muna's probably, the two of them having become fast friends. I lay down and fell into sleep, as deep as any I'd had.

My dream is confusing. I am again in a place I know to be London, familiar because the dream itself is so familiar. I see the bright red jackets and black bearskin hats of soldiers, hear the tolling of Big Ben, smell the slightly rancid odour of the Thames. Yet I am sitting on the patio of a café near Beirut's *Maghen Abraham* Synagogue, sipping espresso. And to my right and left, the tall steel and glass towers of Tel Aviv loom above, reflecting the sun. At the next table, a quartet of familiar faces: the blind sheikh, the marksman Abu Minon, the British attaché Reginald Hastings, his driver Bakr. At another table, looking elegant and aloof, the art dealer Francine Proust, tea in a fine china cup cooling in front of her. Beside her, Yusef Safieh's eldest son, Juda.

I can see the blue blur of ink on the woman's wrist, what I take to be a smirk on Juda's face.

Then, as I hold my breath, the explosion – again, so familiar – my eyes burning with light, my ears throbbing with sound, my nostrils bitter with the smell of smoke and burned flesh.

Now, my eyes are flooded with images – places and faces – and soon drenched with tears. Places I've been, lived in. Faces of people I know and loved, my mother bending over me as an infant, my father patting me on the back as he sent me off on my first day of school. My mind is abuzz with names, dates, a whole cornucopia of detail that has for so long eluded me.

The unforgettable voice of the first mate, exhorting me: "Be a man, Carpenter."

How I miss *that* man.

And Mohan, the riddle-maker – he and the mate and Maryam, of course, and the Safiehs... these were the people who meant the most to me in my short life.

I find myself suddenly awake, and yet feel as if I'm still in the dream – awake and dreaming at the same time. I'm on my feet, brushing dust from my clothes, inspecting my limbs, patting at my body for tell-tale wet spots of blood, and all is as it should be, I'm unharmed. And my head is still filled with familiar images, *familiar*. I turn and see Maryam, standing in the doorway, sunlight streaming in behind her. "Are you all right?"

"Yes. Only a dream. So real, though, and..."

"No, not a dream," Maryam says. "There was a small earthquake. And then an explosion. Didn't you hear it?"

"Yes, but it was in my dream. The clock..." I raise my hands in bewilderment, although already an explanation is beginning to present itself at the edge of my mind. "But..."

"No," she insists. "There was an explosion. And an earthquake. Look."

My eyes follow her gesture and I see the room is in disarray, chairs tumbled over, books and a lamp on the floor.

Just then Yusef Afieh appears in the doorway behind Maryam, who moves aside to let him by. His hair is wild, his face black with soot.

"Don't be alarmed," he says, "just a little accident. That tremor knocked over a propane tank, my welding torch..." He pauses to take a breath. "More sound than fury. Knocked me off my feet but I'm all right, no real harm done. So strange, I had the radio on, the news, there was an explosion in Tel Aviv, at the British embassy, several people dead. And then, *kablooey*, an explosion here." He peers at me. "Yusef Najjar, you appear shaken up as well."

Maryam puts her hand on my arm. I can see she is alarmed at my appearance, the dazed expression on my face, the tears streaming unchecked from my eyes. "You *are* hurt," she says.

"No, I'm not. Really. Something else has happened. I...I remember."

Again, the flashing of images, my father, mother, brothers, a favourite sister....

"What do you mean, Yusef? Remember what?"

"No, you don't understand. My memory has come back. I *remember*."

She looks at me, as stunned as I am.

"Remember what, Yusef?" Her voice is soft now, not demanding. I think of Sister Mark, her gentle questions as I emerged from fever. "Can you tell me?"

"Everything. I remember *everything*."

We look at each other, as if seeing each other for the first time, as perhaps we are. Then I'm overcome with dizziness, and I have to sit down, breathing deeply. Maryam and Yusef Safieh help me to a chair. My ears are still ringing and now new images are flashing through my mind, new faces and places, new names and dates. And splinters of some of the dreams that have haunted me since my time on the island, my empire of sand: the broken bicycle beside the synagogue, bloody footprints in the sand beside the inflatable boats. I never understood those dreams, but now I do, with a sharpness and clarity that startles me.

Maryam sits down beside me and takes my hand. I raise my head and look at her again for the first time. This time, I realize, I am someone new.

"I know," I say. I give my head a shake to clear it, yet the newsreel behind my eyes continues to roll.

I hear again Sister Mark's voice admonishing me: "Life is full of mystery, my dear Adam, and God is the greatest of them.... We don't know what's in God's mind, His plan. He works His wonders in mysterious ways."

"Know what?" Maryam asks. A small half smile forming on her lips.

"I know who I am."

ACKNOWLEDGEMENTS

This novel, like all my novels, had a long journey from start to finish. Along the way, it was the beneficiary of writing time supported by the Canada Council for the Arts, the former Saskatchewan Arts Board (now SK Arts) and the Saskatoon Public Library, for which I am exceedingly grateful.

Work on the novel began on Labour Day, 2001, the day after I moved into a rented apartment in Saskatoon. I'd moved there from Regina to spend the next nine months as the writer in residence at the Saskatoon Library. I hadn't brought the idea for a new novel with me – it arrived on its own. That day, the opening scene came to me, unbidden, and I sat down at my computer and began to write. Over the next few days, I continued writing as the successive scenes opened up in my mind.

I was working on it early in the morning of Tuesday, Sept. 11, when my telephone rang. A friend who I was going to be seeing later that day was calling to tell me to turn on the news.

Although I didn't yet have a clear idea where the story was heading, I did know that it was set in the Mideast and would involve terrorists. After the events of 9/11, a novel about terrorism didn't feel palatable, and I set it aside. But in subsequent years, the pages of novels and movie and TV screens became flooded with terrorists, and I saw that there was a future for this story after all.

Eventually, I returned to it.

My thanks to my writing colleagues David Carpenter and Dwayne Brenna for their suggestions and encouragement; to my sharp-eyed editor, Susan Musgrave, who helped to fine-tune the novel; to the terrific people, Debra Bell and John Kennedy, at my publisher, Radiant Press; and to my colleagues Sharon Butala and Guy Vanderhaeghe for their words of praise (see the back cover.) And to my partner, dee Hobsbawn-Smith, for being there for me, always.

Dave Margoshes

DAVE MARGOSHES is a poet and fiction writer. Most of his adult life has been spent in western Canada, for 35 years, in Saskatchewan. He began his writing life as a journalist, working as a reporter and editor on a number of daily newspapers in the U.S. and Canada, and has taught journalism and creative writing. His *Bix's Trumpet and Other Stories* won two prizes at the 2007 Saskatchewan Book Awards, including Book of the Year. His collection of linked short stories *A Book of Great Worth*, was named one of Amazon.ca's Top Hundred Books of 2012. Other prizes include the City of Regina Writing Award, twice; the Stephen Leacock Prize for Poetry in 1996 and the John V. Hicks Award for fiction in 2001. In 2022 he was the recipient of the Lieutenant Governor's Lifetime Achievement Award. Dave lives on an acreage near Saskatoon.